The Half-Stitched Amish QUILTING CLUB

WANDA E. BRUNSTETTER

BARBOUR
PUBLISHING

Print ISBN 978-1-60260-811-5

eBook Editions:
Adobe Digital Edition (.epub) 978-1-60742-832-9
Kindle and MobiPocket Edition (.prc) 978-1-60742-833-6

Note: The words to the following songs used in this book were written by Wally Nason: "Never," "Falling Star," and "You Saw Me." Used with permission by Nasun Music Group, 2011.

Scripture is taken from the King James Version of the Bible.

Scripture is also taken from the HOLY BIBLE, NEW INTERNATIONAL VERSION®. NIV®. Copyright © 1973, 1978, 1984, 2011 by Biblica, Inc.™ Used by permission. All rights reserved worldwide.

All German-Dutch words are taken from the *Revised Pennsylvania German Dictionary* found in Lancaster County, Pennsylvania.

This book is a work of fiction. Names, characters, places, and incidents are either products of the author's imagination or used fictitiously. Any similarity to actual people, organizations, and/or events is purely coincidental.

Cover photography: Bradon Hill Photos

Interior cover photography: Doyle Yoder Photography

Special thanks to Little Helpers Quilt Shop in Shipshewana for allowing us to use their quilt and costumes.

For more information about Wanda E. Brunstetter, please access the author's website at the following Internet address: www.wandabrunstetter.com

Published by Barbour Publishing, Inc., P.O. Box 719, Uhrichsville, OH 44683, www.barbourbooks.com

Our mission is to publish and distribute inspirational products offering exceptional value and biblical encouragement to the masses.

 Member of the
Evangelical Christian
Publishers Association

Printed in the United States of America

Dedication

To all my dear Amish friends who live in Indiana.
Each one of you is special to me.

A special thanks to Wally Nason, Mel Riegsecker, Dan Posthuma, and
Martha Bolton for your creative suggestions.

The Lord is nigh unto them that are of a broken heart;
and saveth such as be of a contrite spirit.
Psalm 34:18 kjv

F
Brunstet

Brunstetter, Wanda
E.

The half-stitched
Amish quilting
club.

DATE			

PROLOGUE

Shipshewana, Indiana

Emma Yoder's hands shook as a single thought popped into her head. *What if I fail?*

She eased into a chair at the kitchen table and drank from her cup of chamomile tea, hoping it would calm her jangled nerves. When she glanced at the battery-operated clock on the far wall and realized it was 9:45 a.m., her stomach tightened. Half an hour from now she would begin teaching her first quilting class—and to folks she had never met. Some she'd spoken to on the phone, but a few of the reservations had been made by relatives of those who'd be attending.

Emma had made many quilted items to sell on consignment at one of the local quilt shops and had taught several of her family members how to quilt. But teaching strangers would be different. Those who'd signed up for her six-week class could be from all walks of life. Would they understand everything she taught them? Would her instructions be clear enough? When the classes were complete, would she be able to find more students? All these questions swam around in her head, but she refused to let doubt take over.

The back door opened, bringing Emma's thoughts to a halt. Her daughter, Mary, who'd recently turned thirty-two, stepped into the room and sniffed the air. "Umm. . . Do I smell peanut butter cookies?" Mary asked, pulling out the chair beside Emma and taking a seat.

Emma nodded. "I baked a few dozen this morning. I'm just waiting on the last batch." She motioned to the cooling racks, filled with fresh cookies. "I'm planning to serve them to my quilting class, but feel free to have a couple if you like."

"No thanks. I'm still full from breakfast." Mary's brow wrinkled. "Are you sure you really want to do this, Mom?"

In an effort to keep Mary from knowing how apprehensive she felt, Emma smiled and said, "*Jah*, I'm very sure. Learning to quilt will give my students an opportunity to create something beautiful and lasting." She took another sip of tea, letting the smooth taste of chamomile roll around on her tongue and then settle her uneasy stomach. "Perhaps after my students learn the basics of quilting and make a small wall hanging, they might want to try something larger." Emma felt more optimistic as she talked. The thought of sharing her love for quilting gave her a sense of excitement and purpose.

Mary opened her mouth to say something more, but a knock on the front door interrupted them.

Emma jumped, nearly knocking over her cup of tea. "That must be one of my students. Surely none of our friends or relatives would use the front door."

"Would you like me to answer it?" Mary asked.

"Jah, please do. Show them into my sewing room, and as soon as I take the cookies from the oven, I'll be right in."

Mary, looking a bit hesitant, pushed her chair away from the table and hurried from the room.

Emma opened the oven door and took a peek. The cookies were a nice golden brown, perfectly shaped, and smelled as good as they looked. She slipped on her oven mitt, lifted the baking sheet from the oven, and quickly transferred the cookies to a cooling rack.

As she stepped out of the kitchen, she nearly collided with Mary. "Are my students here?" Emma asked.

"Jah, but Mom, are you truly certain you want to teach this quilting class?" Mary's face was flushed, and her dark eyes reflected obvious concern. "I mean, you might reconsider when you see how—"

"Of course I want to teach the class." Emma gave Mary's arm a gentle pat. "Now go on home to your family. I'll talk to you later and tell you how it all went."

"But, I—I really think you should know that—"

"Don't worry, Mary. I'll be just fine."

Mary hesitated but gave Emma a hug. "Come and get me if you need any help," she called as she scooted out the back door.

Drawing in a quick breath, Emma entered her sewing room and halted. A man and a woman who appeared to be in their midthirties sat in two of the folding chairs, scowling at each other. To the couple's left sat a middle-aged African-American woman with short, curly hair. On their right, a pleasant-looking Hispanic man held a baby girl on his lap.

Sitting across from this group of people was a young woman wearing a black sweatshirt with the hood pulled over her head. A look of defiance showed clearly in her dark eyes, accentuated by her heavy black makeup. On the young woman's left sat a big burly man with several tattoos and a black biker's bandana on his head.

Feeling a bit overwhelmed, Emma grabbed the edge of her sewing machine to steady herself. *Ach, my! No wonder Mary looked so flustered. Such a variety of unexpected people have come here today! What in the world have I gotten myself into?*

Chapter 1

Three weeks earlier

As Emma stepped into the spacious sewing room her late husband had added onto their house, a sense of nostalgia settled over her. Ivan had passed away thirteen months ago after a massive heart attack. Emma still missed his cheerful smile and easygoing ways, but she was getting on with her life—keeping busy in her garden and flower beds, working on various quilting projects, and of course, spending time with her beloved family. One thing that bothered her, though, was feeling forced to rely on her grown children so much. Mary and her family lived on the property next door, and ever since Ivan's death, they'd been helping Emma with numerous chores, not to mention contributing money toward her financial obligations. But Mary and her husband, Brian, had five children to support, and Emma's oldest daughter, Sarah, who lived in LaGrange, Indiana, had eight children. Emma's sons, Richard and Ethan, had moved their families to Oklahoma two years ago, and they each had two boys and four girls. All of Emma's children had been giving her money, even though none of them could really afford it. Emma had sold only a few quilts lately, so with the hope of earning enough money to be self-sufficient, two weeks ago she'd placed an ad in a couple of local newspapers and put some notices on several bulletin boards in the area, offering to give quilting lessons in her home. So far, she'd only had one response, and that was from a woman who wanted to reserve a spot for her granddaughter. But Emma was hopeful that more reservations would come in.

Pulling her thoughts aside, Emma took a seat at her sewing machine to begin piecing a quilted table runner. Sewing gave her a sense of peace and satisfaction, and as her foot pumped the treadle in a rhythmic motion, she began to hum. While many of the Amish women in the area had begun using battery-operated sewing machines, Emma preferred to sew the old-fashioned way, as her mother and grandmother had done. However, she did have a battery-operated machine as well, which she would let her quilting students use when she was teaching them. She also planned to borrow one of Mary's sewing machines.

Emma had only been sewing a short time when she heard the back door open. "I'm in here!" she called, knowing it was probably Mary.

Sure enough, Mary entered the room. "Brian's off to work at the trailer factory, and the *kinner* just left for school, so I'm free to help you pull weeds in your garden or flower beds today."

"I appreciate the offer," Emma said, "but I'd planned to get some sewing done today. I also want to line out everything I'll need when my quilt classes begin."

Tiny wrinkles creased Mary's forehead as she took a seat in one of the folding chairs near the table Emma used to cut out material. "Are you sure you want to do this, Mom? What if no one else responds?"

Emma shrugged. "I'm not worried. If the good Lord wants me

to supplement my income by giving quilting lessons, then He will send students. I'm trusting, waiting, and hoping, which to me are all connected like strands of thread that form strong stitches."

Mary's lips compressed as she twirled around her finger the ribbon strings attached to her stiff white head covering. "I wish I had your unwavering faith, Mom. You're always so sure about things."

"I just try to put my confidence in the Lord. Remember, Hebrews 11:1 says, 'Now faith is the substance of things hoped for, the evidence of things not seen.'" Emma smiled, feeling more confident as she spoke. "I believe God gave me the idea to teach quilting, and if my choices and desires are in His will, then everything will work out as it should. And if for some reason no one else signs up for this class, then I'll put another ad in the paper."

Mary leaned over, and her fingers traced the edge of the beautiful Double Wedding Ring quilt draped over one of Emma's wooden quilting racks. Emma planned to give it to a friend's daughter who'd be getting married this fall, and it was nearly finished. "You do such fine work, Mom. Thanks to your patient teaching, all the women in our family have learned to quilt, and I'm sure the younger girls will learn from you as well."

Emma started the treadle moving again as she pieced another strip of material to the runner that was nicely taking shape. "It gives me pleasure to teach others, and if teaching quilting classes will add to my income so I won't have to rely on my family for everything, then so much the better."

"Families are supposed to help each other," Mary reminded. "And we don't mind at all, because we love you."

"I love you, too, and I appreciate all the help you've given me since your *daed* died, but I feel guilty taking money from all of you when you have growing families to raise. I really want to make it on my own if possible."

"If you're determined not to let us help you financially, then I suppose you could consider getting married again. I think Lamar Miller might be attracted to you, and from what I've seen, I believe he'd make a good—"

Emma held up her hand. "Please, don't even go there. I loved your daed very much, and I'm not the least bit interested in getting married again."

"You may feel that way now, but someday you might feel differently. Lamar's a lonely widower, and I don't think he'll wait forever to find another *fraa*."

"I'm not asking him to wait. Maybe he'll take an interest in Clara Bontrager or Amanda Herschberger. I think either of them would make Lamar a good wife."

"Aren't you interested in him at all?"

Emma shook her head.

"Well, I'm sure he's attracted to you. Why, it wasn't more than a few weeks after he moved here from Wisconsin to be close to his daughter that he started coming around to see you."

"I know, and I wish he would quit." Emma peered at Mary over the top of her metal-framed glasses, which she wore for reading and close-up work. "It's time for me to make a new start, and I'm excited about teaching the quilting classes. Fact is I can hardly wait to see who God sends my way."

CHAPTER 2

Goshen, Indiana

The mournful howl of the neighbor's dog caused Ruby Lee Williams to cringe. The infuriating beagle had been carrying on all morning, and it was grating on her nerves. Of course, everything seemed to irritate her these days: the phone ringing, a knock at the door, long lines at the grocery store, the TV turned up a notch too loud. Even a simple thing like the steady hum of the refrigerator could set her teeth on edge.

Ruby Lee poured herself a cup of coffee, picked up the morning's newspaper, and took a seat at the kitchen table, determined to focus on something other than the dog next door, now alternating its piercing howls with boisterous barks. It was either that or march on over to the neighbors' and demand that they do something with their mutt.

"But that wouldn't be the neighborly thing to do," she murmured. For the past two weeks, the Abbots had attended the church Ruby Lee's husband, Gene, pastored, and she didn't want to say or do anything that might drive them away. It was bad enough that Ruby Lee felt like running away.

Inside their newly purchased home, everything was finally in its place after moving a month ago from the parsonage, which was owned by the church. Both Ruby Lee and Gene were in their late forties, and thinking a new house would be where they would retire, they'd decided that a one-story home would be the most practical. But they'd instantly fallen in love with this older brick house, even though it was a two-story and would mean climbing stairs to their bedroom. Compared to all the homes they'd looked at over the winter months, it was hard to pass up a place that was in such good condition and so reasonably priced. The house was solid, and the freshly painted rooms cheerful— not to mention the hardwood floors that shined like a basketball court. Ruby Lee was thrilled with the large windows throughout the house and the charming window seats that had been built into most of the rooms. With the exception of the kitchen and two bathrooms, she could sit on the seats in any of the rooms and enjoy looking out at different parts of their yard. The front and back yards were neatly manicured, and the lovely flower beds were weed free—at least for the moment. With the exception of the sometimes-noisy neighbors' dog, this house was perfect for her and Gene's needs. Now if everything else in their life would just fall into place as nicely as the moving and unpacking had done, Ruby Lee could finally relax.

This morning Ruby Lee had e-mailed her friend Annette Rogers, who lived in Nashville. She'd intended to unburden her soul but had ended up sending a casual message, asking how Annette and her family were and mentioning the beautiful spring weather they'd been having in northeastern Indiana. Ruby Lee had been there for Annette when she'd gone through breast cancer surgery five years ago, but things were now going well in her friend's life, and Ruby Lee didn't want to burden Annette with her own problems. Besides, she hoped the issues they were facing at church might soon work themselves out.

Maybe I just need a diversion, she thought. *Something other than directing the choir, playing the hymns and choruses every Sunday, and heading up the women's ministries. What I need is something fun to do that's outside of the church.*

Ruby Lee turned to the ad section of the newspaper and scanned a few columns, stopping when she came to a small ad offering quilting lessons. *Hmm. . . I wonder if this might be something I should do. I could make a quilt for one of our elderly shut-ins or maybe a quilted wall hanging for our home. Now that all the boxes are unpacked and I've arranged the rooms, I need something—anything—to take my mind off of the church troubles.*

Elkhart, Indiana

"Hey, sweet girl," Paul Ramirez said to his nine-month-old daughter, Sophia, as he carried her from the Loving Hands Daycare Center out to his van. "Were you a good little girl today?"

Sophia looked up at him with her big brown eyes and grinned. "Pa-pa-pa."

"That's right, I'm your papa, and I love you very much." Paul smiled. He knew Sophia was pretty young to be talking yet and figured she was probably just imitating him because he said *Papa* to her so often. Then, too, from what he'd read in her baby book, some children started saying a few words at an early age.

Paul opened the back door of the van and secured Sophia in her car seat. Then, handing the little girl her favorite stuffed kitten, he went around to the driver's side. With just a few weeks left until school was out for the summer, Paul was looking forward to the time he'd have off from teaching his second-grade class. He could spend more time with Sophia and more time with his cameras, as well. Perhaps he could combine the two. Maybe when he took Sophia to the park or out for a walk in her stroller, he'd see all kinds of photo opportunities. It would be good not to have to worry about who was watching Sophia during the day when he was teaching, too. It'd be just the two of them spending quality time together.

Paul swallowed around the lump in his throat. *If Sophia's mother were still alive, it would be the three of us enjoying the summer together.* Lorinda had been gone six months already. Every day he missed seeing her pretty face and listening to her sweet voice. Yet for Sophia's sake, he'd made up his mind to make the best of the situation. Thanks to his faith in God and the support of his family and friends, he'd managed to cope fairly well so far, despite his grief over losing his precious wife. The hardest part was leaving Sophia at the day care center every day. This morning when he'd dropped her off, the minute he'd started walking across the parking lot, she'd begun to cry. By the time they'd reached the building, Sophia was crying so hard, the front of Paul's shirt was wet with her tears, and it was all Paul could do to keep from shedding a few tears of his own. It nearly broke his heart to leave her like that. He wished he could be with her all the time, but that simply wasn't possible.

Paul looked forward to spending this evening with his sister, Maria, and her family. Maria had invited Paul and Sophia to join them for supper, and he was sure that whatever she fixed would be a lot better than anything he could throw together.

By the time Paul pulled into Maria's driveway, his stomach had begun to growl. He hadn't eaten much for lunch today and was more than ready for a substantial meal. If not for Maria's frequent supper invitations, he would have almost forgotten what a home-cooked meal tasted like.

When he stepped into his sister's cozy home a few minutes later, he was greeted with a tantalizing aroma coming from the kitchen.

"Umm. . . Something smells awfully good in here," he said, placing Sophia in the high chair Maria had bought just for the baby to use whenever they came for a meal.

Maria turned from the stove and smiled, her dark eyes revealing the depth of her love. "We're having enchiladas tonight. I made them just for you."

Paul gave her a hug. "I know I've said this before, but you're sure a good cook, Maria. Your enchiladas are the best. All I can say is *gracias* for inviting Sophia and me here for supper this evening."

"You're more than welcome." Maria patted Sophia's curly, dark head. "It won't be long and she'll be off baby food and enjoying enchiladas, tamales, and some of our other favorite dishes."

Paul gave a nod. "How well I know that. She's growing much too fast."

"That's what kids do," Maria's husband, Hosea, said, as he strode into the kitchen, followed by three young girls. "Just look at our *muchachas*." He motioned to Natalie, Rosa, and Lila, ages four, six, and eight. "Seems like just yesterday and we were changin' their *pañal*."

Lila's face reddened as she dipped her head. "Oh Papa, you shouldn't be talkin' about us wearin' diapers like that, 'cause we don't wear 'em no more."

"That's right," Maria agreed. "And can't you see you're embarrassing our girls?"

"Aw, they shouldn't be embarrassed in front of their uncle Paul," Hosea said with a chuckle.

Maria handed him a platter full of enchiladas, and he placed it on the table.

"You know, Paul, you're absolutely right about Maria bein' a good cook. She's always liked spendin' time in the kitchen, so I knew soon after I met her that she'd make a good wife." Hosea winked at Maria, and she playfully swatted his arm.

"Lorinda enjoyed cooking, too." Paul's throat tightened. Watching Hosea and Maria together and thinking how much he missed his wife made him almost break down in tears. Even during a pleasant evening such as this, it was hard not to think about how Lorinda had died after a truck slammed into their car. Paul had only received minor bumps and bruises as a result of the accident, but the passenger's side of the car had taken the full impact, leaving Lorinda with serious internal injuries. She'd died at the hospital a few hours later, leaving Paul to raise their daughter on his own. Fortunately, the baby hadn't been with them that night. Maria had been caring for Sophia so Paul and Lorinda could have an evening out by themselves. They'd eaten a wonderful meal at Das Dutchman in Middlebury and had been planning to do a little shopping on their way home to Elkhart. That never happened.

"Paul, did you hear what I said?" Maria gave his arm a gentle tap.

"Huh? What was that?"

"I asked if you've talked to any of Lorinda's family lately."

"Her mama called the other day to see how I'm doing, and said she'd be sending a package for Sophia soon," Paul replied. "Ramona sends a toy or some article of clothing to Sophia on a regular basis. I know it's hard for her and Jacob to be living in California, with us so far away, but they're good about keeping in touch, same as our folks do."

"Yes, but Mom and Dad only live in South Bend, so you get to see them more often," Maria said.

"That's true."

"Are Lorinda's folks still planning a trip here sometime this summer?" Maria asked.

Paul nodded. "As far as I know."

"That'll be nice." Maria smiled. "It's good for Sophia to know both sets of her grandparents."

"What about Lorinda's sister? Have you heard anything from her since the funeral?" Hosea asked.

Paul shook his head. He wished Carmen's name hadn't been brought up. "I doubt that I'll ever hear from her again," he murmured.

"Well, that's just ridiculous! That young woman's confused, and she's carryin' a grudge against you for no reason." Hosea shook his head. "Some people don't know up from down."

Paul went to the sink to get a glass of water, hoping to push down the lump that had risen in his throat. "Can we talk about something else—something that won't ruin my appetite?"

Maria's eyes brightened as she leaned against the counter and smiled. "I saw an interesting ad in the newspaper the other day."

"What was it?" Paul asked.

"It was put in by a woman named Emma Yoder. She's offering to give quilting lessons in her home in Shipshewana."

"What got you interested in that?" Hosea asked. "Is my pretty little *esposa* plannin' to learn how to quilt?"

Maria shook her head, causing her short, dark curls to bounce around her face. "You know your wife doesn't have time for that. Not with my part-time job at the bank, plus taking care of our girls." She winked at Paul. "I was thinking you might want to take the class."

Paul's eyebrows shot up. "Why would I want to take a quilting class?"

"Well, Lorinda liked to sew, and since she started that pretty pink quilt for Sophia and never got it finished, I thought maybe—"

Paul held up his hand. "It would be nice to have the quilt done, but I sure can't do it. I can barely sew a button on my shirt, and I'd never be able to make a quilt."

"But you could learn, and it might even be fun," Maria said.

"Huh-uh. I don't think so. Besides, I have enough to do with my teaching job and taking care of Sophia."

"Say, how about this?" Hosea thumped Paul's shoulder. "Why don't you let Maria sign you up for the class? Then when you get there, you can see if the Amish woman, or maybe one of her students, might be willing to finish the quilt Lorinda started."

Paul rubbed his chin as he mulled the suggestion over a bit. With a slow nod, he said, "I'll give it some thought, but right now I'm ready to eat."

Goshen

Star Stephens sat at the kitchen table, staring at the words of a song she'd begun working on earlier this week. *Can't seem to look behind the right door; maybe that's 'cause I don't know exactly what I'm looking for. Can't seem to shake the hand that I've been dealt; a road of bitter regret, headed straight to hell. And it doesn't really matter to those who really matter. . . .*

Star tapped her pen as she thought about her life and how she and Mom had left their home in Minneapolis and moved to Goshen, Indiana, six months ago. Mom needed to take care of Grandma, who'd been having health problems because of emphysema. From what Mom had told Star, Grandma had been a heavy smoker for a good many years. As time went on, Grandma got worse, and two weeks ago she'd passed away, leaving her rambling old house and all her worldly possessions to Star's mom, her only child. Star had never met her grandfather, whom she'd been told had drowned in a lake when Mom was three years old. Grandma never remarried. She'd raised her only daughter alone and supported them by working at a convalescent center as a nurse's aide. Star hadn't met her own father either. All she'd ever had was Mom to rely on, and their relationship had never been all that good. They'd moved around a lot during Star's childhood, and Mom had held more jobs than Star could count. She'd done everything from waitressing to hotel housekeeping but never kept one job very long or stayed in one place more than a few years. Mom seemed restless and had drifted from one boyfriend to another. She'd also been self-centered and sometimes had lied to Star about little things. Star had learned to deal with Mom's immaturity, but it irritated her nonetheless.

"What are your plans for today, Beatrice?" Mom asked when she entered the room wearing a faded pink bathrobe and a pair of floppy, lime-green bedroom slippers that were almost threadbare and should have been thrown out months ago.

"My name's Star, remember?"

Mom blinked her pale blue eyes as she pushed a wayward strand of shoulder-length bleached-blond hair away from her face. "I know you've never liked the name Beatrice, but I don't see why you had to change your name to Star. Couldn't you just be content with being called Bea for short?"

Star shook her head determinedly. "For cryin' out loud! I'm twenty years old, and I have the right to do as I want. Besides, I like the name Star, and that's what I want to be called—even by you."

Mom scrutinized Star and then slowly shook her head. "You need to get over the idea that you're going to be a star, because that's probably never gonna happen."

Star's jaw clenched as she ground her teeth together. Mom had never understood her desire to sing or write songs. In fact, she'd actually made fun of some of the lyrics Star had written, saying she should get her head out of the clouds and come down to earth. Well, what did Mom know about all that, anyway? She could barely carry a tune and didn't care for the kind of music Star liked. Other than appreciating the roof over their heads, the two of them really had very little in common.

Mom stared at Star a little longer. "I wish you hadn't gotten that stupid star tattooed on your neck. It looks ridiculous."

"I like it. It's who I am."

"And I suppose you like those ugly purple streaks in your hair?"

"Yep."

"What about that silly nose ring? Doesn't it bother you?"

"Nope."

Star could see that Mom was about to say something more, so she grabbed up the notebook and headed for her room, stomping up the stairs and slamming the door. She tossed the song lyrics on the dresser and flopped back onto the bed with a groan. As she lay there, staring blindly at the cracks in the ceiling, she thought of Grandma and all the times Mom had brought her here to visit. She'd say she was leaving Star at Grandma's for a few weeks because Grandma had asked her to, but Star had a hunch it had been more for Mom's benefit. She figured Mom had just wanted her out of her hair for a while so she could be with whichever boyfriend she had at the time. A woman as pretty as Mom never had any trouble finding a man, and it was no surprise when she'd married Wes Morgan shortly after Star turned eight. Tall, blond-haired, good-looking Wes had turned on the charm and promised everything but the moon.

Star clutched the edge of her bedspread tightly between her fingers. *I hated that man, and I'm glad he's dead!*

Tears stung her eyes as she thought back to the times she'd spent with Grandma, which she now realized had been the happiest days of her life. *Oh Grandma, I miss you so much.*

Grandma had been pretty ill the last two weeks before her death, and it had grieved Star to watch her suffer. But at least they'd been able to share some special moments, talking about the past and the fun times they'd had. Star had even shared with Grandma her dream of getting some of her songs published, and Grandma had never once put her down. She missed the words of encouragement Grandma had offered, even in her weakened condition. She longed to see Grandma's cheerful smile and be held in her loving arms.

Three days ago, Star had been looking through Grandma's room, searching for Grandma's old photo album. She remembered it being filled with pictures of Mom when she was young and a few older photos of Grandma and Grandpa when they were newly married. There'd also been some pictures of Star from when she'd come to visit. Star had finally found the album in Grandma's dresser, and when she'd opened the drawer, an envelope had fallen out. Written on the outside in Grandma's handwriting was Star's name. Grandma had never hesitated to call her only granddaughter *Star*, because she knew how much Star disliked her given name.

Inside the envelope, Star had found a note stating that Grandma had paid for a six-week quilting class in Star's name. It had puzzled Star at first, but then she'd read the rest of Grandma's note and realized that since Grandma had always enjoyed quilting, she wanted Star to learn how to quilt as well. She'd even said she hoped if Star learned to make a quilt that she would think of her and remember all the happy times they'd had together.

At first Star thought learning to quilt was a dumb idea, but after contemplating it for a while, she'd decided to give it a try. Maybe Mom would appreciate her quilting instead of nagging all the time about Star needing to do something sensible with her life. Not that Mom had ever done anything levelheaded with her own life. It seemed as though Mom was always searching for something she couldn't find.

As Star shook her negative thoughts aside, a few more song lyrics popped into her head. She leaped off the bed, grabbed her pen and notebook, and took a seat at the desk. *I'll never give up my desire to become a songwriter,* she thought. *And someday I'll show Mom that I can be a real star.*

CHAPTER 3

Shipshewana

L ook over there, Stuart! Do you see that colorful Amish quilt hanging on the line in the yard across the road?" Pam Johnston nudged her husband's arm.

"Don't poke me when I'm driving. You might cause an accident," he grumbled, adjusting his baseball cap.

Pam wished he hadn't worn that ugly red cap today. It looked ridiculous! Of course Stuart didn't think so. He wore the dumb thing a good deal of the time. She was surprised he hadn't tried to wear it to work. Truth was the only time Stuart dressed halfway decent anymore was when he was at work, managing the sporting goods store in Mishawaka.

"I really wanted you to see that quilt," Pam said, rather than bringing up the subject of Stuart's baseball cap.

"Yeah, it was nice."

"How would you know that? You didn't even look when I called your attention to the quilt, and now we've gone past it."

Stuart shook his head. "I can't look at everything and keep my focus on the road ahead. You want us to get in an accident?"

"Of course not, but you could have at least glanced at the quilt. I'll bet you would have looked if it had been something you'd wanted to see."

Stuart mumbled something unintelligible in response.

Pam sighed. "I wish I could make an Amish quilt. It would give me a sense of satisfaction to be so creative."

No comment. Not even a grunt.

She nudged his arm again. "Did you hear what I said, Stuart?"

"I heard, and if you don't stop poking me, I'm going to zip right out of Shipshewana and head back to Mishawaka."

"I'm not ready to go home yet. Besides, you said we could stop by Weaver's furniture store and look for a new coffee table."

"Yeah, okay, but that's the last stop I'm going to make. There are other things I'd rather be doing than shopping for furniture."

"Like what?"

"There's gonna be a baseball game on TV this evening, and I don't want to miss it."

Pam looked at Stuart with disgust. It was always the same old thing with him. "When you're not working, you're either hunting, fishing, watching some sports event on TV, or putting your nose in one of those outdoor sportsman's magazines. You obviously would rather not be with me."

"That's not true. I'm here with you right now, aren't I?"

"Well, yes, but—"

"I've spent all morning and part of the afternoon traipsing in and out of every shop in Shipshewana just to make you happy."

She glared at him. "It's kind of hard for me to be happy when in almost every store you said you were bored and wished we could go home."

Stuart tapped the steering wheel with his knuckles. "Never said I was bored. Just said I could think of other things I'd rather be doing."

"Oh, I'm sure you could."

For the next several minutes, Pam said nothing, but as they turned into the parking lot of Weaver's store, she reached into the plastic sack at her feet and pulled out a newspaper she'd picked up when they'd first arrived in town. "Before we go inside, I want to talk to you about something."

Stuart turned off the engine and looked at her, blinking his hazel-colored eyes. "What's on your mind now?"

"Remember how our marriage counselor suggested we do more things together?"

"Yeah. . .yeah. . .What about it?"

"She said I should do something you like, and then in turn, you should do something I like."

"Uh-huh."

"I went fishing with you two weekends in a row." *Which I absolutely hated*, she mentally added. "So now it's your turn to do something I want to do."

"Just did. Came here so you could do some shopping."

"Shopping doesn't count. All we've bought so far are some bulk foods items at E&S."

"But we went into nearly every other store in town just so you could look around."

Ignoring his sarcastic comment, Pam held the newspaper in front of Stuart's face and pointed to the ad she'd circled. "An Amish woman who lives here in Shipshewana is offering a six-week quilting class."

"So?"

"I've always wanted to make an Amish quilt, and I really would like to take the class."

"Go right ahead; I have no objection to that."

"I thought maybe we could attend the classes together."

He tipped his head and looked at her as though she'd lost her mind. "You want me to go to a quilt class?"

She nodded. "It would be fun."

"Oh, you think? You'd better speak for yourself on that, 'cause I think it would be boring." Stuart shook his head forcefully. "No thanks. I'll pass. It's not the kind of thing a man like me would do."

"Oh, so do you think sewing is just for women?"

"Yeah. That's exactly what I think." Stuart drummed the steering wheel with his fingers, emphasizing his point.

"Well, if sewing's only for women, then fishing's only for men."

He shrugged.

"I hated fishing, Stuart," she said resentfully. "Now it's your turn to do something with me that you think you'll hate."

He gave an undignified snort. "Give me a break, Pam!"

"I went fishing to make you happy. Can't you do the same for me?"

His eyebrows furrowed. "Six weeks? Do you really expect me to sit in some dumb quilting class for six whole weeks with a bunch of women I don't even know?"

"You'll know me, and I don't expect you to just sit there."

"What then?"

"You can learn to quilt, same as me."

His eyes narrowed as he stared at her in disbelief. "I can't believe you'd expect me to learn how to quilt. That's the dumbest thing you've ever asked me to do."

She folded her arms and glared at him. "I can't believe you would expect me to hire a sitter for the kids so I could sit in your boat at the lake and hold a fishing pole all day. But I did it for you, so why can't you do this for me?"

"You only went fishing two Saturdays. If I went to the quilting class for six weeks, it wouldn't be fair."

"What are you saying? Do you expect me to go fishing with you four more times? Is that what you're saying?"

"Yep. That's exactly what I'm saying."

Pam sat mulling things over. "Agreed."

"Huh?"

"I'll do it."

"You'll go fishing with me four more times?"

"Yes, that's what I said."

"And you won't complain about anything?"

Pam nibbled on her lower lip. No complaining? Now, that would be really difficult; especially since she hated the bug-infested woods.

"Well, what's it gonna be?"

"If you promise to go to the quilt classes every Saturday for six weeks, then for the next four Saturdays after that, I'll go fishing."

"And you won't complain?"

"I'll try not to."

"It's a deal then. Now are we done with this discussion?"

Pam swallowed hard as she gave a slow nod. She couldn't believe what she'd just agreed to do. Maybe after the quilting classes were over, she could think of some excuse not to go fishing with Stuart. Better yet, maybe she could talk him out of going fishing, period. Well, for now, at least, she'd be getting her way. As soon as they got home, she planned to call the number in the ad and reserve two spots for Emma Yoder's quilting classes.

CHAPTER 4

Stuart couldn't believe Pam would even want to make an Amish quilt, much less expect him to make one, too. Some women were hard to figure out, and his wife was certainly one of them. Maybe the idea of quilting was just a passing fancy. Could be that after she'd attended a class or two she'd change her mind and decide that quilting wasn't something she really wanted to do.

Six whole weeks! That's just plain dumb. I catch on to things really fast, though. Bet I'll have the whole process down pat after the first couple of weeks, and then I won't have to go anymore. 'Course, if Pam does decide to stick it out, she'll expect me to go along, even if I am able to quilt something sooner than that.

Stuart gripped the steering wheel a little tighter. This was really a no-win situation—at least for him. On the other hand, if he stuck it out the entire time, then Pam would have to keep her end of the bargain and go fishing with him four more times. It might be worth it just to watch her try to deal with the whole fishing scene again.

Stuart chuckled to himself. The last time they went fishing, it had been comical to watch Pam swatting at bugs, primping with her hair, and struggling with the line on the fishing pole when she'd caught a fish. He could still hear her hollering when she'd tried to reel it in: *"Help! Help me, Stuart! I don't know what to do with this fish!"*

That day could have been kind of fun if Pam hadn't whined and complained about every little thing. Why couldn't she just relax and enjoy the great outdoors the way he did? If he'd known she was too prissy to get dirty and deal with the bugs once in a while, he'd have thought twice about marrying her. Of course, during their dating days he'd been attracted to her beauty and brains and hadn't thought much about whether they had a lot in common. He just felt good being with her back then.

Just look at her now, Stuart told himself. *She's sitting over there in the passenger's seat, looking so prim and perfect. Not a hair out of place on her pretty blond head, and I'll bet there isn't one wrinkle on her slacks or blouse. We're sure opposites in what we like to do, how we dress, and in so many other ways. No wonder our marriage is in trouble. Even with the help of our counselor, I have to wonder if there's really any help for me and Pam.*

Topeka, Indiana

"How'd it go with your probation officer yesterday?" Jan Sweet's employee Terry Cooley asked as Jan climbed into the passenger side of Terry's truck.

Jan shrugged and clipped on his seat belt. "Went okay, I guess. During our sessions, she always asks me a bunch of stupid questions, but I'm just keepin' it real."

"That's probably the best way, all right. So, are you ready to head home now or what?"

"Yeah, sure thing." They'd just completed a roofing job at a home near Tiffany's Restaurant, and Jan knew it was too late in the day to start tearing the roof off the Morgans' house in LaGrange. "Guess we'll get an early start on Monday mornin'," he told Terry.

"Sounds good to me. I'm kinda tired anyways."

"Same here."

They rode in silence for a while, and then Jan brought up the subject that had been on his mind all day. "You know, I really hate relyin' on you for rides all the time. Sure will be glad when I get my license back, 'cause I like drivin' my own truck to work." Jan thumped his knee. "And man, I sure do miss ridin' my Harley. I like the feel of the wind in my face and the freedom I have when I'm sailin' down the road on my motorcycle. Know what I mean?"

Terry nodded. "Just hang in there, buddy. As long as you don't do anything to blow it, you won't have too much longer to go."

"Three more months seems like forever." Jan groaned. "In the meantime, when I don't have far to go, I'll keep ridin' that old bicycle I bought at the secondhand store. And when I need to travel farther, I'm thankful for friends like you who are willin' to give me a lift."

"Hey man, it's no big deal." Terry grinned and pushed his shoulder-length, flaming red hair away from his face. "If the tables were turned, I'm sure you'd do the same for me."

"You got that right." Jan appreciated a friend like Terry, who was not only a hard worker, but liked to ride motorcycles, as well. The two of them, both single, had become good buddies despite their age difference. Although Terry was only twenty-eight and Jan had recently turned forty, they had a lot in common and saw eye to eye on many things. When Jan moved to Shipshewana and started his roofing business three years ago, he'd been glad to find Terry.

"So what'd your probation officer have to say during your session yesterday?" Terry asked.

Jan squinted his eyes almost shut. "Said I should try to find some kinda creative outlet."

"How come?"

"She thinks I'm uptight and need to find somethin' that'll help me relax."

"You mean somethin' other than a few beers?"

Jan grimaced. "It was a few too many beers at the biker bar that caused me to lose my license, remember?"

"Yeah, but if you hadn't gotten picked up for drivin' your motorcycle too fast, you wouldn't have gotten nailed for driving under the influence."

"True, but I've learned my lesson. No more drinkin' and drivin', and no more speedin'." Jan pointed to a grocery store on his left. "Would you pull in over there? I'm thirsty, and I'm all out of bottled water."

"Sure thing." Terry put on his signal and turned into the store's parking lot. "Guess I'll go with you, get some water, and see what I can find to snack on."

"I'll grab us the waters while you look for whatever you wanna munch on."

"Okay. Thanks, bud."

When they entered the store, Jan went to the cooler and grabbed two bottles of water. As he waited for Terry, he studied the bulletin board on the wall near the front entrance.

His gaze came to rest on a handwritten notice offering quilting classes. Learning to quilt would sure be creative, and it might even help him relax. Jan had never admitted it to anyone, but he'd done a bit of sewing in the past and had even embroidered a few pictures he had hanging in his bedroom where no one else could see them.

He pulled off the section of paper with the phone number on it and stuck it in his shirt pocket. He didn't know if he'd take the quilting class or not, but he'd give it some thought.

CHAPTER 5

Shipshewana

I still think this is a really dumb idea, and even though I agreed to come here with you, if this class is boring, don't expect me to do anything but sit and listen," Stuart mumbled as he pulled his black SUV onto the graveled driveway leading to a large white farmhouse on the outskirts of town.

Pam wrinkled her nose. "That's not fair. I shouldn't need to remind you that I went fishing with you not once, but twice."

"That was different." He scowled at her. "It's easy to fish, and it's something both men and women do."

"Some men sew, and some men cook. We've been through all this before, Stuart."

"I cook every time you want something barbecued."

"That's not the same thing, and you know it."

"It is to me."

"By the way, have you looked in the mirror lately?"

"Yeah, this morning when I was brushing my teeth. Why?"

"Well, you didn't look close enough, because you obviously forgot to shave."

Stuart rubbed his stubbly chin. "Guess I did."

"I'm not real pleased with your choice of clothes, either. You could have worn something more appealing than that stupid red baseball cap, faded jeans, and a red-and black-plaid flannel shirt. Oh, and I hope you won't tell any corny jokes today. We're here to learn how to quilt, not put on a show or try to make people laugh."

When Stuart and Pam had begun dating and he'd joked around, she'd thought it was funny, but not anymore. Now it irritated her—not to mention that when he did it in public, she was embarrassed.

"All right, already! Would you stop needling me?" Stuart yelled.

Pam frowned. They sure weren't starting off on the right foot today. She hoped Stuart didn't humiliate her during the quilting class. Since he didn't want to go, no telling what he might say or do.

"It looks like you're not the only man here," she said, motioning to an attractive-looking Hispanic man with a dark-haired, rosy-cheeked baby exiting the silver-colored minivan parked beside Stuart's SUV. Although he was dressed in a casual pair of jeans, his pale blue shirt looked neatly pressed. That was more than she could say for Stuart.

Stuart grunted. "The guy's obviously not with his wife. I wonder what's up with that."

"Maybe she couldn't come today. Maybe he cares about her so much that he's willing to take the class in her place."

"You think so?"

"I guess we'll soon find out." Pam opened the passenger door and stepped down, being careful not to let her beige-colored slacks brush the side of their dusty vehicle. It really needed a good washing.

She'd just closed the door when a blue, midsize car pulled in. A few minutes later, a middle-aged African-American woman stepped out of the vehicle. "Are you here for the quilting class?" she asked, smiling at Pam.

"Yes, I am," Pam replied, admiring the pretty turquoise dress the lady wore. "I'm eager to learn how to quilt, and being taught by an Amish woman is a good guarantee that I'll be taught well. From what I understand, most Amish women are expert quilters."

The woman nodded. "That's what I've heard, too."

Pam glanced over at Stuart, thinking he might be talking to the Hispanic man, but no, he stood in front of their vehicle with his arms crossed, staring at the ground. *Maybe I made a mistake forcing him to come here,* she thought. *I probably should have come up with something else I wanted to do that he would enjoy, too. Well, it's too late for that. We're here now, so we may as well go in.*

Pam went around to the front of the car and took hold of Stuart's arm. "Are you ready to go inside?"

"Ready as I'll ever be," he muttered.

"Well, hold that thought," she whispered, again hoping he wouldn't embarrass her during the class.

They started for the house, and as they stepped onto the porch, a small red car in dire need of a paint job pulled in. When a slender young woman dressed in a pair of black suede boots, black jeans, and a black sweatshirt with the hood pulled over her head climbed out of the car and headed their way, Pam couldn't help but stare. The girl didn't seem like the type who'd want to learn about quilting, but then neither did the Hispanic man. She guessed everyone who'd come must have their own reasons, and she hoped Stuart would now see that quilting wasn't just for women.

Pam was about to knock on the door when Stuart nudged her arm. "Look who's joining us now." He motioned toward a tall, burly-looking man with a short brown beard, riding in on a bicycle, of all things! He wore blue jeans; a tight white T-shirt; and a black leather vest. A black biker's bandana was tied around his head, and his brown ponytail hung out from the back of it. The man had a mean-looking black panther tattooed on his left arm and the name *Bunny* on his right arm. He wore black leather boots—the kind motorcyclists wore—and looked like he belonged on the back of a Harley instead of on a beat-up blue and silver bike.

When I signed us up for this quilting class, Pam thought, *I certainly never expected there would be such an unusual group of people taking the class.*

The young woman wearing the hooded sweatshirt barely looked at Pam as she stepped up to the door and knocked before Pam even had a chance to lift her hand. A few seconds later, a thirty-something Amish woman answered the door. She wore a very plain dark blue dress and a stiff white cap perched on the back of her dark brown hair, which had been parted in the middle and pulled into a bun at the back of her head. The woman stood staring at them with a strange expression. After several awkward moments, she said she was Emma Yoder's daughter, Mary, and then she led the way into an unexpectedly large room, which she told them was where the quilt class would be held.

Pam tried to take it all in with one swooping look. The room held a long table, several folding chairs, some wooden racks with colorful quilts draped over them, and three sewing machines. One of them was a treadle and appeared to be an antique. The four gas lamps flickering overhead completed the picture of plain, simple living.

"If you'll all take a seat, I'll get my mother," Mary said before hurrying from the room. The poor, red-faced woman looked about as uncomfortable as Pam felt right now.

Pam and Stuart quickly found seats, and everyone else did the same. Stuart turned to Pam and glared at her. "Why didn't you tell me it would be like this?"

"I didn't know." She glared right back, grabbing Stuart's ball cap and plunking it in his lap. Didn't he have any manners at all? Between the angry look on Stuart's face and the stony expression from the biker, as well as the young woman dressed in black, the room seemed to be permeated with negative vibes.

Pam glanced over at the dark-skinned woman and was relieved when she smiled. At least someone in the room seemed friendly. She couldn't tell much about the demeanor of the Hispanic man, because he was occupied with his baby.

They all sat quietly for several minutes until a slightly plump, rosy-cheeked Amish woman with gray hair peeking out from under her stiff white cap and wearing a plain rose-colored dress and a pair of metal-framed glasses, entered the room. She looked a bit overwhelmed as she stood beside the antique sewing machine, gripping the edge until her knuckles turned white. Maybe she, too, hadn't expected such an unusual group.

Emma released her grip on the sewing machine and took a deep breath, hoping she could find her voice. When she'd placed the ads and bulletin board notices for the quilting classes, she hadn't expected those who came would be from such varied walks of life. And she certainly hadn't figured any men would attend her classes! No wonder Mary had looked so worried when she'd come to get her.

Thinking back to the phone calls she'd received, there had been one from a man, but he'd said he wanted to make a reservation for Jan. Emma had assumed it was for the man's wife or a friend. And come to think of it, another woman who'd called had said she wanted to reserve a spot for her brother; although at the time Emma had thought maybe she'd misunderstood and that the woman had said, "her mother."

"Hello," she said, smiling despite her swirling doubts and the reeling in her stomach from the nervousness she felt. "I'm Emma Yoder. Now would each of you please introduce yourself, tell us where you're from, and state the reason you signed up for this class?" Maybe the introductions would put them all at ease.

The English woman with golden-blond hair hanging slightly below her shoulders was the first to speak. "My name's Pam Johnston. That's Johnston with a *t*. I enjoy sewing and have always wanted to learn how to quilt." She turned in her chair and motioned to the man with thick brown hair sitting beside her. "This is my husband, Stuart, and we live in Mishawaka. Stuart manages a sporting goods store, and I'm a stay-at-home mom to our children: Devin, who's eight, and Sherry, who is six." Pam wore an air of assurance, but Emma sensed it might be just a cover-up for a lack of self-confidence.

Stuart gave a nod in Emma's direction then glanced at his wife as though seeking her approval. "She's the one who actually wanted to come here. I just came along for the ride."

"That's not true." Pam shook her head. "My husband also wants to learn how to quilt."

"Yeah, right," Stuart mumbled. His tone was clipped, and the look he gave his wife could have stopped any of Emma's clocks from ticking.

Emma quickly turned to the African-American woman wearing a full-length turquoise dress with a loosely knit brown sweater. "What's your name, and what brings you to my class?"

"I'm Ruby Lee Williams, and I live in Goshen, where my husband pastors a church. We have twin sons who are twenty and attending a Bible college in Nampa, Idaho. Of course, they'll be out of school for the summer in a few weeks, but they've both founds jobs there, so they won't be coming home until Christmas." She grinned, looking a bit self-conscious. "I guess that's a lot more than you asked me to share."

"No, that's okay," Emma said. After all, Ruby Lee really hadn't shared any more than Pam. "Would you mind telling us why you're taking this class?"

"I came here to learn how to quilt because I thought maybe—"

"What church does your husband pastor?" Pam interrupted.

"It's a community church," Ruby Lee replied.

Pam gave a brief nod. "Oh, I see."

"So what brought you to my class?" Emma asked Ruby Lee.

"Well, I just thought it would be kind of fun and that maybe I could make something for our new home or perhaps a quilt for someone I know."

Emma smiled and turned her attention to the young woman wearing black jeans and a black hooded sweatshirt, which she kept firmly in place on her head. It was really too warm to be wearing a sweatshirt—especially indoors. "Why don't you go next?"

"I'm Star, and I also live in Goshen. My grandma used to quilt, and before she died, she paid for me to take this class because she wanted me to learn how to quilt, too."

"You have a very pretty name." Ruby Lee smiled at the young woman. "What's your last name, Star?"

Star lifted her gaze, as though studying the cracks in the ceiling. "You can just call me Star."

"Is that your real name?" Pam asked before Emma could voice the question. She'd never met anyone named Star before. Besides the dark clothing she wore, her coffee-colored eyes were accentuated by heavy black eyeliner.

"It's real enough for me." Star lowered her gaze, and when she gave a nod, the shiny gold ring on the side of her nose caught the light coming through the window.

"I thought maybe it was a nickname," Pam said.

Star lifted her chin and stared straight ahead. It didn't take a genius to see that the young woman had some issues she needed to deal with.

Feeling even more uncomfortable, Emma turned to the tall muscular man with the short-cropped beard and tattoos on his arms. "And who are you?"

"Name's Jan Sweet. Now ain't that sweet?" He slapped the side of his leg and chuckled, a rich, warm sound. "I live here in Shipshewana and have my own roofin' business. I got a DUI three months ago when I was ridin' too fast on my Harley; had my driver's license suspended for six months; had to do thirty days jail time; and paid a hefty fine. I'll be on probation for three more months, at which time I'll get my license back." Jan paused to draw in a quick breath. "My probation officer suggested I do somethin' creative, so when I saw your notice on a bulletin board, I signed up for the class."

"Jan Sweet? What kind of a name is that for a man?" Stuart, who had been staring at the tattooed man, snickered. "Sounds more like a girly girl's name to me."

Jan's brown eyes narrowed as he eyeballed Stuart. "Better watch what you're sayin,' buddy, or I might just have to show you how much of a man I can be." His tone had grown cold, and the muscles on his arms rippled slightly.

"Oh, I–I'm sure my husband was only kidding," Pam was quick to say. She bumped Stuart's arm with her elbow. "I think you owe Mr. Sweet an apology, don't you?"

"Sorry," Stuart mumbled without looking at Jan.

"Yeah, well, some people oughta keep their opinions to themselves," Jan growled. "You hear what I'm sayin'?"

Emma could tell by the smirk on Stuart's face that he still thought his comment about Jan's name was funny. And Jan looked downright miffed. How on earth would she handle things if the animosity kept up between these two men? Did she have the nerve to ask one or both of them to leave? Would that even be the right thing to do? Could God have sent this group of unlikely folks to her home for another reason besides learning how to quilt?

Emma turned her attention to the Hispanic man holding the baby. "What's your name, and who's the cute little girl on your lap?"

"I'm Paul Ramirez, from Elkhart. I teach second grade, and this is my daughter, Sophia. She's nine months old." Paul bent his head and kissed the top of the baby's head. "My wife, Lorinda, started a quilt for Sophia, but she was killed in a car accident six months ago, so the quilt was never finished. I came here hoping someone might be able to finish it for me." He removed the small pink quilt from the paper sack he'd brought along.

"Oh, I think you should be the one to finish it," Emma said, understanding the look of pain she saw on the young man's face. Perhaps completing the quilt his wife started would give him some sense of peace.

"I—I don't know a thing about sewing, but I guess with your help I can try." Paul motioned to the baby. "I won't bring Sophia with me when I come next week, but I couldn't find a babysitter today. Since I didn't think I'd be staying for the whole class, I brought her along." One look and Emma could see how much that adorable little girl meant to Paul.

"She's a cute little tyke," Jan spoke up. For such a big, tough-looking man, he sure had a tender expression when he smiled at Paul's baby.

Emma still couldn't believe she'd ended up with such an unusual group of people, but Lord willing, she would teach them all how to quilt, and maybe a bit more besides.

CHAPTER 6

When Emma took a seat in a rocking chair and draped a colorful quilt across her lap, everyone gathered around. Then, as Emma began to explain the history of Amish quilts, Star glanced over at the biker dude. In so doing, the hood of her sweatshirt slipped off, and she quickly put it back in place. She couldn't believe that Jan had blabbed all that information about himself, or for that matter, that he'd been stuck with a girl's name. It didn't fit his rough exterior. But then, the fact that he kept smiling at the baby girl sitting on her daddy's lap didn't fit the way Jan looked either. Maybe he wasn't as tough as he appeared. Maybe he had a soft spot for kids. He sure didn't seem the type who'd want to learn how to quilt, but then neither did the other guy, Stuart.

Guess I don't really fit the mold either. Even though I told them about Grandma signing me up for this class, some still might be wondering what a girl like me is doing here.

Star pulled her gaze away from the biker and focused on the Amish woman holding another colorful quilt she said was the Lone Star pattern. *Now that one fits me,* Star thought. *I'm a lone Star who no one but Grandma has ever really loved.*

To keep from giving in to self-pity, Star studied her surroundings. While she'd seen many Amish people when she'd gone to the Shipshewana Flea Market, this was the first time she'd been in one of their homes. Upon first entering Emma's house, she'd noticed how neat and clean it was. From what she could tell, not one thing was out of place. A wonderful aroma permeated this home, too—like freshly baked cookies—which gave the place a homey feel. In some ways, Emma's house reminded Star of her grandmother's place but with one big distinction—the absence of electricity. The oversized sewing room was dimly lit with only the light coming from the windows and the few gas lamps suspended from the ceiling.

How weird it would be for me to live without electricity, she thought. *No TV, computer, dishwasher, hairdryer, or microwave.* Star was sure she'd be bored if she couldn't go online and post messages on forums to people she didn't really know or download favorite songs to her computer. Yet something about being here in this simple, plain home, gave Star a sense of peace. She was glad she'd followed through with Grandma's wishes and come to the class. If nothing else, it would be a nice diversion.

"And this colorful quilt is called the Double Wedding Ring," Emma said, breaking into Star's musings. "It's a quilt that's often given to young couples when they get married."

"I wish someone would have given me and Stuart a lovely quilt like that when we got married," Pam spoke up. A look of longing showed on her perfectly made-up face.

"Perhaps after you learn how to quilt, you can make one of your own," Emma said, as though to offer encouragement.

"That would be nice." Pam looked over at her husband. "Don't you think so, Stuart?"

"Uh-huh. Whatever," he mumbled, pulling one of the newer type smartphones out of his pocket.

"There seems to be a sense of unity in the balance and blending of the many parts and colors in your quilts," Ruby Lee interjected.

Emma nodded, peering at Ruby Lee over the top of her glasses. "I believe you're right about that. Also, quilting not only holds the layers of fabric together, but it's important for the design and appearance of the quilts."

Emma showed the class a few more quilts, including Weaver Fever, Ocean Waves, and one called Dahlia. "The Dahlia pattern has a three-dimensional effect from the gathered petals surrounding the center of each star-shaped flower," she went on to explain. "Since I have a love for flowers, Dahlia-patterned quilts are one of my favorites."

"That's the one I like," Ruby Lee said cheerfully, "because since we moved into our new home, I'm enjoying all the pretty flowers blooming in my yard this spring."

"I like flowers, too," Pam agreed, "but I still favor the Double Wedding Ring quilt."

"This one might fit you, Jan," Emma said, holding up a quilt made with both light and dark brown material, which she identified as the Log Cabin pattern. "Now this quilt is often made from various scraps. Its narrow, log-shaped pieces often vary in length, and smaller pieces of material can be used that aren't large enough for other patterns."

Jan shrugged his broad shoulders. "Well, I ain't much into campin', but I guess the house I live in could be considered my cabin."

"I like to camp," Stuart interjected. At least he was paying attention again.

Emma reached for another quilt. "This is called Tumbling Blocks, and it's also referred to as Baby Blocks. By using a single diamond shape, with varied placement of colors, the quilt creates an optical illusion of hexagons, cubes, stars, or diamonds." She motioned to the small quilt Paul had brought along. "My Tumbling Block pattern is similar to the quilt Paul's wife started for Sophia."

Paul's forehead wrinkled. "I'm still not sure I'll ever be able to finish that quilt."

"Don't worry about it for now," Emma said patiently. "You may feel differently once you learn how to quilt."

Star glanced at Stuart. He was back to fiddling with his phone. The guy was probably surfing the web or playing some game. She looked away, and her mind began to wander again as she continued to peruse her surroundings. Across the room sat an old treadle sewing machine. Star knew this because she'd seen one in an antique shop when she and Grandma had gone shopping during a visit to her home a few years before she'd become so ill. Grandma had been interested in antiques, and the strange-looking milk bottles on her kitchen counter were some of the old things she'd collected. An antiquated roll-top desk sat in the bedroom where Star slept. In the attic, she'd also seen several old pieces of furniture in dire need of repair, as well as a battered-looking trunk, which she hoped to go through someday.

When Stuart exhaled a noisy, deep breath, Star looked at him in disgust. Slouched in his chair with his eyes half closed, still holding his phone in one hand, he looked about as bored with all of this as she used to feel during high school math. The poor guy obviously did not want to be here. His wife, on the other hand, sitting straight in her chair with an expectant look, was no doubt eager to learn everything there was about quilting. The prissy little blond's makeup was perfectly done, as were her fingernails, painted with a pale lavender polish that matched her gauzy silk blouse.

I wonder if she paints her nails to match everything she wears, Star thought with disdain. *I can't figure out why some people have to look so perfect, while others don't seem to care how they look at all.* She glanced back at Stuart, noting a dark stain—probably from coffee—on his shirt. He and Pam sure didn't fit—at least not in the way they dressed. Emma and the others were okay, she guessed. At least they seemed more down-to-earth than Pam, although Star would have to wait until she'd spent more time with these people before drawing any real conclusions.

"Now that I've explained some of the history of quilts and shown you several of the designs I have here, I'll explain what we're going to do with the quilted wall hangings you'll be learning to make," Emma said. "I have lots of material you can choose from, and I think it would be good for everyone to use the same simple star pattern for your first project. Then hopefully, once you know the basics of quilting, you'll be able to make a larger quilt on your own. Or in Paul's case, he should be able to finish the baby quilt his wife started. Of course you may all use whatever color material you like, which will make each of your wall hangings a bit different and unique."

When Paul's baby started to fuss a bit, Star jerked her attention to him, noticing how attentive he was to the little girl, as he gently patted her back. It couldn't be easy for Paul, losing his wife and having to raise their child alone. Star hoped he would do a better job of it than Mom had done with her. A baby needed to know she was loved and that her needs came first, not the other way around.

During Star's childhood, she'd felt more like Mom was her big sister, rather than her mother. Mom sometimes seemed like a silly schoolgirl—especially when she was around one of her boyfriends. Maybe Mom's immaturity stemmed from the fact that she'd only been eighteen when Star was born, but by now she should have grown up and quit acting so self-centered.

Emma set aside the last quilt she'd shown them and had just risen from the rocking chair when a thumping noise drew everyone's attention to the window behind Emma. A white goat with its nose pressed against the glass stared in at them. *Ba-a-a-a! Ba-a-a-a!*

"Get away, Maggie! Go on now, shoo!" Emma tapped on the window and flapped her hands at the goat. When the critter didn't budge, Emma turned to the class, her cheeks turning red. "I'm sorry for that interruption. Maggie can be a real pest sometimes. She often gets out of her pen and causes all kinds of trouble. Even pulled some clothes off my line the other day, and then I had to rewash them."

"Want me to put her away for you?" Stuart asked, practically leaping out of his seat. "I'm a sportsman, and I know a lot about animals."

Emma looked a bit hesitant but nodded. "You can try if you like. My grandchildren next door helped me plant a small garden two weeks ago, and I would hate to see Maggie running through and ruining it."

"Sure, no problem. I'll put her right back in the pen." Stuart slapped his ball cap on his head and moved quickly across the room.

Pam followed and grabbed hold of his arm. "I don't think that's a good idea, Stuart."

"Why not?"

"Chasing after a goat isn't the same as shooting a deer. The animal might butt you."

Stuart pried Pam's fingers loose from his arm and adjusted his ball cap, which was slightly askew. "Duh! I'll just catch the critter and put her back in the pen."

"Be careful," Pam called as he sauntered out the door.

Star exchanged glances with the biker. Did he know what she was thinking?

Jan grinned tightly and gave her a wink.

Smothering a giggle, Star moved over to the window, eager to see how the know-it-all hunter would go about capturing the goat. Everyone else followed, including Emma, all jockeying for a position at the window.

As soon as Stuart stepped onto the porch, the goat leaped over the railing and darted across the yard. Stuart did the same.

I wonder what that guy's trying to prove, Star thought. *He could have just as easily taken the stairs.*

Star glanced back at Jan, who now stood beside her wearing a big grin. Like Star, he probably thought they were in for a pretty good show. Amused and a bit skeptical, she was eager to see what would happen next, although she kept her thoughts to herself.

As Stuart approached the four-legged creature, Maggie let out a loud *Ba-a-a-a!* and leaped onto the picnic table. Stuart leaned forward with his arms outstretched. He was almost touching the goat's neck when it jumped into the air, nearly hitting Stuart's head with one of its hooves. Fortunately, the ball cap took the brunt of the impact and flew into the air. After Maggie's feet hit the ground, she looked back at Stuart as if to say, "All right now. Catch me if you can!"

Red-faced and shaking his fist, Stuart scooped up his hat and raced across the grass in hot pursuit of the goat. Round and round the yard they went until Stuart made a sudden leap for the critter. It darted between Stuart's legs, and he ended up facedown on the ground, unfortunately in a puddle of water—no doubt from last night's rain.

Everyone but Pam started laughing; it really was a comical sight. Star thought it was worth coming here just to see that.

Pam gasped as the goat turned around and made a quick lunge for Stuart's ball cap. A few seconds later, Maggie was running across the yard with the cap in her mouth.

"I'm real sorry about this," Emma said, turning to Pam with an apologetic expression.

Pam slowly shook her head. "It's not your fault. My husband should never have gone out there thinking he could capture your goat."

"If someone will hold Sophia, I'll go out and see if I can help Stuart round up the goat," Paul said.

"I'll hold the baby." Jan eagerly spoke up before any of the women could respond.

"Why don't you let one of us hold the baby and you can go help the men catch the goat?" Pam suggested.

Jan shook his head. "I ain't in the mood to chase after some stupid goat that obviously don't wanna be caught." He glanced at Paul's little girl and smiled. "Besides, I'd much rather hold the baby."

Paul hesitated but then handed Sophia to Jan. As Paul went out the door, Jan took a seat in the rocker and began rocking the baby while gently patting her back.

Star vacillated between watching the burly biker speak in soft tones to the baby and Paul out in the yard helping Stuart chase after the goat. It seemed odd that Jan would rather be holding a baby than helping the men prove their valor, but something about seeing Jan's tender look as he held little Sophia touched a place in Star's heart. Growing up, no one other than Grandma had looked at her in such a gentle way.

Having never known her real father and being stuck with a jerk for a stepfather, she hadn't experienced what it was like to have loving parents. She supposed in her own way, Mom loved her, but she'd never expressed her love so that Star believed or felt it. Mom had always seemed to care more about meeting her own needs than she did Star's. If it hadn't been for Grandma, Star might never have known what it felt like to be loved at all. Maybe if Mom could have been at home more with Star, things might have been different. Then again, she doubted it.

After Mom married Wes, Star had thought that her mother's days of working as a waitress would be over, but the lazy bum never held a steady job, so Mom had been forced to continue working full-time in order to pay the bills. *I never liked that man,* Star thought bitterly. *He was abusive to Mom and treated me like I wasn't even there. He probably wished I wasn't so he could have Mom all to himself. The two years he lived with us were horrible, and I hope Mom never gets married again!*

"Well, would you look at that!" Ruby Lee shouted. "Paul almost has that ornery goat eating right out of his hand."

Star turned her gaze to the window again. Paul stood near the edge of the yard, holding several pieces of grass, and Maggie the goat was moving slowly toward him. When Maggie drew closer and took the grass in her mouth, Paul put his hands around the goat's neck and led her easily to the pen. Meanwhile, Stuart stood near the porch holding his battered-looking baseball cap and shaking his head. So much for the great white hunter!

When the men returned to the house, Emma, still chuckling a bit, apologized to Stuart for the rumpled cap. "I think maybe we all need a little break," she said. "Let me go to the kitchen and get some refreshments."

"I'll go with you," Ruby Lee said, quickly following Emma out of the room. Star figured their teacher probably needed a break as much as those in her class did right now. Hopefully after some refreshments, everyone would calm down and relax.

Jan seemed reluctant to give the baby back to Paul, but when Paul sniffed the air and said the baby's diapers needed to be changed, Jan scrunched up his nose and quickly handed Sophia to her father.

"Babies will be babies." Pam nudged her husband's arm. "Isn't that right, Stuart?"

"Huh?" He was fooling with his phone again.

"I said, 'Babies will be babies.'" Pam glared at him and pointed to the phone. "Would you please put that thing away? I suppose you're checking the scores on some stupid sporting event."

Stuart shrugged and put his phone back in his pocket. Star hadn't expected him to give in so easily. Was he always so compliant or merely trying to avoid a fight?

"So what do you do for fun?" Star asked, turning to Jan.

"I ride my Harley." He gave her a sheepish grin. "Well, I did before I lost my license."

"I've never ridden a motorcycle," she said.

"You oughta try it sometime. It's really a lot of fun." He frowned as he slowly shook his head. "Sure beats ridin' a beat-up bike that you have to pedal everywhere."

"Well then, maybe you ought to get one that's not so beat-up," Stuart interjected.

Star held her breath, waiting for Jan to make some wisecrack, but he just ignored the man. Didn't even glance his way. It was probably a good thing, because if he'd said something derogatory, the two men might have ended up going toe-to-toe again.

It would serve Stuart right if Jan punched him in the nose, Star thought. *He's got a big mouth and oughta know when to keep quiet. Maybe Mr. High and Mighty needs someone bigger than him to put him in his place.*

Paul returned from the bathroom, where he'd gone to change the baby, just as Emma and Ruby Lee entered the sewing room, bringing with them a plate full of peanut butter cookies, a pot of coffee, and a pitcher of iced tea. They also had cups, glasses, and napkins, which they set on the table. The atmosphere in the room seemed more relaxed after everyone had been given a treat.

Emma smiled at Paul and then Stuart. "I want to thank you both for rounding up my goat, which I'm sure saved my garden."

"No problem," Paul said.

"Yeah, I was happy to do it," Stuart added with a satisfied smile. Had he forgotten so quickly that the goat had gotten the best of him? Didn't he care that they'd all been laughing as they'd watched his antics from the window?

What a jerk, Star thought. *He's right up there with Mom's boyfriend, know-it-all Mike. Only I think Stuart likes to show off so he'll get attention.*

As they ate their refreshments, everyone shared a little more about themselves. Star was surprised to learn that Jan liked the same kind of music as she did, and that he was a self-taught harmonica player. Of course, she didn't think playing the harmonica was all that difficult. One of the geeks at the coffee shop in Goshen had a harmonica, and he'd told her once that it was really nothing more than knowing when to suck in air and when to blow it out.

When everyone had finished their cookies and drinks, Emma showed the class how to use a template and begin marking the design on the fabric, using dressmaker's chalk or a pencil.

"When you're done marking, you'll need to cut out the pattern pieces," Emma said. "In the next step, which is called 'piecing,' the pieces you've cut will be sewn together, and then onto the quilt top, which will also need to be cut," she continued. "Now, the pattern pieces are usually pieced onto the quilt top by machine. Then the backing, the batting, and the quilt top are layered, put into a frame, and quilted. When that is done, the binding will be put on, and the project will be finished."

Stuart, still obviously disinterested in the whole process, leaned back in his chair, which he'd positioned near the wall. With his arms behind his head, he closed his eyes and dozed off. Star was sure he was sleeping, because she heard soft snores coming from his side of the table.

That guy shouldn't even be here, she thought. *He oughta be home taking a nap or doin' whatever he does to occupy his time. He's probably one of those geeks who likes to sit around watching some game on TV and doesn't help his wife at all.*

"Wake up!" Pam bumped Stuart's arm, jolting him awake so he nearly fell out of his chair. "We didn't come here so you could sleep."

"I can't help it. Chasing that stupid goat wore me out." His face still shone with the sweat of his exertion.

Pam wrinkled her nose. "You shouldn't have gone out there then. All you succeeded in doing was getting your ball cap nearly ruined and your jeans wet and dirty. Oh, and by the way, you'd better give me your handkerchief so I can wipe those smudges off your face. I can't believe you didn't wash up before you ate Emma's cookies."

Like an obedient little boy, Stuart reached into his jeans pocket and handed her his hanky, but he didn't look the least bit happy about it. Star almost felt sorry for the poor sap. Of course, if Stuart had stood up to Pam and put her in her place, they'd have probably had a blowup.

Star's forehead wrinkled as she frowned. All married couples seemed to do was fight—just one more reason she was never getting married. It wasn't worth the pain and disappointment.

"Hey, Stuart, I want to thank you for givin' us all such a good laugh," Jan said with a smirk. "You were quite entertaining with that goat out there in the yard. In fact, you looked downright silly."

"Well, no thanks to you! At least Paul was man enough to help out."

Stuart stood and took a step toward Jan. "You chose to sit in here with the women and a baby in your arms. So you shouldn't be laughing at me."

Jan stood, too, and moved toward Stuart until they were almost nose to nose. "So you think me sittin' in the house holdin' Paul's baby is funny, do ya?"

"Well, since you asked. . ."

Jan bristled. "Hey, I'm talkin' here, and I wasn't done, so kindly don't interrupt!"

"You're totally out there, you know that?"

"Oh, you should talk. You know why guys like you have to prove their manhood?" Jan's eyes narrowed as he pointed at Stuart. "Because you're afraid."

"Oh yeah, right," Stuart said gruffly, shifting his stance. Then he drew his shoulders back and stood to his full height, which Star figured probably wasn't more than five feet ten. "For your information, Mr. Tattoo Man, I'm not afraid of anything."

Jan's face reddened, and he took another step toward Stuart. Like the ferocious-looking black panther on his arm, Jan looked ready to attack. "Why, I oughta—"

"What are you gonna do—sit on me?"

"If that's what it takes to shut you up."

Emma's eyes widened; Pam's mouth dropped open, as did Paul's. Ruby Lee folded her hands as though praying, and Star just sat there shaking her head. Men could be so juvenile sometimes—always having to prove how tough they were. Well, if she had to choose sides, she'd go with the biker. The baseball-cap geek acted like a big know-it-all. He probably thought he was smarter and better than Jan. At least Jan seemed real and down-to-earth. He'd proven that when he'd spilled his guts about driving under the influence and doing time in jail. It was doubtful that Stuart ever had so much as a speeding ticket, and even if he had, he'd probably never admit it.

Star leaned forward, waiting to see who would land the first blow, but before either man could raise a hand, Ruby Lee left her seat and stepped between them. "I think you both should calm down. We came here to learn about quilting, not watch the two of you act like a couple of silly schoolboys trying to one-up each other."

The men, both red-faced, stood a few more seconds looking peeved, but finally returned to their seats.

Emma, talking fast and appearing to be quite shaken, began explaining more of the things they'd be learning over the next several weeks. Everyone listened, and thankfully there were no more nasty comments from either Stuart or Jan. Star really felt sorry for poor Emma.

I'll bet she never expected anything like this would happen during her quilt class.

By the time class was over, Emma had given each person some material and a template for their star-shaped pattern, along with instructions on how during the week they should mark, cut, and pin the pieces together.

Everyone told Emma good-bye, and as they headed out the door, Jan looked over at Paul and said, "You're a lucky man to have such a cute baby."

Paul smiled and nodded. "Yes, I feel very blessed."

Star glanced at Stuart and Pam, who were arguing again about the goat escapade as they headed to their car. *I'll bet that man's wishing he didn't have to come back here again. Maybe he's wondering what sort of excuse he can make up to get out of learning how to quilt. It'll be interesting to see whether he shows up for the class next week. Bet he doesn't. Bet prissy Pam comes alone.*

CHAPTER 7

"I can't believe you," Pam said through tight lips.

"What's that supposed to mean?" Stuart asked as he directed his SUV onto the highway.

"The way you acted during the quilt class was absolutely inexcusable!" She narrowed her eyes as she stared at him, hoping he'd realize how angry she was. "Emma Yoder seems like a very nice lady, but after today, she's probably wondering why she ever agreed to teach us quilting."

"If you're talking about the goat escapade, I was only trying to help. It wasn't my fault that crazy critter thought my baseball cap would make a great morning snack. Besides, if you'll recall, Emma thanked me for helping out."

"I wasn't just talking about the goat or your stupid cap. I was mostly referring to the fact that throughout the entire class you were either nodding off or saying something rude."

His thick eyebrows furrowed. "What are you talking about, Pam?

I never said anything rude."

"You most certainly did."

"Such as?"

"For one thing, the way you talked to the biker was terrible. When he introduced himself, it wasn't right to make fun of his name. Why did you have to insult him like that?"

Stuart gave a nonchalant shrug. "Well, what can I say? Jan's a dumb name for a guy. Besides, he had it coming, the way he was ribbing me about how I chased after the goat."

"When you made an issue of his name, you had no way of knowing he was going to say anything to you about the goat. And even if you think Jan's name is dumb, you didn't have to make a big deal about it and say it sounded like a girly girl's name." Pam gripped the straps of her purse tightly, trying to keep her emotions under control. "Then getting on his case about staying in the house with the women while you were trying to round up the goat made things even worse. In fact, the way you acted today made you no better than him."

"I was only stating the obvious. Do you have a problem with it?"

"As a matter of fact, I do."

"Yeah, well, I wasn't gonna let some tattooed bully push me around."

"Jan hardly seems like a bully. I think he was just defending his pride."

"Oh, and I wasn't?"

She sighed. "You're impossible, Stuart."

"Give me a break. I'm no more impossible than you." He glanced over at Pam and frowned. "I can't believe you'd expect me to learn how to quilt or sit in that boring class with a bunch of weird people."

"They're not weird; they're just different. And you need to get over your prejudices."

"I'm not prejudiced."

"Whatever you say." Pam knew she should stop right there, but she couldn't. "So, let me ask you something, Stuart. How does it feel to be Mr. Right twenty-four hours a day?"

He stared straight ahead. "I think we should find something else to do together. Something other than quilting."

"Like what?"

"I don't know. Anything that doesn't involve sitting in some dimly lit room, listening to an Amish woman bore us about the history of quilts. I'm surprised everyone wasn't sleeping."

"Emma was only giving us some background on quilting so we'd have a better idea of what makes up the different quilt patterns. We've got homework to do this week, and next Saturday she'll be teaching us the next step involved in making our wall hangings, so I'm sure the class will be more interesting."

"For you, maybe," he mumbled. "Wish now I'd never taken you fishing!"

"You know what?" Pam shot back. "That's one thing I can agree with you about. I wish you'd never taken me fishing either!"

Soon after her quilting students left, Emma went to the kitchen to fix some lunch. The morning hadn't gone at all the way she'd planned, and she couldn't get the thought out of her mind that God had sent her some very unusual people to teach.

Am I really up to the task? Emma asked herself as she removed a loaf of whole-wheat bread from the bread box. *Is there more than quilting I should teach these people?* With the exception of Ruby Lee, who'd appeared to be fairly bright and cheerful, the others in the class seemed to have some serious issues they were dealing with. She was concerned about Star and

Paul because they'd both recently lost a family member, although, from what Emma could tell, Paul seemed to be dealing with his wife's death fairly well. Perhaps he'd found comfort in his baby girl, and maybe he had a strong faith in God. When he'd leaned forward to pick up a toy the baby had dropped, Emma had noticed a silver chain with a cross around his neck. She figured he probably wore it as an indication of his religious beliefs.

Star, on the other hand, had been dressed almost completely in black. Was it because she was mourning her grandmother's death, or did she just prefer to dress that way? With the exception of the goat incident, when nearly everyone had been laughing, Emma hadn't seen Star laugh or smile during the two-hour class.

Emma paused to chuckle, thinking how funny Stuart had looked, running around the yard chasing Maggie after she'd grabbed hold of his hat. For Pam's sake, Emma had tried not to laugh, but with everyone else laughing as they watched out the window, she just couldn't help herself.

"A day without smiling is a wasted day," Emma murmured as she took a can of tuna fish from the pantry. That used to be one of Ivan's favorite sayings, and he'd lived up to it by looking on the brighter side of life and having a cheerful smile and a good sense of humor. Emma tried to be cheerful, too—especially since Ivan died. Laughter was good medicine for the soul, and looking for things to be joyful about had helped Emma through the worst of her grief.

Turning her thoughts to Star again, Emma wondered if the somber young woman might be angry with someone. Or perhaps she was just unsure of herself. Whatever the reason, Emma hated to see Star or anyone else look so sad.

It touched Emma's heart to know that Star had come here because her grandmother had wanted her to learn how to quilt as a remembrance of her.

Emma knew all about things that made a person remember a loved one. She thought about Ivan and how he'd died a few weeks before her sixty-fifth birthday. He'd made something special for Emma—a finely crafted quilt rack, which she'd found three days after her birthday, hidden in the barn behind a stack of hay. Ivan had attached a note to the gift, telling Emma how much he loved her. The love and respect she and Ivan had felt for each other would always be with her, and every time she looked at the quilt rack he'd made, she would think of him fondly.

Knowing she needed to finish making her lunch, Emma removed a jar of mayonnaise from her propane-operated refrigerator, letting her thoughts go to the muscular man with the black leather vest and tattoos who'd come to her class to learn how to quilt. With the exception of his encounters with Stuart, Jan had seemed nice enough. And he'd certainly looked content when he'd held Paul's baby. However, Emma had a feeling the man with the girl's name had a painful and perhaps shameful past.

Then there was the married couple, Stuart and Pam. Not once during the morning had they said a nice word to each other. Stuart seemed to have a need to prove his manhood, and he'd obviously been bored and probably felt forced to come to the class.

I wish Stuart could have met my Ivan and heard how kindly he spoke to me. Emma grimaced. *Of course, Pam wasn't very kind to Stuart either. Those disgusted looks she gave him, not to mention her unkind words, makes me wonder if she loves her husband at all.*

Perhaps after a few weeks of getting to know each of her students, Emma could get them to open up and share what was on their hearts. If she knew more about these people, she would know what things from her own life she could share that might help them, too.

With her sandwich made, Emma took a seat at the table and bowed her head. *Dear Lord,* she silently prayed, *if I'm supposed to do more than just teach this group of people how to quilt, then please give me wisdom, a sensitive heart, and of course, Your direction.*

The back door opened, and Mary stepped into the room just as Emma finished her prayer.

"*Wie geht's?*" Mary asked.

"I'm a little tired but otherwise fine."

"How'd the class go?"

Emma motioned to the chair beside her. "If you'd like to take a seat while I eat my sandwich, I'll tell you about it. And you're welcome to join me. I can make another sandwich for you."

"No, you go ahead. I had a bowl of soup before I came over here." Mary pulled out a chair and sat down. "So how'd it go with the class? Were you able to teach that. . .uh. . .rather unusual group anything today?"

"I'll admit I was taken aback when I saw the people who'd come to my class. From the phone calls I'd received, I'd really thought I would be teaching all women."

"And I bet you didn't expect one of them to be dressed all in black with a ring in her nose."

"No, I sure didn't."

"When I answered the door for you this morning, I was more than a little surprised by the group waiting on your porch."

Emma took a bite of her sandwich and sipped some water. "I was, too. And I certainly never expected someone like Jan Sweet to join the class."

Mary tipped her head. "Jan Sweet?"

"Jah. He was the big, tall, muscular man dressed in biker clothes."

"Oh, so his name is Jan?"

Emma nodded. "One of the other men, Stuart, teased Jan about his name. Said it was a girly girl's name, and Jan didn't take that too well."

Mary's eyes widened. "What happened?"

"Jan pretty much told Stuart to keep his opinions to himself." Emma frowned. "For a minute there, I was afraid Jan might hit Stuart or something."

With a worried frown, Mary placed her hand on Emma's arm. "*Ach,* Mom. Do you really think you ought to be teaching these people? I mean, what if—"

Emma held up her hand. "As you well know, God made everyone, and we're all uniquely different."

"Jah, some more than others." The worry lines in Mary's forehead deepened.

Emma chuckled. "Be that as it may, God cares for them just as much as He does you and me. I'm sure that He looks beyond what people are to who they can become, and I have a feeling way down deep in my heart that God brought the people who came here today for more than just learning to quilt."

"What other reason could there be?"

Emma took another drink of water and blotted her lips with a napkin. "Well, after just one meeting, I could sense that most of them are dealing with some kind of a painful or distressing issue. And with God's help and His words of wisdom, I hope I'll be able to say or do something that might help them all spiritually or emotionally, in addition to teaching them how to quilt."

Mary's face relaxed a bit. "One thing I do know is that you have been blessed with the ability to sense when people are hurting. You proved that many times during my childhood, and especially during my teen years when I had a problem and didn't share it until you wormed it right out of me."

Emma grinned. "Well, I hope I won't have to worm anything out of my students, but I would ask you to pray that the Lord will give me insight and wisdom in knowing what to say and when to say it."

Mary nodded. "I'll be praying for you, as well as your students."

CHAPTER 8

For the last three days, Jan and Terry had been roofing a house in LaGrange, and by the time Jan got home from work each evening, he was too tired to do anything but fix a quick bite of supper, play a few tunes on his harmonica, and fall into bed. The roof on the house in LaGrange had been steep, and he was glad to have it done. Every muscle in his legs seemed to hurt from the energy it took to keep his balance on that high-pitched roof.

But Thursday morning it was raining too hard to begin his next job in Middlebury, so Jan was at home, just him and his dog, Brutus. He'd acquired the black and tan German shepherd two years ago when it was a pup. Brutus had proved to be a good companion, although due to Jan's busy work schedule during the warmer months, he didn't spend much time with the dog.

A roll of thunder sounded in the distance as Jan poured himself a cup of coffee and took a seat at the kitchen table. Brutus, sleeping peacefully under the table, didn't budge; he just began to snore.

Jan decided that today would be a good opportunity for him to begin working on his quilting project. With Saturday only two days away, he wanted to be sure he'd done his homework as Emma had instructed. What she'd asked them to do seemed easy enough, so he was sure he could get it done quickly. He figured once he finished the wall hanging, he might try to make a full-sized quilt. He could donate it to one of the local benefit auctions. There always seemed to be plenty of those going on in the area, since that's how many of the Amish raised money to help with medical expenses. One thing for sure: Jan couldn't wait to tell his probation officer when he saw her next week that he'd found something creative to do.

He thought about Emma and smiled. Through his job and living in Shipshewana, he'd met other Amish people, but he hadn't gotten to know any of them very well. Emma Yoder seemed like the type of person who easily made friends, and her patience with those in the class last Saturday made him think she was easygoing and accepting of others.

Emma kinda reminds me of Mom, God rest her soul, Jan thought as he gulped down his lukewarm coffee and headed to the living room to get the material he needed. *She's even got that same perky smile and soft way of speaking Mom had. Wish I could say the same for my dad.*

Jan's mother had died from a brain tumor when he was seventeen. A year later, his dad split for parts unknown, never to return. Jan was an only child, and since he had no intention of living with his drunken uncle, Al, he lit out on his own, doing whatever odd jobs he could find and living in the back of his beat-up van. Jan ended up in Chicago for a time, where he'd bought a motorcycle, joined a club, and met the girl he thought he would marry. When things went sour, he stuck around for a while but finally moved on, doing everything from slinging hash at a diner in Sturgis, South Dakota, to boring factory work in Springfield, Missouri. Several years later, while living in Grand Rapids, Michigan, Jan learned the roofing trade under the guidance of a motorcycle buddy who had his own business. After a few years, Jan became restless, so he moved on and eventually ended up in Shipshewana, where he'd opened his own business. It was the first time he'd stayed in one place for more than a year, and since he really liked it in this quiet, quaint little town, he felt sure he would stay.

Jerking his thoughts back to the present, Jan was about to grab his sack of material when someone knocked on the front door.

"Now I wonder who that could be," Jan mumbled, ambling across the room. With the rain coming down as hard as it was, he couldn't imagine anyone being out in this weather. He could hear the rain from inside as it pelted his roof.

When Jan opened the door, he was surprised to see Selma Nash, the elderly woman who lived in the house next door, standing on his porch. She held a black umbrella in one hand, but it hadn't done much to protect her clothes, because the skirt of her dress and sleeves on her light-weight jacket were wet.

" 'Mornin', Selma. What brings you to my door on this rainy spring day?" he asked, offering her a smile and hoping it would wipe away the deep frown that graced her wrinkled face. "Is everything okay?"

Selma's frown deepened. "No, young man, everything's not okay."

"No?"

She shook her head.

"What's wrong?"

"I'm getting sick and tired of your dog tearing up my flower beds. If you don't do something about it, I'm going to call animal control and have that mutt hauled off to the pound!"

Jan's eyebrows shot up. "Brutus is here in the house with me. Fact is, he's sleepin' under the kitchen table right now, so I don't see how he can be diggin' in your flower beds."

Selma lowered her umbrella and gave it a little shake. "Now don't you play games with me, Mr. Sweet. I know the mess Brutus made wasn't done just now. He did it yesterday while you were at work."

"How do you know it was my dog and not someone else's?" Jan questioned. "There's several other dogs in this here neighborhood, you know."

"Humph! I know it was Brutus."

"How can you be so sure? Did you actually see him diggin' up the flowers?"

"No, but I saw him wandering around my yard soon after you left for work, and it wasn't long after that when I noticed that my flower beds had been torn up." She shook the umbrella a little harder this time, sending a spray of water in Jan's direction.

He stepped back, but not before getting hit in the face with a few drops of liquid sunshine. "I ain't believin' that my Brutus tore up your flower beds, but I'll do my best to keep my eye on him from here on out."

She pursed her lips and tipped her head back as she stared up at him, her milky blue eyes narrowing into tiny slits. "And just how are you planning to do that? With you working all day, that mangy mutt of yours is free to do whatever he wants. You know, there are laws about controlling your pets."

Jan couldn't argue with any of that. When he put Brutus outside every morning, he had no idea what the dog was up to all day. But he didn't think Brutus wandered very far, because when he arrived home from work, the dog was usually lying on the front porch waiting for him. Since the house he'd bought a few years ago was in the country and on nearly an acre of land, Jan had never felt the need to chain the dog up or build him a pen. Now, with Brutus being under suspicion with the neighbor, Jan figured he'd better do something about the situation. He sure didn't want the old lady calling animal control and having Brutus hauled off to the pound.

"I'll tell you what," he said, smiling at Selma. "I'll build Brutus a dog pen just as soon as I find the time. Until then, I'll keep him in the garage when I'm gone. Is that okay with you?"

"Yes, I suppose that will keep him from digging up my flowers again, but what about the pansies he's already ruined? Are you going to buy me some new ones?"

Jan hated to shell out money for flowers he wasn't sure his dog had wrecked, but he didn't want to rile the old lady anymore than she already was. So rather than argue about it, he reached into his jeans' pocket and pulled out a twenty-dollar bill. "Think this'll cover the cost of some new posies?"

She gave a quick nod. "It was pansies your dog destroyed, Mr. Sweet, and you'd better see that it doesn't happen again."

"No, it sure won't."

Selma lifted the umbrella over her head and hurried away, muttering something under her breath about wishing she had a better neighbor— someone without a dog.

When Jan returned to the living room, now out of the mood to work on the wall hanging, he spotted Brutus lying on the sofa. "Mrs. Nash would probably pitch a fit if she knew I allowed you to be on the furniture." Jan plopped down beside Brutus and reached out to stroke the dog's silky ears. "Lucky for you I didn't invite her in."

Brutus grunted and nuzzled Jan's hand with his wet nose. Jan was glad for the loyalty of the dog, because he knew some people couldn't be trusted. With the exception of his biker buddies, Jan didn't allow himself to get close to many people—especially women. He hadn't lived forty years without learning a few things about the opposite sex. He'd been burned once by a cute little thing who'd promised to love him forever, and he'd vowed sometime ago that he'd never let it happen again.

Deciding to watch TV for a while, he reached for the remote under his sleeping dog's paw. As he did, he looked closer and noticed some dirt caked on the pads of Brutus's front feet.

"Brutus, was that you diggin' up the flower beds next door?"

Oblivious to the words of his master, Brutus started making muffled barking noises as he continued to sleep.

Jan smiled to himself as he watched the dog, still dreaming and now making digging motions with his two front feet. How comical it looked with those paws moving while his muzzle quivered as if he was trying to bark. All Jan could do was chuckle as he thought, *Think I'd better get that dog pen built as soon as I can.*

Goshen

Ruby Lee stepped into the sanctuary to practice the songs she'd picked out for Sunday. A knot formed in her stomach. It was hard to believe she and Gene had been here for ten years already. It was also difficult to believe that the joy they'd felt when Gene had been asked to take this church was now far removed. At least for Ruby Lee. Gene went about his ministerial duties, acting as though nothing was wrong, but she was sure that deep inside he was hurting—probably more than her, truth be told. She'd seen her husband's pained expression when he'd come home from the last few board meetings. She'd heard his concern when he talked about the future of their church. If she only knew of something that might make things better. If she could just take away the pain and frustration tugging at her and Gene's hearts.

Ruby Lee knew she should go to the altar and leave her burdens there, but she didn't feel like praying today. Oh, she'd brought this problem to the Lord many times already. Nothing had changed, and it was beginning to affect her ability to minister to others. She felt as if her faith was being tested and wondered if an end was in sight.

With a sigh of resignation, Ruby Lee took a seat at the piano and opened the hymnbook. Besides the lively choruses they sang every Sunday to open the worship service, they always did a few traditional hymns. Ruby Lee's favorite was "Rock of Ages," one of the songs she'd decided to play this Sunday.

" 'Rock of ages,'" she sang as she played along, " 'cleft for me. Let me hide myself in thee.'"

She certainly felt like hiding these days—hiding from the church people—hiding from her friends—and yes, even hiding from God. With the problems the church had been having, her faith in those who called themselves Christians had begun to dwindle little by little, week by week. But she couldn't let on. She had to keep her chin high and put a smile on her face so no one would know about the deep ache in her heart. After all, she was the pastor's wife, and it was her duty to set a good example to others. It wouldn't be right to let anyone in the congregation know how truly miserable she felt. It might jeopardize Gene's ministry.

As Ruby Lee's fingers glided easily over the piano keys, she continued to play the rest of the song. No longer able to sing, her thoughts went to the quilting class she'd attended last Saturday. Emma Yoder seemed like such a pleasant, patient person. The kind she could easily make her friend.

In two days she would be going to Emma's house for another lesson, and Ruby Lee wondered how things would go. *Too bad I'm not Emma's only student,* she thought wistfully. *It would be easier to learn quilting if the others weren't there, asking so many unnecessary questions and making catty remarks, the way Stuart Johnston did last week.*

It didn't take a genius to see that Pam and Stuart's marriage was strained—maybe even in deep trouble. During Gene's years of preaching, he'd counseled many couples with marriage problems. Some listened to his advice, and others continued down the same old path that had brought them to his office for counseling. A good marriage took commitment and a desire to meet the needs of one's spouse. When selfishness and always wanting to have one's own way took over, it spelled trouble. And from what Ruby Lee had seen during the quilt class, both Pam and Stuart had issues they were dealing with—issues that had affected their marriage.

Then there was the young woman who called herself Star. From the way she talked, and her whole demeanor, it had been obvious to Ruby Lee that Star had a chip on her shoulder and probably needed to let her defenses down. Ruby Lee wondered why Star had worn a black sweatshirt with the hood up on her head the whole time they'd been in class. Was she trying to make some kind of statement, hiding something under that hood? Or could the defiant young woman be one of those "gothic" people Ruby Lee had seen around town? Star was a pretty girl, so why she would hide her natural beauty was a bit baffling to Ruby Lee. Perhaps Star needed some counseling, too.

The biker with the big biceps probably had a few issues as well. But with the exception of his encounter with Stuart, Jan had seemed fairly easygoing. And even though Jan looked like the type who might punch someone in the nose if they looked at him the wrong way, Ruby Lee had a hunch that he was a really just a big ole softy with a heart of gold.

The young Hispanic schoolteacher who'd recently lost his wife seemed fairly stable, yet Ruby Lee figured he must still be hurting pretty bad. Who wouldn't hurt if they'd lost their spouse and been left with a baby to raise? It was a shame that Paul's little girl would grow up never knowing her mother.

I should be very kind to these people, she thought. *I'm a pastor's wife, and it's my duty to set a good example to others. But how can I do that when I feel so angry and depressed myself?*

Ruby Lee leaned forward, resting her forehead on the piano keys. *If You will, God, please give me a sense of peace.*

As Star left the Goshen Walmart after working the early-morning shift where she stocked shelves, she frowned. It was raining hard, and by the time she reached her car, she was soaking wet.

Well, let it rain, she thought. *I have no place but home to go today anyway.* Still, she didn't care for this drenching wet weather. It was depressing, and when it rained, she didn't like being cooped up inside.

Star thought she might spend the rest of the day cutting out the pieces for the star pattern that would be in the center of her wall hanging. After that was done, she hoped to get some more lyrics written on the song she'd started a few weeks ago. Maybe someday she would find a way to get some of her music published. Maybe someday her musical abilities would be recognized. But for now, she'd have to be content with playing her guitar and singing her songs at the coffee shop in downtown Goshen on Friday nights. Some of the kids from the local college hung out there, and a few performed on the little stage; although no one but Star sang original songs.

Who knows? Star thought as she started her car's engine and pulled out of the parking lot. *Maybe the right person will be sitting in the coffee shop some night, and I'll get discovered.*

She let go of the steering wheel with one hand and slapped the side of her head. *Dumb. Stupid. Like that's ever gonna happen. I'm just a nobody who no one cares about. It's just like Mom always says: I'm full of big ideas that will never come true. And now that Grandma's gone, I'll probably never find anyone who truly loves me for the person I am. I'll always be lost—like a falling star that nobody ever noticed.*

Some new words to one of the songs she'd been working on popped into Star's head, and she began to sing in a whispered tone: "It's hard to breathe; it's hard to sleep; it's hard to know who you are when you're a lost and falling star."

CHAPTER 9

Mishawaka, Indiana

I'm ready to work on my quilt project now," Pam called to Stuart, who sat on the sofa in the family room watching TV with his feet propped on the coffee table.

No reply.

"Stuart, are you listening to me?"

Still no response.

Pam pushed her son's toy truck out of the way with her foot and stepped in front of the TV.

"Hey! You're blocking my view." Stuart gave Pam a determined, angry look and waved her away.

She stood firm, both hands on her hips. "It's the only way I can get your attention."

"What do you want?" He peered around her to look at the TV.

She moved to the right so his view was still blocked. "I said I'm ready to work on my quilting project now."

"That's nice. Would you please move out of my way?"

Pointing a finger in his direction, Pam felt her face heat. "The next quilt class is only two days away, and you promised we could work on our wall hangings together this evening."

Stuart shook his head. "I never promised anything of the sort. You said you wanted to work on your quilt project, and I said that was fine with me." He pointed to the TV. "I'm watching a baseball game. At least I was until you interrupted me."

Pam's irritation mounted. "If you don't work on your project tonight, you won't have the first phase of your wall hanging done before Saturday."

"I'll work on it tomorrow night."

"Tomorrow's Devin's piano recital, and afterwards, we're taking the kids out for ice cream. Remember?"

"Oh yeah, that's right. Okay then, I'll work on the stupid wall hanging Saturday morning—before we head to Shipshewana." He yawned and stretched his arms over his head. "Or maybe I won't work on it at all. Maybe I won't even go this week. I might sleep in on Saturday."

She narrowed her eyes. "You'd better not go back on your word."

He leaned to the left, craning his neck to see the TV again. "Oh, great! I missed that last play, and now the other team is up to bat."

Pam gritted her teeth. "Why is it that baseball is more important than me?"

"It's not."

"Yes it is. If it wasn't, you'd turn off the TV, come into the dining room, and cut out the material for your star pattern. We can visit while we cut and pin the pieces in place."

Stuart's face tightened and tiny wrinkles formed across his forehead. "Look, Pam, when you went fishing with me, you didn't have to do anything before we went."

"And your point is?"

"I didn't expect you to dig worms for bait or even get the fishing gear out of the closet. I did all those things for you. All you had to do was sit in the boat and fish."

Her irritation increased. "Are you saying you think I should work on my quilt project and yours, too?"

A smile played at the corners of his mouth. "That'd be nice."

"Oh sure! Then you can just show up at Emma's on Saturday with a big smile on your face and let everyone think you'd done what she asked."

He shrugged.

"If you don't want to do your homework, that's up to you, but don't expect me to do it for you!" Pam turned on her heels and stomped out of the room. She didn't think any amount of counseling or doing things together would save their marriage. They were heading down a one-way street, and unless a miracle transpired, she feared their journey might end in divorce.

Elkhart

"Could this week get any worse?" Paul grumbled while his daughter fussed in her playpen. A parent/teacher conference one night and a meeting with the school principal the next evening was just too much for one week. Both times Paul had asked Carla, a teenager from church, to watch Sophia. Carla seemed capable enough, but both evenings when he'd arrived home, Sophia had been sobbing. It was bad enough that he had to drop his little girl off at the day care center every morning before school. He wished he didn't have to leave her with a sitter whenever he had to be away during the evening. He wished, too, that his sister, Maria, could watch Sophia all the time, but with her part-time job at the bank, plus caring for her three active girls, that just wasn't possible. On the days Paul took Sophia to day care, she still cried as soon as he pulled up in front of the building. It nearly broke his heart when she reached her little arms out, as though begging him to stay.

Paul hoped Maria could watch Sophia on the remaining Saturdays he'd be attending the quilt classes so he wouldn't have to take her along, like he'd done last week, or worse yet, leave her with a sitter she didn't know. Even though Sophia had been good during the two hours they were at Emma's, it had been hard for Paul to concentrate on all that Emma had been trying to teach them. It was important for him to learn some quilting techniques, since he'd decided that he would definitely try to finish the quilt for Sophia, and he hoped by doing so it might bring him some closure.

Tonight, Paul was thankful to be home, but he had some papers to grade. Sophia was in the dining room with him, but she wasn't happy being in the playpen rather than on her daddy's lap, like she was accustomed to doing most evenings. Still, it was better than having someone else watch her.

"Oh Lorinda," Paul whispered, rubbing a sore spot on his forehead. "How I wish you were here with me right now, holding our precious baby daughter."

Shipshewana

Emma had just taken a seat in front of her treadle sewing machine when she heard the back door swing open. A few seconds later, her eight-year-old granddaughter, Lisa, skipped into the room.

"*Daadi* built a bonfire out back, and we're gonna roast hot dogs and marshmallows soon," the blond-haired, blue-eyed little girl announced. "Would you like to come over and eat with us, *Grossmammi?*"

Emma smiled and gave Lisa a hug. "I appreciate the offer, but I've already had my supper."

"Then come for some marshmallows." Lisa grinned up at Emma and smacked her lips. "They taste *wunderbaar gut*."

"I think marshmallows are wonderful good, too, but I'm busy sewing right now. Maybe some other time when your daed builds a bonfire I can join you," Emma said.

Lisa's lower lip protruded in a pout. Emma hated to disappoint the child, but if she didn't get the piecing done on this quilt, she'd never have it finished in time for the benefit auction that would be held in a few months. She also hadn't quite completed the quilt for the fall wedding she would attend. Still, she didn't want to pass up an opportunity to be with some of her family.

She patted her granddaughter's arm. "I'll be over later on, after I get some sewing done. How's that sound?"

A wide smile stretched across Lisa's face. "Sew real fast, grossmammi!"

Emma smiled as the rosy-cheeked little girl scampered out of the room. It was nice living so close to Mary and her family. Not only could they be there whenever she had a need, but almost always someone was at home next door for Emma to visit when she felt lonely. Other times, especially during the warmer months when her windows were open, it was nice just hearing her grandchildren on the other side of the fence, laughing and playing in their yard. It made her feel connected to them.

For the next hour, Emma worked on the quilt. As she sewed, she thought about her upcoming quilt class. She hoped it would go better than last week's had, and that everyone would take an active interest in the things she planned to teach. Last Saturday, when Stuart had fallen asleep, she'd been worried that he might be bored or hadn't understood what she'd been trying to explain. Even though Emma knew a lot about quilting, she wasn't sure she'd presented the information clearly or interestingly enough. She would make sure to go a little slower this week and not let her nerves take over. And hopefully there would be no interruptions, like Maggie getting out of her pen, or Stuart and Jan exchanging heated words and nearly getting into a fight. Emma had found that most unsettling.

Emma's thoughts came to a halt when she heard the wail of a siren, which seemed to be drawing closer all the time. When she saw red lights flashing through the window and realized they were coming up the driveway that separated her home from Mary's, she became very concerned.

She sniffed the air. *Is that smoke I smell?*

Hurrying to the window, Emma gasped as two fire trucks pulled in. Moving to the side window, she noticed smoke and flames coming from the shed where her son-in-law kept their wood and gardening tools. The shed wasn't far from the barn, and Emma feared that if they didn't get the fire out soon, the barn might also catch on fire.

With a quick yet fervent prayer for everyone's safety, Emma rushed out the back door as the sound of crackling wood reached her ears.

CHAPTER 10

Goshen

Star had just sat down at the kitchen table to cut out her pattern pieces when Mom entered the room.

"I just looked over the movie schedule," Mom said, holding the newspaper out to Star. "That new romantic comedy we've seen advertised on TV is playing at Linway Cinema 14. Would you like to go?"

Star shook her head. "No, I'm good. I'm just gonna hang out here tonight."

"Doing what?"

"I'll be busy cutting out the pattern pieces that will make up my wall hanging. Gotta have this first part done before Saturday." She pointed to the black-and-gold material she'd chosen.

Mom's eyebrows drew together as she frowned. "I still think it's a dumb idea for you to waste your time on that quilt class."

Star gritted her teeth. *Not this again. So much for trying to impress Mom with something I'm doing.* "Grandma wanted me to go, or she wouldn't have reserved a spot for me."

Mom looked at Star like she still didn't get it.

"I miss Grandma, and taking the class so I can learn how to quilt makes me feel closer to her," Star said.

"You can miss her all you want, but I'm the only parent you have, and you ought to appreciate me and be willing to spend some time together when we have the chance."

"I'd spend more time with you if we liked more of the same things." What Star really wanted to say was, *"Yeah, like all the time you spent with me when I was growing up?"* But she couldn't get the spiteful words out of her mouth.

"What kind of things are you talking about?" Mom asked.

Star placed her scissors on the table and looked up at Mom. "I like to play the guitar, sing, and write songs, and you don't like music at all," she said, trying to sound nonchalant. One thing she didn't need this evening was a blowup with Mom. They had those too often as it was.

"That's not true. I just don't care for the kind of music you sing and play."

Star's defenses began to rise, despite her resolve to keep things calm. "And just what do you think's wrong with my music?"

"It's slow and the lyrics you write are depressing."

"Maybe that's because I feel depressed a lot of the time."

Mom folded her arms and glared at Star. "You have nothing more to be depressed about than I do, but I don't go around singing doom and gloom."

Star clenched her piece of material so tightly that her knuckles turned white. "It's not doom and gloom. I'm just expressing the way I feel."

"And how is that?"

"Alone and unloved."

"You have no call to feel unloved. Ever since you were a baby, I've taken care of you. That's more than I can say for—"

Star lifted her hand. "Let's not even go there, Mom. I've heard the old story so many times I know every word by heart."

"Well, good. Then you ought to appreciate the sacrifices I've made for you and get that chip off your shoulder."

"Yeah, okay, whatever." Star figured there was no point in saying anything more. Mom had raised her single-handedly and thought she deserved the Mother-of-the-Year award. Anything more Star had to say would only fall on deaf ears.

Deciding this might be a good time to change the subject, Star said, "You know, Mom, it wouldn't hurt you to do something creative, something different for a change. I've actually met some rather interesting people at the quilt class. I really think I'm gonna enjoy getting to know them all better, too—especially Emma; she really seems nice."

"You, making friends? You've pushed people away most of your life. What's different now?"

"Well, there must be a reason Grandma wanted me to learn how to quilt. Who knows—maybe it goes beyond quilting; and to tell you the truth, I'm kind of anxious to find out."

"Is that so?" Mom put her hands on her hips. "Well, we'll just see how long that lasts."

"Boy, Mom, you can be so negative." Star flipped the ends of her hair over her shoulder. "I really don't care what you think. I have a feeling that Emma's classes are just what I need right now. Learning to quilt could even be a positive thing for me."

"You've got to be kidding! It sounds to me like you're putting more faith in this Amish woman than you ever have with me."

It's kinda hard to put your faith in someone who thinks more about themselves than she does her daughter, Star thought. With all the little lies Mom had told over the years, Star didn't see how she could be expected to have much faith in her. Of course, in all fairness to Mom, Star had to admit that since they'd moved to Goshen, Mom had seemed a bit more settled and not quite so flighty. Star hadn't caught her telling any white lies either, so at least that much was good.

Mom tapped her foot as she continued. "You really don't know the half of it. I gave up a lot to give you a decent life, and—"

"Before you say anything more and get yourself in an uproar, just listen to what I have to say," Star interrupted.

"Okay, sure; go right ahead."

"As I was going to say about Emma. . .she truly listens when people talk, and she seems genuine, too. She reminds me of Grandma in a lot of ways. She alone would give me a reason to continue going to the classes."

Seeing that she had Mom's attention, Star rushed on. "Then there's this biker dude, who I'm pretty sure is nothing more than a big ole teddy bear. There's also a very pleasant African-American woman who's a preacher's wife, and a Hispanic schoolteacher who has the cutest baby girl. It's a shame the poor guy's wife passed away six months ago. Oh, and there's a married couple attending the class. I can't figure them out yet, but they made the time in class quite interesting. It's almost funny to watch 'em pick on each other."

"Those people sound unique all right, but I still think you're all talk about this and won't follow through." Mom shrugged. "But you go ahead and do what you want; you always have."

Star's defenses rose. "Just forget it, Mom. You can't see past your own issues, but mark my words: I'm gonna prove you wrong about this, because I'll not only finish the class, but I'm gonna learn to make a beautiful quilted wall hanging, 'cause that's what Grandma wanted me to do!" Star picked up her scissors and started cutting another pattern piece.

"So are you going to see the movie with me or not?" Mom asked, waving the newspaper in front of Star's face.

"Didn't you hear me the first time? I said no. I'm going to spend the evening working on my quilt assignment."

Mom stared at Star with a look of disgust. "Fine then; I'll see if Mike wants to see the movie with me!"

"That's a really great idea," Star mumbled as Mom hurried from the room. "He's probably better company than me anyway." Trying not to let the tears clouding her vision spill over, she squared her shoulders. *Boy, just once I'd like to be the one who says, "I told you so."*

Shipshewana

By the time Emma reached Mary's yard, she was out of breath and panting. She gasped when she saw how the fire had gotten out of control. And if the wind started to blow, the house could be in danger. Maybe Emma's own home, as well.

Don't borrow trouble, Emma told herself as she hurried to Mary and her family watching the firemen battle the flames. *We just need to trust God and pray for the best.*

"Is everyone okay?" Emma asked, touching Mary's arm.

"Jah, we're all fine," Brian said before Mary could respond. "I'm afraid I wasn't watching close enough, and some of the sparks from our bonfire caught the shed on fire." He wiped the sweat from his forehead and pushed a lock of sandy brown hair aside. "I tried putting it out with the garden hose, but it didn't take long for me to realize that I needed the fire department, so I sent Stephen to the phone shack to make the call while I kept the water going."

"After the fire trucks got here," Mary continued, "Brian and the boys wanted to help, but they were told to stand aside and let the fireman take care of the situation." Tears gathered in the corners of her dark eyes. She appeared to be terribly shaken.

"While one group of men works at getting the fire out, another group is keeping the house and barn wet so they don't catch fire," Brian added.

Emma was glad the fire department wasn't too far from where they lived. Remembering back to the time in her early marriage when she and Ivan had lost their barn and several of the livestock because they'd lived so far from help made her glad that they'd moved closer to town several years ago, where help during a crisis was readily available.

"Where are the little ones?" Emma asked Mary, noting that the children were nowhere in sight.

"Lisa and Sharon were frightened, so I sent them next door to our neighbors," Mary replied.

"You could have sent them to my house." Emma felt a little hurt that Mary had chosen to send the children to their English neighbor's rather than over to her.

"I knew as soon as you heard the sirens you'd be coming over here," Mary explained.

Emma nodded. Even if the children had been at her house, she probably would have come. But she would have told them to stay put while she went to check on things. She'd never been one to sit around and wait to find out how things were going. She guessed it was just her curious nature, coupled with the need to help out whenever she could.

"Mary, why don't you go with your *mamm* back to her house?" Brian suggested, wiping more sweat from his brow. "There's no point in you both standing out here in the cool evening air."

Mary shook her head determinedly. "I'm not going anywhere until I know that our house and barn are safe from the fire."

CHAPTER 11

When Emma woke up on Saturday morning, she felt so tired she could hardly keep her eyes open. She'd spent most of yesterday helping Mary clean her house and get rid of the lingering smell of smoke. They'd also fed the men who'd come to help Brian clean up the burned wreckage left by the fire. They'd lost the shed, but thankfully, the barn and house hadn't caught fire. Sometime next week a new shed would be built, and Brian planned to move the fire pit farther from their outbuildings.

Emma had been glad to hear that. The thought of losing a house to a fire sent chills up her spine. When she was a girl, one of her friends had died in a house fire, and several others in the family had been seriously burned. Emma had never forgotten that tragedy and hoped no one she knew would ever have to go through anything like that.

A knock sounded on the front door. Emma glanced at the clock on the kitchen wall. It was ten minutes to ten, so she figured one of her quilting students had arrived a little early.

When Emma answered the door, she was surprised to see Lamar Miller on her porch, holding his straw hat in one hand.

"*Guder mariye*, Emma," he said with a friendly grin.

"Good morning," Emma replied without returning his smile. She didn't want to appear rude, but at the same time, she didn't want to encourage Lamar in any way.

"I heard about the fire at Brian and Mary's and wanted to make sure everything was okay," Lamar explained.

"Except for some frazzled nerves, everyone's fine. It could have been so much worse. Brian will have to replace their shed, of course, but other than that, nothing was damaged."

"That's good to hear," Lamar said with a look of relief. He shifted his weight slightly and cleared his throat. "The other reason I came by is I'm heading to the bakery to get some doughnuts and wondered if you'd like to go along."

She shook her head. "My quilt class begins at ten o'clock, and my students should be arriving soon, so I'll be busy all morning. But *danki* for asking," she quickly added.

Lamar placed his straw hat on his head and pushed it down, as though worried it might fall off. "Guess we could wait till this afternoon, but by then there may not be any doughnuts left."

"That's okay; you go ahead. I'll be busy with other things this afternoon, too."

"Oh, I see." Lamar's shoulders drooped.

"Maybe another time," Emma said, although she didn't know why. She really had no intention of going anywhere with this persistent man. "Oh, and danki for your concern about the fire next door."

"I'm glad it was only minor damage." Lamar's face brightened a bit. "Maybe I'll stop by the next time I'm heading to the bakery."

Oh, great, Emma thought as she watched Lamar amble across the yard toward his horse and buggy. *I hope I have a good excuse not to go with him the next time he drops by.*

Lamar had just pulled out of Emma's yard when the Johnstons' SUV pulled in, followed by Ruby Lee's car. A short time later, Star's dilapidated-looking vehicle came up the driveway, and then Jan pedaled in on his bicycle. Everyone was there but Paul.

"Let's all go inside and take a seat," Emma suggested. "As soon as Paul gets here, we'll begin today's lesson."

Everyone agreeably pulled up a chair at the table.

"How long do we have to sit here waiting for the school teacher?" Stuart asked, glancing at his watch with a look of agitation. "I don't have time to twiddle my thumbs all day, and I'm sure not going to stay past noon because we've gotten a late start."

Pam's eyebrows squeezed together as she shot him a disgruntled look. "Oh, stop your complaining. I'm sure Paul will be here soon."

Stuart folded his arms. "Well, he'd better be."

Pam looked at Ruby Lee and scrunched up her nose. "All he ever does is complain."

Ruby Lee quickly changed the topic of conversation to the weather they'd been having this spring. That seemed to help the atmosphere some.

Emma was about to suggest that each person show what they'd done on their quilt project this week when a knock sounded on the door. She was relieved when she opened it and found Paul on the porch.

"Where's your baby girl?" Jan asked when Paul entered the room with Emma and took his seat. "I was kinda hopin' she'd be with you again."

"My sister, Maria, is taking care of Sophia today," Paul replied.

"Maria and her family were out of town last week, so that's why I brought Sophia along."

"Oh, I see."

Emma couldn't help but notice Jan's disappointment. He was obviously hoping Paul would bring the baby with him. Emma would have enjoyed seeing little Sophia again, too, but she knew it would be easier for Paul to concentrate on learning if he didn't have the baby to care for.

"Sorry I'm late," Paul said. "We were almost ready to go out the door when Sophia made a mess in her diaper. Of course, in all fairness to Maria, I had to change the baby before I dropped her off. Never thought there'd be so many messes to clean up with a baby in the house." He shook his head. "And none of those messes are fun."

"I've always figured that God gives us children to make us humble," Emma said with a chuckle. "I can't count all the times one of my children made a mess on either their clothes or mine, and it was usually on a Sunday morning when we were almost ready to leave for church."

"Where's your church located?" Paul asked.

"Oh, we don't worship in a church building the way Englishers do," Emma said. "We hold our services every other week, and the members in our district take turns hosting church in their home, barn, or shop."

"You have church in a barn?" Star asked.

Emma nodded. "Sometimes, if that's the biggest building available and we know a lot of people will be attending."

Stuart snickered and plugged his nose. "I imagine that must smell pretty raunchy with all those dirty animals in there. Do the horses' neighs and the cows' moos accompany your singing?" he asked with a smirk.

Pam's elbow connected with her husband's ribs, causing him to jump. "Stuart, don't be so rude! I'm sure there are no animals in the barn when the Amish hold their worship services."

"That's right," Emma agreed. "If we do choose to hold a service in one of our barns, the animals are taken out and everything is cleaned before the wooden benches are brought in."

Ruby Lee quirked an eyebrow. "You mean you sit on wooden benches, not padded chairs?"

"Yes. We have backless benches that are transported from home to home in one of our bench wagons whenever we have a church service, wedding, or funeral."

Tiny lines formed across Pam's forehead when she frowned. "I can't imagine sitting in church for a whole hour on a backless wooden bench."

"Actually, our services last more than an hour," Emma said. "They usually go for three hours, and sometimes longer if we're having communion or some other special service."

"Three whole hours?" Stuart groaned. "I could never sit that long on a wooden bench with no back."

"You sit that long on the bleachers when you go to some stupid sporting event," Pam said, her elbow connecting with Stuart's ribs once more.

Not only must the poor man's ribs hurt after all that jabbing, Emma thought, *but he's probably embarrassed by his wife's behavior. Should I say something or just ignore it?*

"Sitting on bleachers can't be compared to wooden benches." Stuart stood and moved his chair away from Pam. "When I'm watching a game, I jump up and down a lot. Besides, there's more to see at a baseball or football game than there would be in a barn." He shook his head slowly. "Sure am glad I'm not Amish."

"Stuart!" Pam's cheeks turned bright pink; she looked absolutely mortified.

Emma wanted to say something right then, but for the life of her, she couldn't think what. She noticed how uncomfortable the others looked, too, as they squirmed in their chairs.

"Say, why don't you just keep your opinions to yourself?" Jan spoke up. "The Amish have their way of doin' things, and we Englishers have ours. And who says anyone has to have cushy padded pews in order to worship God?"

"What would you know about it?" Stuart shot back. "When was the last time you stepped foot in a church?"

Jan leaned forward and leveled Stuart with a look that prickled the hair on the back of Emma's neck. "I might ask you the same question, buddy. So you wanna make somethin' of it?"

Oh no, not more trouble between these two men. Emma knew she'd better say or do something before things got out of control.

"Now, now," Ruby Lee said, before Emma could find her voice. "We didn't come here to talk about church. We came to learn more about quilting." She looked at Emma and smiled. "Isn't that right?"

Emma nodded, relieved that after Ruby Lee's comment both men seemed to relax a bit. "Before we begin the next step in making your wall hangings, did you all get your pattern pieces cut out this week?"

Everyone but Stuart nodded. "With all my responsibilities at the sporting goods store, I didn't have time to get anything done on the quilt project this week," he mumbled.

Pam crossed her legs, and her foot bounced up and down as she shot him a look of disdain. "That's not true, and you know it! You would have had plenty of time to get all your pattern pieces cut out if you hadn't watched so much TV. But no, just as soon as you came home every night, on went the stupid sports programs."

"Well, at least I'm not sitting around all day watching a bunch of melodramatic soap operas," he shot back.

"I don't do that!" Pam said with a huff. "When I'm not cleaning, cooking, or doing laundry, I'm in the car running the kids to and from school. Oh, and don't forget, I drive Devin to and from his piano lessons and soccer practice every week."

"I go to all his games."

"Sure you do, but it's not the same as—"

Emma cleared her throat loudly, hoping to put an end to the Johnstons' bickering. "Shall we begin with the next phase of making your wall hangings?"

"How's he gonna begin the next phase when he hasn't done the first phase?" Star asked, pointing at Stuart. It was the first time the young woman had said more than a few words since she'd entered Emma's house this morning. "I hope we don't have to sit here and watch while he does what he should've done during the week."

"That's for sure," Jan spoke up. "We all paid good money to take this class so we could learn how to quilt." He leveled Stuart with a look Emma thought could have stopped a runaway horse in its tracks.

Before Stuart could respond, Emma intervened. "Now if everyone will please lay their pattern pieces on the table, I'll be able to see how things are progressing."

Emma wasn't surprised at how neatly Pam's pink and Ruby Lee's blue pieces had been cut out and pinned, but she never expected Jan's dark green pieces to have been done with such precision. Paul's pieces were yellow, and both his and Star's black and gold pieces were a little off-center, but nothing a little readjusting and pinning wouldn't fix.

Emma smiled. "You've all done quite well."

"All but him." Pam motioned to her husband. "He did nothing at all."

Stuart's eyes squinted as he sneered at her. "That's it. Just keep on reminding me about it!" His face turned red, and his voice rose with each word he said. "Things always go so much better between us when you throw things up in my face. And it's even better when you have an audience, isn't it? I'm sure it makes you feel real good if you can get others to take your side."

"You're impossible," Pam mumbled, turning her head away.

Emma squirmed nervously. A lot of anger and tension seemed to be going on between Pam and Stuart. She knew she had to say something to help ease the tension, and her mind grappled for the right words. Then, remembering something Ivan had told her once, she looked first at Pam and then Stuart. "Tolerance is what we all need for each other. Things go smoother if we're kind to everyone we meet."

Neither of them said a thing in response.

"Love God, yourself, and others. That's what the Bible teaches," Ruby Lee put in.

Paul gave a decisive nod; Star rolled her eyes toward the ceiling; Jan shrugged his broad shoulders; and Stuart and Pam both stared at the table. Emma figured not all her students went to church or had a personal relationship with God. Although most Amish didn't evangelize the way many English believers did, most, like Emma, tried to set a Christian example through their actions and words. Emma determined in her heart that she would try to show her students the love of Jesus and would begin doing that today.

CHAPTER 12

E mma was about to show the class what they needed to do next when she heard a knock on the back door. "Excuse me a minute while I see who that is," she said, hurrying out of the room.

When Emma opened the door, she was surprised to see Lamar holding a rectangular cardboard box. *Oh dear, what does he want now?* She'd told him earlier that she would be teaching her class until noon, so she couldn't imagine what he was doing here again.

Before Emma could voice the question, Lamar smiled and held the box out to her. "I know you still have guests, and I didn't mean to interrupt, but when I got to the bakery and discovered they had chocolate and powdered-sugar doughnuts on sale, I bought a dozen of each. Knowing it was more than I could eat, I decided to bring most of the doughnuts here, thinking you could share them with the people in your quilting class."

Emma, still feeling a bit put out for the interruption, took the box of doughnuts, thanked Lamar, and said she needed to get back to her students.

"Oh, of course. Sorry for the intrusion. I'll be on my way."

Emma nodded and stepped back into the house, almost shutting the door in his face.

"Who was that?" Pam asked when Emma returned to her sewing room.

"Oh, it was just Lamar Miller—a man in my community. He was on his way home from the bakery and stopped by to give me these." She lifted the box of doughnuts. "We can take a break soon, and I'll share them with you."

"Yum. . .doughnuts sure sound good," Stuart said.

"I'd better pass," Paul said. "I had some of my sister's homemade tamales for breakfast this morning, and I'm still feeling kind of full."

Jan's eyebrows shot up. "You had tamales for breakfast?"

Paul nodded. "I could eat them any time of day."

"Did you invite the nice man who brought the doughnuts to join us?" Ruby Lee asked Emma.

Emma's face heated as she shook her head. So much for setting a good example for her quilting students. They probably thought she'd been rude for not asking Lamar if he wanted to come in and share the doughnuts. Well, they didn't understand. If she'd invited him in, he would have seen it as an invitation to come here again—maybe even during one of her classes. It was bad enough that he'd been hanging around so much lately—doing little chores she hadn't asked him to do and trying to have conversations she'd rather not get into. A few weeks ago, Lamar had stopped by when she wasn't at home and mowed her lawn. Emma knew he had done it because he'd left his straw hat on one of the fence posts, and she'd discovered his name on the underside of the brim. Emma figured she'd better do something to discourage him soon or she might be looking at a marriage proposal.

"Are you all right, Emma?" Ruby Lee asked. "You look upset."

"I'm fine," Emma said, not wishing to discuss her thoughts. "I'll take the doughnuts to the kitchen until it's time for our break." She hurried from the room, feeling more flustered than ever.

When Emma returned, fully composed, she overheard Paul talking to Jan about Sophia and how he hoped the quilt he wanted to finish after he learned the basics of quilting would be a keepsake for the baby. He explained that when Sophia was old enough he planned to tell her what a wonderful mother his wife had been.

Paul paused and reached into his pocket for a handkerchief as several tears trickled onto his cheeks.

Everyone in the room got deathly quiet. Obviously no one knew what to say.

"I'm sorry. I know Lorinda's in a better place," Paul said after he'd dried his tears and blown his nose. "But I—I miss her so much, and it pains me to think that Sophia will never know her mother." Pausing to take a deep breath, he continued. "Then this past week was sort of a nightmare, with meetings, grading papers, and Sophia protesting through it all. The weekend just couldn't get here fast enough."

Emma stepped forward and placed her hand on Paul's shoulder. "It's never easy to lose a loved one. My husband's been gone a little over a year, and I still miss him and wish he could come back to me." She swallowed hard, hoping she wouldn't give in to her own threatening tears. "When the death of a loved one occurs, everything changes, and you find yourself doing things you never thought you could do."

"I miss my grandma, too." Star's forehead creased, and she opened her mouth like she might say more, but then she closed it and dropped

100

her gaze to the floor.

Emma's heart ached for the members of her class who were so obviously grieving. Even though she still missed Ivan, she'd found joy in life again. She hoped she could share some of that joy with her class.

As Emma showed the class how to stitch the patterned pieces together, using one of the battery-powered sewing machines, Ruby Lee thought about how flustered Emma had seemed right after the Amish man brought the doughnuts by. At least she assumed he was Amish. While Ruby Lee hadn't actually seen the man, she'd heard the distinctive *clippety-clop* of horse's hooves and the rumble of wheels as the buggy pulled away.

Could there be something going on between Emma and that man? Ruby Lee wondered. *If so, I guess it's really none of my business.*

Ruby Lee's role as a pastor's wife often put her in a position to know other people's business—sometimes more than she wanted to know. She always kept quiet about the things she heard, knowing it wouldn't be good to start any gossip. But there were others in the congregation who didn't seem to care about that. Some, even those with well-meaning intentions, spread gossip like wildfire.

Ruby Lee winced. For the past several months, Gene had been the subject of gossip within their church, yet he wouldn't do anything to stop it. He just continued to turn the other cheek and tried not to let the rumors and grumblings bother him. It was all Ruby Lee could do to keep from stepping into the pulpit some Sunday morning and chastising those who had gossiped and complained. The congregation needed to know that Gene had the church's best interests at heart and that he didn't deserve to be unjustly accused.

"And now I'd like each of you to spend the next half hour working on your quilt project," Emma said.

With a sense of determination not to think about anything church-related, Ruby Lee picked up one of her pattern pieces and pinned it to another, making sure it was positioned correctly. She'd signed up for this class so she could forget about the church and its problems and was determined to do just that.

"Hey, watch out there, junior," Jan said, pointing at Stuart. "You're gonna stick yourself with a pin if you're not careful."

Stuart frowned. "Just worry about yourself; I'm doing fine over here."

Jan shrugged his shoulders. "Whatever. I'm just sayin'—"

"How does this look?" Ruby Lee asked, holding up the two pieces of material she'd sewn together and hoping to diffuse any more arguments between the men.

"That's exactly right." Emma smiled. "You know, I just thought of something."

"What's that?" Pam asked.

"My grandmother used to say that God stitches the fabric of our lives according to His purpose and perfect pattern in order to shape us into what He wants us to be, just as you are all shaping your quilt patterns here."

"That's a little over the top, don't you think?" Star spoke up. "I mean, comparing God—if there really is a God—to us making a quilted wall hanging? That seems pretty far-fetched to me."

"Of course there's a God," Ruby Lee was quick to say. While her faith in other Christians may have dwindled in the last few months, she'd never doubted God's existence.

"I think anyone who doesn't believe in God must have a problem," Paul put in. "Why, I can see the hand of God everywhere."

"That's right," Emma agreed. "God's hand is in the flowers, the trees..."

"A baby's sweet laugh," Paul said, picking a piece of thread off his jeans.

Star shrugged her shoulders. "You can think whatever you like, but I'm not convinced that God exists, and I *don't* have a problem."

"Everyone has some kind of problem or somethin' they're tryin' to hide," Jan said. "Some of us just hide it better than others." He looked right at Star. "What's your problem, anyway?"

"I just told you, I don't have a problem." Star stared back at Jan defiantly. "Even if I did, I wouldn't discuss my personal life with a bunch of strangers."

"We're not really strangers," Pam interjected. "This is our second time together, and—"

"And with the exception of you and me, none of us knows each other at all." Stuart removed the green baseball cap he'd worn today and pulled his fingers through the top of his hair, causing it to stand straight up. "Of course, there are days when I'm not sure I really know you all that well either."

Pam blinked a couple of times. "I hope you're kidding, Stuart. We've been married ten years, and we dated two years before we got married. If you don't know me now, then I guess you never will."

Oh no, here we go again. They're going to start arguing now. These two really do need marriage counseling. Ruby Lee pushed her chair away from the table. "I don't know about anyone else, but I'm hungry. Is it all right if we have those doughnuts now, Emma?"

"Yes, of course. I'll get them right away." Emma scurried out of the room, and Ruby Lee was right behind her.

"What can I do to help?" she asked Emma as they stepped into her cozy kitchen.

"You can get some napkins and the box of doughnuts, and I'll get the coffee and cups." Emma smiled. "Maybe these doughnuts will sweeten everyone up and we'll end our class on a pleasant note today. Oh, and be careful not to get any of that powdered sugar on yourself." Nodding toward the doughnuts, she added, "There must be a hole in the bottom of the box, because I see some powder drifting out from underneath, and I'd hate to see any of it get on that pretty pink blouse you're wearing today."

Ruby Lee nodded, appreciating the warning and, even more, the compliment from Emma.

When they returned to Emma's sewing room, Ruby Lee was glad to see that with the exception of Paul, who was talking on his cell phone, everyone was visiting. It seemed like they all might be warming up to each other a bit. She placed the doughnuts and napkins in the center of the table and took a seat.

"I have coffee to go with the doughnuts," Emma said as she set a tray with the coffeepot and cups beside the doughnuts. "Go ahead and help yourselves."

"I don't really care much for coffee," Pam said. "Do you have something else to drink?"

"There's chocolate milk in the refrigerator, or you can have water," Emma replied.

"Chocolate milk sounds good to me." Pam started to rise from her chair, but Emma shook her head.

"Help yourself to a doughnut while I get the milk."

By the time Emma returned from the kitchen with a glass of chocolate milk, Paul was off the phone and everyone had begun eating their doughnuts. Paul mentioned that he'd called his sister to check on Sophia and was relieved to hear that she was doing just fine. Then the talk around the table turned to the weather.

"Sure has been raining a lot this spring," Ruby Lee commented. "I hope the sunshine we're having today keeps on, because I would hate to have flooding like we did two years ago."

"I remember it was so bad that some of our roads were closed," Emma said. "One of my friends had so much water at her place that she couldn't even get to her phone shack."

"Phone shack?" Pam looked surprised. "Don't you have a phone in the house?"

Emma shook her head. "Most of us share a phone with other family members or two or three close neighbors, and it's in a small wooden building we call our 'phone shack.'"

"Oh, I couldn't handle not having a phone in the house," Pam said, slowly shaking her head.

"And I couldn't do without my cell phone." Stuart reached across Pam to take another doughnut and bumped her arm just as she was about to take a drink.

The glass tipped, and chocolate milk spilled all over the front of Pam's creamy-white blouse. "Oh no!" she gasped. "Just look what you've done now! My new blouse is ruined!"

"I–I'm sorry," Stuart sputtered. "I didn't mean to bump your arm."

Red-faced, Pam jumped up from the table, her eyes flashing angrily. "Get up, Stuart; it's time to go home!" With that, she raced out the front door.

Stuart, looking thoroughly embarrassed, grabbed his and Pam's quilt projects, stuffed them into the canvas tote Pam had brought along, and turned to Emma. "Sorry, but I'd better go." Before Emma had a chance to respond, he hurried out the door.

CHAPTER 13

Tears burned Pam's eyes as she slid into the car feeling humiliated and angry with Stuart. How could he have been so careless and bumped her arm like that? Didn't he ever watch what he was doing?

"Are you okay?" Stuart asked as he took his seat behind the wheel and fastened his seat belt.

"No, I'm not okay!" She sniffed and blotted the tears from her cheeks. "I just bought this beautiful blouse, and now it's ruined."

"I'm sure it'll be fine once we get home and you've washed it."

"I. . .I doubt it. Chocolate's hard to get out, and it'll probably leave a nasty stain."

"If it does, you can buy a new blouse."

"No, I can't. This was the last one they had in my size in this style."

"Then buy one in another style."

She shook her head. "I like this one. Besides, I'm not like you. You'd be happy if the baseball cap, faded jeans, and red-checkered flannel shirt you wear so much of the time were the only pieces of clothing you owned. Don't you ever get tired of wearing those things? Wouldn't it be nice if just once in a while you'd dress in clothes that are a bit more tasteful—especially when we go someplace together?"

"You're exaggerating, Pam. I don't wear a flannel shirt and ball cap all the time. I sure don't wear 'em to work."

"Don't you realize how embarrassing it is for me when you dress like a slob?"

"It's all about you, isn't it?" Stuart slashed back. "Did it ever occur to you that I just might be comfortable in these clothes? Or should I say *rags*, which is probably what you think of them anyway. Now buckle up. We're heading home."

Pam said nothing as he started the engine and pulled out of Emma's yard. What was the point? She was sure her blouse was ruined and equally sure that Stuart didn't really care. He didn't care about his sloppy appearance either.

They rode in silence until they were almost out of Shipshewana; then Stuart looked over at Pam and said, "This isn't working out. I want—"

Pam's heart hammered and her mouth went dry. "A divorce? Is that what you want?" She knew they were just holding on by a thread.

"Whoa! Who said anything about a divorce?"

"You said things aren't working out, so I assumed you meant—"

"I was talking about the stupid quilting class." He gave the steering wheel a whack. "I'm bored with the class, I'll never catch on to sewing, and I'm getting sick and tired of hearing you talk about me to anyone who'll listen. You make it sound like I'm the world's worst husband, and you're saying it to a bunch of people we don't even know." He groaned. "Why do you always have to make me look bad? Is it so you can make yourself look good?"

"Certainly not." She folded her arms and stared straight ahead. "You're just too sensitive, that's all."

For a few seconds, their conversation ebbed as traffic came to a halt in both directions. Pam watched as a mother duck, followed by seven scurrying ducklings, crossed the road in front of them to get to the area where water had formed a small pond after the recent rain. *If only life were as simple as crossing the road to get to the other side, where something good awaited you.*

Picking up their conversation as if they'd never seen the ducks, Stuart continued talking as traffic moved once again. "Humph! You think I'm too sensitive? You're the one who lost it when I bumped your arm and the chocolate milk spilled on your blouse. It's not like I did it on purpose, you know."

"So you said."

"Look, Pam, this whole quilting thing is only adding more stress to our marriage, and it's sure not helping our relationship any. I think you should go without me next week."

She sat quietly for several seconds, letting his words sink in; then with a quick nod she said, "Okay, I'll go by myself, and you can stay home and watch the kids instead of asking our neighbor girl to babysit them."

"Why can't Cindy watch them again? She said she'd be available to sit with the kids for all six weeks."

"It would be a waste of money to pay her when one of us isn't going."

A muscle on Stuart's right cheek quivered, the way it always did whenever he was irritated with her. "Fine then. I'll watch the kids!"

Pam was pretty sure Stuart wanted to do something else next Saturday—probably go fishing with one of his buddies. Well, that was too bad. If he wasn't going to keep his promise and take the quilting class with her, then he could stay home and deal with the kids.

She leaned her head against the seat and closed her eyes, allowing her thoughts to drift back to her childhood. Back then, the only thing she should have been worried about was having fun with her friends— deciding what to do for the day and what games they would play. Those should have been days filled with mindless entertainment, doing things kids enjoyed, like lying in the grass with no cares in the world and watching the clouds overhead form into all sorts of characters and shapes. It was a phase in her life when time schedules shouldn't have been that important yet. Unfortunately, Pam's childhood wasn't that simple. As far back as she could remember, she'd felt like she had the weight of the world on her back. She'd never had those carefree days of youth. Instead, Pam constantly had her nose in a book and strived to be a straight-A student so Mom and Dad would be proud of her and say something that would let her know they approved. The hope of gaining their approval gave Pam the determination and drive to keep striving for perfection.

School books make lousy friends, she thought. Even with all the studying Pam had done, none of it seemed to have really mattered to anyone. The good grades were rewarded, but with money or clothes, not words of affirmation or a loving hug.

During Pam's childhood, she'd never even had a close friend. Heather Barkely, whom she'd met at aerobics class a few years ago, was the first real friend she'd ever had.

What was worse than not having any close friends, and the one thing she'd really despised about school, was going back in the fall after summer vacation. When the teacher would ask if the students wanted to share their summer adventures with the rest of the class, Pam envied hearing about the family outings most of them had. Sure, her parents had given her many things, and she'd learned at a very young age how to put on a good front. Pam had been clever about fooling her parents and others when she'd pretended to be pacified with the so-called treasures they'd bought for her. And she appreciated that she'd been given nice clothes. At least that was something she was complimented for during her teenage years—that, and her good looks—especially from the boys.

Maybe this is why it bugs me so much about the way Stuart dresses, she thought. *I just want him to look as nice as I do so people will be impressed.*

Stuart hadn't been such a slob before he'd married her. What had happened between then and now to make him change in his appearance?

Focusing on the scenery as they continued the drive home, Pam kept all those forgotten feelings from the past to herself. If she told Stuart any of this, he wouldn't understand. He didn't seem to want to communicate with her on any level these days.

———

Star noticed that as soon as Stuart and Pam stormed out of Emma's house, the sewing room had become so quiet she probably could have heard a needle drop on the floor. Even Ruby Lee, who was usually quite talkative, sat drinking her coffee with a strange-looking stare.

Emma, looking more flustered than she had when the man with the doughnuts came by, stood near the window, looking out at her yard.

Star watched outside as a wasp flew around the overhang above the window, no doubt trying to find a place to build its nest.

Several more minutes went by; then Jan leaned close to Star and said, "I can't say as I care much for know-it-all Stuart, but that wife of his is sure one whacked-out chick. You know what I'm sayin'?"

She gave a nod, glad that Jan saw things the way she did—at least where prissy Pam was concerned.

"I guess she had a right to be upset, but I'm sure Stuart didn't bump her arm on purpose," Paul spoke up. "Although I think she could have been a little more understanding when he said he was sorry."

Would you have been understanding if someone had spilled chocolate milk all over your clean shirt? Star thought, although she didn't voice the question. Seeing the way Pam and Stuart argued only confirmed in her mind that she was never getting married. Most of the men she'd known had been jerks, and even though Star didn't care for Pam's uppity ways, she'd actually felt a bit sorry for her when she dashed out of the house in tears.

"Women like Pam Johnston are never understanding; they're just high maintenance," Jan muttered. "Believe me; I know all about whacked-out, high-maintenance chicks."

"Biker babes?" Star asked.

"Some yes, some no." Jan reached for a doughnut and took a bite, followed by a swig of coffee. "The first biker babe I ever met was probably the most whacked-out chick of all."

"In what way?" Star asked, her curiosity piqued.

"She could never make up her mind. One minute she wanted to get married; the next minute she didn't." A pained expression crossed Jan's face as he slowly shook his head. "She took off one day without a trace—just like my old man did after my mom died."

"How old were you when that happened?" Star questioned.

"I was seventeen when Mom died from a brain tumor." Jan went on to tell that his drunkard father had split a year later, and then he'd lit out on his own. "I eventually learned the roofing trade and ended up in Shipshewana, where I started my own business," he said.

"Losing your mother, and then having two people you loved run away must have been very painful." Ruby Lee reached over and touched Jan's arm. Her eyes, the color of charcoal, looked at him with such compassion that it made Star feel like crying.

It wasn't bad enough that the burly biker had lost his mother, but then some fickle woman hurt him so badly that he still carried the scars of her rejection. To top it all off, having his dad take off had probably left Jan feeling a lot of animosity. Star could sure relate to that, since her own dad had done the very same thing. The only difference was Jan had known his dad for seventeen years, whereas Star had never known her dad at all.

"Yeah, it was all very painful, but I learned how to cope." Jan swiped some crumbs from the front of his T-shirt. "You know Bunny was the only girl I ever really loved." He pointed to the tattoo on his right arm. "I even had her name put here. But of course, that was when I thought she was gonna marry me. Now I realize what a jerk I was for believin' her. Shoulda never got involved with her in the first place."

Guess I'm not the only one in this room with hurts from the past, Star thought. *It's too bad people have to disappoint each other. If everyone had a heart of love the way Grandma did, the world would be a better place. I'm thankful I had her, even though we didn't get to spend nearly enough time together.*

Emma turned from the window and joined them at the table again. "No one is perfect. We all make mistakes, but we have to forgive and move forward," she said.

Star grimaced. *That's easy enough for you to say. You've probably never made a mistake in your life. Well, walk in someone else's shoes for a while, and then see what you have to say about forgiveness.*

CHAPTER 14

As Jan pedaled home from the quilting class, he thought about his comments concerning the woman he'd once loved and wondered if he'd said too much. The way everyone had looked at him made him wonder if they thought he was some dumb guy who'd never gotten over his first crush. Or maybe they'd felt sorry for him because he'd been jilted. Either way, he figured it would be best if he didn't say too much more about his personal life during the quilting classes. It was bad enough that during their first class he'd told them about his DUI. He'd signed up to learn how to quilt, not spill his guts about the past and hash things over that couldn't be changed. Looking back on it, he figured he'd blabbed all that because he'd been uncomfortable the first day, unsure of what to expect and a bit embarrassed because he didn't know how people would respond to a guy like him taking a quilting class.

Jan knew that he needed to quit worrying about what others thought. He also needed to forget his former life and look to the future.

He'd been doing a pretty good job of that until he'd started blubbering about Bunny.

"Yikes, I'd better watch what I'm doin'," he muttered, nearly losing his balance as he caught sight of some pretty azaleas blooming in a yard along the way. "Better pay closer attention to handlin' this stupid bike and quit gawkin' around, or I might end up on my backside."

Continuing on, Jan pictured some azalea bushes around his small house. Maybe a few flowers would help it look a little homier and not so plain. He had a lot of yard space he could work with and really needed something to give the place some charm.

Vr. . .oom! Vr. . .oom!

"Now that there's what I really need to be thinkin' about," Jan said as a motorcycle roared past. He could hardly wait to get his driver's license back so he could take his Harley out and start riding again. He missed the exhilaration of zooming down the road with the wind at his back. He missed the power of the motorcycle underneath him.

Hang on, he told himself. *Just a few more months and I'll be home free.*

When Jan pedaled up the driveway to his house, he noticed right away that his garage door hung open. He glanced toward the house and grimaced when he saw Brutus lying on the front porch.

"Oh, great," he muttered as the dog greeted him with a welcoming bark and a wagging tail.

Jan parked his bike, stepped onto the porch, and bent to pet the dog's silky ears. "Hey, boy. How'd you get out of the garage, huh?"

Brutus whimpered and nuzzled Jan's hand with his nose.

Jan took a seat on the top porch step as he contemplated the situation. When he'd put Brutus in the garage this morning before leaving for Emma's, he'd thought he had shut the door.

I either must've forgot or didn't close it tight enough. Should've paid closer attention, I guess.

Brutus ambled across the porch and picked up an old dilapidated slipper in his mouth. Then he plodded back and dropped it at Jan's feet.

"Now where'd that come from?" Jan scratched his head. "Sure isn't mine. Brutus, did you steal this from someone in the neighborhood?"

Brutus gave a deep grunt as he flopped onto the porch and stuck his nose between his paws.

Jan squinted. "Well, if you did steal it, then I guess I'd better get started buildin' that dog pen right away, 'cause I can't have you gettin' me in trouble with more of the neighbors."

Goshen

As soon as Ruby Lee stepped into the house, she knew something was wrong. The newspapers that had been scattered on the coffee table when she'd left for the quilting class were still there, as well as Gene's empty coffee cup, which sat in the middle of the strewn-out papers. Gene was a perfectionist and rarely left things lying around. His motto was "When you're done with something, put it away." He'd started a rule in their house back when the boys were small that when a person was finished with their dishes, they were to take them straight to the kitchen sink.

Gene was so meticulous that whenever he finished his coffee, he would rinse the cup out and put it right in the dishwasher. Since he'd obviously not done that this morning, nor had he picked up and folded the newspaper he'd been reading after breakfast, he'd either been called out because of an emergency or was upset about something and forgot.

Ever since they'd been having problems at church, Gene hadn't been acting like his usual self at home. He seemed less talkative, became easily distracted, rarely played his guitar, and had become moody and despondent. At church, though, he went about his business, unwilling to let anyone in the congregation know how he really felt. Ruby Lee had tried talking to him about it but couldn't get him to open up. If something didn't happen to change the church situation soon, she feared he might have a nervous breakdown from holding his emotions inside.

I wish I could get through to him, Ruby Lee told herself as she bent to pick up Gene's cup. *I need to convince him that he should leave the ministry or at least seek a new church.*

Ruby Lee took the cup to the kitchen, and as she was placing it in the sink, she spotted Gene out the window. He was sitting on the grass in the middle of the backyard with his legs crossed, staring up at the sky. It wasn't like him to do that. For that matter, since he usually called on members of their congregation most Saturdays, it seemed strange that he was home at all.

Ruby Lee went out the back door and knelt on the grass beside him. "What are you doing out here?" she asked, touching Gene's arm.

His forehead gleamed like polished ebony as he lowered his head and gave her a blank stare. "What do you mean?"

"Well look at you, hon. How come you're sitting here on the grass staring up at the sky?"

"I was talking to God. Oh, yes, indeed."

Ruby Lee tried not to act surprised by his statement, but she'd never known him to talk to God in this manner. Not that it mattered where, when, or how a person talked to God, but with the exception of the prayer they said at meals, Gene usually went to the church to pray. He'd told her on more than one occasion that he felt closer to God when he was on his knees in front of the altar. Ruby Lee would sometimes join him there, and they'd pray and meditate together, but she hadn't done much of that lately. Maybe, like her, Gene just needed a change of pace. That was why she'd decided to take the quilting class. So far it had been a nice diversion, giving her something other than their church problems to focus on.

"Gene, I've been thinking about something," she said softly.

"What's that?"

"I think we should consider looking for another church. Or better yet, let's get out of the ministry altogether. Now that we've moved from the parsonage and are in our own home, we're not tied to the church. Since we both like to sing and each of us plays an instrument, maybe we could teach music lessons."

Gene shook his head. "I'm not leaving the ministry, Ruby Lee. God called me to it, and I'm not going back on my promise to serve Him."

"I'm not suggesting you stop serving God. I just think there are other ways you can serve besides pastoring a church full of ungrateful people. Even moving from the parsonage to our own place here, we can't seem to escape all the gossip. And if things keep going as they are, you're bound to cave in." *And so will I.*

" 'Though he slay me, yet will I hope in him,'" Gene quoted from Job 13:15.

Ruby Lee swallowed hard. "Yes, that's what I'm afraid of."

He gave her arm a gentle pat and lifted his gaze to the sky again.

Sighing deeply, Ruby Lee rose to her feet and headed back to the house. *Sweet Jesus, we need Your help in this. Please protect my man and make everything all right for us again.*

CHAPTER 15

Shipshewana

Emma had spent a good deal of Wednesday afternoon shopping in Shipshewana, and had also stopped to see her friend Clara Bontrager. During their visit, the subject of Lamar came up, and Emma dropped a few hints about Clara and Lamar maybe getting together. She'd even gone so far as to say she thought they would make a good couple. Clara had completely vetoed that idea, however, saying that she'd been corresponding with Emmanuel Schrock, an Amish man from Millersburg, Ohio, whom she'd met when they'd both visited Sarasota, Florida, the past winter.

"I actually think Lamar is interested in you," Clara had said.

"Jah, I know," Emma mumbled, talking out loud, as she flicked the reins to get her horse moving a bit faster. "I just hope he realizes that I'm not interested in him."

Not quite ready to go home, she decided to stop by a place she and Ivan used to go when they were courting. It was near a pond about four miles from where she lived. If she went there now and didn't stay too long, she should still have plenty of time to get back before supper. Besides, she'd only be cooking for herself this evening, so it really didn't matter what time she ate.

Heading on down the road, Emma slowed her horse to watch an English man on his tractor mowing his acreage. She smiled, noticing the tree swallows as they swooped and dove at the bugs flying out of the grass from the mower. The birds brought up another scene in her mind from long ago. This scene was of Ivan, strong and capable, walking behind their mules as he worked in the fields. She couldn't help smiling back then, either, as the birds followed after her husband, looking for an easy meal.

As Emma guided her horse and buggy off the main highway and onto a narrow, graveled road, more memories flooded her mind. When she and Ivan had come here, either alone or with friends, they'd often shared a picnic supper, fished in the pond, or taken leisurely walks along the wooded paths. Not too much had changed since then, except the trees were much taller now. Back then everything had been more overgrown, of course, and not nearly as many people used the pond as they did now. Even so, coming here gave her a peaceful, nostalgic feeling.

Emma stopped her horse and buggy in a grassy spot, climbed down, and secured the horse to a tree. She was about to take off on foot in search of her and Ivan's special spot when Lamar pulled up in his open rig.

"Wie geht's?" he called.

Oh no. What's he doing here? Emma forced a smile. "I'm doing fine. How about you?" she asked, a little less enthusiastically.

"Real well, thanks." He climbed down from his buggy and lifted a fishing pole out. "Came here to do a little fishing. Would you like to join me, Emma?" he asked with a twinkle in his eyes.

She shook her head. "I'm going for a walk and need to be alone." *There, that ought to discourage him.*

A look of hurt replaced Lamar's twinkle, causing Emma to regret her choice of words. It seemed like she was always saying the wrong thing when she was with Lamar, and even though she wanted to discourage him, she didn't want to hurt his feelings.

"There's a spot up the path that used to be my husband's and my special place," she said, pointing in that direction. "I like to go there sometimes and spend time alone, thinking about the past and thanking God for the wonderful years Ivan and I had together."

Lamar gave a brief nod. "I understand. My wife, Margaret, and I had a good life, too."

From the look of longing Emma saw on Lamar's face, she figured he probably missed his wife as much as she missed Ivan.

"I'll let you get to your walk now. Nice seeing you, Emma." Lamar flashed her a quick smile and headed off toward the pond.

Emma turned and started up the path, seeking her place of pleasant memories and solace. The afternoon breeze carried the scent of wildflowers, and she noticed several bees dancing on the flower blossoms. What a lovely day it was for a walk.

Emma found what she was looking for a short way up the path. The area was overgrown, but she recognized the leafy branches of the huge maple tree, where several clumps of wild irises grew nearby. A large boulder sat beneath the tree—the perfect place for young lovers to sit and make plans for the future. It was here that Ivan had first declared his love and told Emma he wanted to marry her. It was here that Emma had agreed to become his wife. And yes, it was even here in this very spot that the birds still seemed to sing their sweetest, as if to serenade her every time she came to visit this special place.

Emma took a seat on the rock and looked up. Even after all these years, her and Ivan's initials were still there—carved deep in the wood with Ivan's pocketknife.

Tears welled in Emma's eyes. "Dearest Ivan, oh, I still miss you so much."

As a young woman, Emma had been courted by a few other men— one in particular, whom she'd rather forget. But she'd never loved anyone the way she had Ivan, and she thanked God for the precious years they'd had together. She wished all couples could be as happy as she and Ivan had been.

As Emma continued to contemplate things, she thought about Pam and Stuart Johnston and wondered how they'd been getting along this week. Had Pam managed to get the chocolate stain out of her blouse? Had she accepted Stuart's apology and forgiven him for bumping her arm? Emma was sure Stuart hadn't done it on purpose. *I wonder if they ever have any fun together, without all that strife.*

Emma closed her eyes and whispered a prayer. "Dear Lord, please be with that troubled couple and heal their marriage. When they come to my class next week, help me to be an example of Your love—to Stuart and Pam, as well as the others in my quilting class."

When her prayer ended, she opened her eyes just in time to see a butterfly, with its colorful wings of yellow and black, flitting around her head. Emma smiled, feeling peace and never tiring of God's almighty showcase.

Mishawaka

As Pam stood in the laundry room staring at the ugly chocolate stain on her blouse, a sense of bitterness welled in her soul. Not only had Stuart's carelessness ruined her new blouse, but he'd reneged on his promise to attend the quilting classes with her. It wasn't right to make a promise and then break it, but Stuart didn't seem to care. Well, maybe she'd enjoy the class more without him, and maybe after being stuck at home watching the kids this Saturday, he'd change his mind and agree to go with her for the three lessons after that. If he didn't, she wouldn't be going fishing or camping with him ever again. Not that she wanted to go anyway. She disliked sleeping in a tent, and sitting in a boat for hours on end was just as bad. She hated everything about spending time in the dirty, bug-infested woods.

When Pam first married Stuart, he'd mentioned wanting to go camping together, but she'd had no idea he meant in a tent. She'd suggested they get an RV, which had many of the conveniences she was used to at home, but Stuart shot that idea down, saying he preferred to rough it, and that he thought sleeping in a tent was a lot more fun.

Fun for him, maybe, Pam fumed, tossing her blouse into a bag of cleaning rags. That's all it was good for now. She would never wear it again—not even around the house. *I should go find that stupid flannel shirt of his and throw it in this bag, too. It would serve him right for ruining my blouse.*

The sound of children's laughter drifted through the open window of the laundry room, reminding Pam that Devin and Sherry were playing in the backyard. They'd gone outside shortly after they arrived home from school, and Pam figured they'd stay out there until she called them in for supper.

She glanced at the small clock she kept on the shelf above the dryer. It was almost four. Stuart should be getting home from work in the next hour or so. Since it was a warm spring evening, she hoped he'd be willing to cook some hot dogs and burgers on the grill. Those would be good with the potato salad she'd made earlier. If he wasn't willing to barbecue, she'd have to broil the meat in the oven.

"Gimme that! Gimme that right now!" Devin's angry voice pulled Pam's thoughts aside. When she looked out the window, she saw Sherry running across the yard with a basketball. Devin was right on her heels.

Pam waited to see what her son would do, but when he pushed his sister down and the children started shouting and hitting each other, it was time to intervene.

"What's the problem here?" Pam asked after she'd rushed out the door and up to the children.

Devin pointed to the ball.

"Now, just say what you mean, because I don't understand pointing," Pam said, trying to keep her voice calm.

"She took my ball and won't give it back!" Devin's brown eyes flashed angrily as he glared at his little sister and made a face.

Sherry's lower lip protruded, and her blue eyes filled with tears. "He wouldn't let me play with it."

Devin wrinkled his freckled nose. "You can't play basketball 'cause you can't throw the ball high enough to reach the hoop."

"Can so."

"Can not."

"Can so, you stupid head." Sherry raised her hand like she might slap her brother.

"I'm not a stupid head. You're a—"

Pam stepped quickly between them. "That's enough! There will be no more hitting, and it's not nice to holler and call each other names."

Sherry tipped her blond head back and looked up at Pam with a most serious expression. "You and Daddy holler at each other."

A feeling of shame washed over Pam. Her daughter was right; she and Stuart did argue a lot.

Determined not to set a bad example for Devin and Sherry, Pam decided right then that she wouldn't argue with Stuart anymore—at least not in front of the children. Of course, she would need help controlling her tongue, because Stuart seemed to know exactly how to push her buttons.

Pam crossed her fingers and said a quick prayer. Maybe the two gestures didn't mix, since crossing one's fingers was superstitious, but if she was going to keep from arguing with Stuart, then she'd need all the help she could get.

She took the ball from Sherry and handed it to Devin. Then she reached for Sherry's hand and said, "Why don't you come in the house with me? You can help me bake a cake for dessert tonight. How's that sound?"

The child nodded and walked obediently with Pam toward the house. They stopped to look at the tulips blooming around their deck. Pam was happy to see all the other flowers that were sprouting up and starting to bloom in the various nature gardens she'd created. All the pretty flowers and shrubs added just the right touch to their charming Cape Cod home.

When they stopped on the patio to bring in a plant Pam needed to repot, Sherry pivoted toward Devin and stuck out her tongue.

"That's not nice," Pam scolded, turning the girl toward the door. She couldn't imagine where her daughter had picked up such a bad-mannered gesture.

"I saw you stick your tongue out at Daddy once," Sherry said as they stepped into the kitchen.

Setting the plant near the window, Pam flinched. She really did need to set a better example for the children. Opening the curtains so the plant would get more sunlight, Pam sighed deeply and leaned her head against the window. *It's gotten so bad that even the kids are imitating us now.*

Shipshewana

For the last three days, Jan had been working late, and by the time he got home from work, all he wanted to do was sleep. But Brutus had other ideas. Locked safely away in his new dog pen, which Jan had built a few days ago, the poor dog seemed to want Jan's attention as soon as Terry dropped him off at the house.

"Oh. Oh. Looks like Brutus got out," Terry said as he pulled his truck into Jan's yard that afternoon.

Jan rubbed his tired eyes and squinted. Sure enough—there lay Brutus on the front porch. "For cryin' out loud!" Jan opened the door and hopped out of the truck. When he stepped onto the porch, he noticed a blue cotton shirt lying beside Brutus.

"What's up, man? You look upset," Terry said when he joined Jan on the porch.

Jan grunted and pointed to the shirt.

"Where'd that come from? Is it yours?"

"Nope, but I'll bet somebody's missin' it, and only Brutus knows where it belongs."

Terry's brows lifted high, and then he leaned over the porch railing and spat on the ground. "Not only is your mutt an escape artist, but looks to me like he's also a thief."

Jan reached under his biker's cap and scratched the side of his head. "Guess I'd better find out how he got out of his pen and make sure it don't happen again."

CHAPTER 16

Mishawaka

W hew! That was quite a workout we had today, wasn't it?" Pam asked her friend Heather after they'd finished their aerobics class for the day.

Heather nodded and pushed a loose strand of jet-black hair behind her right ear. "It got my heart pumping pretty good. That's for sure."

"Do you have time to sit at the juice bar and visit a few minutes?" Pam asked. "I really need to talk."

"Sure, no problem. Ron's working late at the office like he usually does on Fridays, so I don't have to be home for a couple more hours."

They both found seats at the bar and ordered cranberry juice over ice.

"What's up?" Heather asked. "Even after that workout we just had, you look kind of stressed."

Pam drew in a quick breath and blew it out with a puff of air that lifted a piece of hair that had stuck to her sweaty forehead. "I've been stressed for several weeks, and it's only gotten worse."

"What's wrong? Are the kids getting on your nerves?"

"It's not the kids; it's Stuart. Despite the fact that we've been seeing a counselor for the last month, things aren't any better between us."

"But you're taking that quilting class together, right?"

"Well, we were, but Stuart hated it so much he said he didn't want to go again."

"Then maybe you shouldn't force the issue."

Pam took a drink of juice and frowned. "I'm not trying to force him to take the class, Heather. At first he agreed to go if I promised to go fishing with him four more times."

Heather's eyebrows squeezed together. "I know how much you hate to fish, so why would you even agree to do such a thing?"

"I agreed to it because our counselor said we should do some things together, and also because I wanted Stuart to learn how to quilt with me."

"But why? You had to know he wouldn't like it. I mean, most men I know wouldn't be caught dead with a needle and thread in their hands. And Stuart sure doesn't seem like the type who'd want to learn how to sew."

Pam wrinkled her nose. "You're right about that. All he ever thinks about is hunting, fishing, and sports. And since I don't enjoy any of those things, I decided it was time for him to do something just for me. . . something that would prove how much he loves me. But I'm beginning to think he doesn't love me at all."

"Has he said he doesn't love you?" Heather asked.

"No, but he rarely says so anymore. And when he does, it's usually because he wants me to do something for him. I can tell by the way Stuart acts that whatever love he used to feel for me has dried up and blown away." Tears welled in Pam's eyes and threatened to spill over. "I cook all his favorite foods, dress in stylish clothes, and work out here every week so I can keep my figure, but he barely notices me. When we were dating, he paid me compliments about my looks, and there wasn't anything he wouldn't do for me. But that's over now—just like our marriage."

"You don't think there's another woman, do you?"

Pam shook her head. "I just think he's selfish and so into himself that he doesn't see me or even acknowledge my needs. Besides, with the sloppy way he often dresses, I doubt any other woman would be attracted to him. I know I wouldn't have been if he'd looked like that before we started dating."

"Have you tried talking to him about the way he dresses and how he treats you?"

Pam flipped the ends of her hair over her shoulder. "Oh, dozens of times. He just shrugs it off and says I'm too demanding. The other day he even said I was a high-maintenance woman and that I should quit putting so many expectations on him."

"What'd you say to that?"

"I said he was insensitive and only thinks of himself."

Heather drank the rest of her juice. "Maybe you and Stuart should go away by yourselves for a few days and see if you can talk things through. A little romance wouldn't hurt either," she added with a grin.

Pam rolled her eyes. "If I suggested going away by ourselves, Stuart would probably want to go camping—in a tent, of all things."

"Just put your foot down and tell him you want to stay at a nice hotel or a bed-and-breakfast. I hear there's some lovely B&Bs between Middlebury and Shipshewana."

Pam shook her head. "I doubt he'd go for that."

"Well, you won't know if you don't ask. A little time alone might do wonders for your marriage."

Pam sighed deeply. "That would be nice, but it would have to be on a weekend, and with the quilting class taking up most of my Saturdays, we couldn't even think about going away by ourselves until the last class is over."

Heather gave Pam's arm a gentle pat. "Well, my good thoughts are with you, and remember, I'm here anytime you need to talk."

"Thanks, I appreciate that."

"Is everything okay?" Blaine Vickers, one of Stuart's employees, asked as he joined Stuart in the break room. "You've been looking kind of stressed-out all day."

"I am stressed," Stuart admitted.

"Did something happen here at work?"

Stuart shook his head. "Everything's going along fine here in the store. What has me stressed is what's going on at home."

"A little trouble in paradise?"

"More than a little; and our home is anything but paradise these days."

"I'm a good listener if you want to talk about it," Blaine said.

"Pam and I started seeing a counselor about a month ago, but it's not helping. Things just seem to be getting worse."

Blaine gave Stuart's shoulder a light thump. "Well, give it a bit more time. There's never been a city built in a day, you know."

"I don't think any amount of time will make Pam enjoy the same things I do." Stuart scrubbed his hand down the side of his bristly face. He really should have shaved this morning. It wasn't good for business to have the store manager looking scruffy, but he'd been upset with something Pam said and left the house in a hurry. Pam was always nagging him about the way he looked and dressed, and even though he knew she was probably right, it irritated him to have her telling him what to do all the time. He had to admit at times he deliberately wore clothes she didn't like just to get back at her for harassing him.

"Maybe if you did more things your wife enjoys, she'd be willing to do some things you like to do."

"I doubt that's ever going to happen, but I did try something she wanted me to do."

"What was that?"

"You're probably not gonna believe this, but Pam actually talked me into going to some quilting classes with her."

Blaine's dark eyebrows lifted almost to his hairline. "Are you kidding me?"

Stuart shook his head. "She promised to go fishing with me four more times if I attended the six-week quilting class."

"I can't believe you'd agree to that. You've got more guts than I do."

Stuart thumped the side of his head. "More to the point, I think I was just plain stupid."

"So you're actually going to learn how to make a quilt?"

"Well, I was supposed to be making a quilted wall hanging, but—"

"What will you do with the wall hanging when it's done?" Blaine asked as he poured himself a cup of coffee.

"If I were to finish mine, it would probably look so horrible I'd end up throwing it in the garbage." Stuart grimaced. "Pam's such a perfectionist; hers will probably be good enough for any wall in our house. You know, I thought at first that quilting would be easy, but after the second lesson, I realized there's a lot more to it than I'd expected."

Blaine sat staring at Stuart, slowly shaking his head. "You must love your wife a lot if you'd be willing to sit through six weeks of classes, playing with a needle and thread."

"We made an agreement that I'd take the quilting classes with her, and then she'd have to go fishing with me four more times, but I—"

"That sounds tough. Besides the sewing thing, which I could never do, I'm not sure I could sit with a group of people I don't even know while they carried on about material and quilts all day."

"The class is only two hours every Saturday, and after the way things went last week, I decided I don't want to go back."

"So you're reneging on your promise to Pam?"

Stuart shrugged. "If you want to call it that, then, yeah, guess I am."

Blaine shook his head. "Oh boy, no wonder your marriage is in trouble."

"What do you mean?"

"It means if I'd made a promise to Sue and backed out, she'd never let me hear the end of it." Blaine took another swig of coffee. "Was it really that bad sitting in class with a bunch of women?"

"This may surprise you, but I wasn't the only man in the class."

"Now that is a surprise. How many other men were there besides you?"

"Two. There's this big biker fellow who likes to throw his weight around and a young Hispanic schoolteacher whose wife recently died. There are also three women taking the class: Pam; Ruby Lee, an African-American woman who's a pastor's wife; and Star."

"Star?"

"She's a young woman with a nose ring and an attitude that reeks of defiance."

"Wow! Sounds like you've gotten yourself hooked up with quite an unusual bunch of people."

"Yeah. That little quilting club is pretty unique." Stuart lifted his coffee mug and took a drink. "And from what I could tell, almost everyone there has some sort of problem."

"Problem with quilting you mean?"

"Nope. A problem with some issue in their life."

"Show me someone who doesn't have problems, and I'll show you someone who's no longer livin' on this earth," Blaine said with a snicker.

"Yeah, you're right, but some problems are more serious than others." Stuart groaned. "I'm just afraid if Pam and I don't get our problems solved soon, we might be headed for a separation—or worse yet, a divorce."

Shipshewana

"You can just drop me off here," Jan told Terry as they approached his driveway late Friday afternoon. "Need to check my mail, and since I know you have a heavy date this evening, you can just be on your way."

"It's not a heavy date. Dottie and I are going bowling and out for pizza." Terry thumped Jan's shoulder. "Want us to fix you up with Dottie's friend Gwen? I think you'd really like her."

"Not tonight, man," Jan said. "I've gotta work on my wall hanging."

Terry looked at Jan with disbelief. "I can't believe you'd pass up a night of bowling and pizza with a fine-looking chick to stay home and keep company with a needle and thread."

Jan shrugged his shoulders. "What can I say? Think I've found my creative self, like my probation officer said I should do. And you know what—it's actually kinda relaxin' and fun."

Terry snorted. "I can think of lots of other creative things to do besides prickin' my finger with the sharp end of a needle."

Jan chuckled. He didn't figure Terry would understand. "I'll see you on Monday mornin'. Have a good weekend, bud."

"Yep. You, too."

As Terry's truck pulled away, Jan headed for his mailbox by the side of the road. He'd just taken out a stack of mail when Brutus bounded up, wagging his tail.

Jan frowned. "You're out again? How in the world are you doin' it, Brutus?"

Woof! Woof! Brutus's fast-moving tail brushed Jan's pant leg.

"Well, come on. Let's see where you dug out," Jan said as he tromped up the driveway with the dog at his side, tongue hanging out. He could have sworn Brutus was smiling, but then, somehow the dog always looked like he was grinning about something. He was one of those dogs that panted no matter what the weather was like. Even on the coldest days of winter, his tongue would often be hanging out the side of his mouth.

When Jan reached the dog pen, he discovered a hole where Brutus had obviously dug his way out. He shook his finger at Brutus. "Bad dog!"

Brutus lowered his head and slunk through the grass until he reached the house; then he leaped onto the porch with a grunt and a thump. When Jan caught up to him a few seconds later, he discovered a canvas gardening glove lying on the porch near the door.

"Now where'd this come from?" he muttered. "Brutus, did you steal this glove from one of our neighbors?"

The dog's only reply was another deep grunt as he flopped down and rolled onto his back.

"This has gotta stop," Jan said with a disgruntled groan. "Before I do anything else, I'm gonna dig-proof your dog pen."

Goshen

"Where are you going, Beatrice?" Mom asked when Star entered the kitchen wearing her favorite pair of jeans and black hooded sweatshirt.

"I'm goin' to the music store to get some new strings for my guitar; then I'll grab a bite to eat someplace and head over to the coffee shop." Star frowned. "And would you please stop callin' me Beatrice?"

Mom emitted a disgusted sound as she lifted her gaze to the ceiling. "Can't you find something else to do on a Friday evening besides hang out with a bunch of wannabe musicians?"

"I wish you'd get off my case. It's what I enjoy, it's the way I am, and it's better than hangin' out here all evening watching you act all sappy when Mike shows up." Star paused and cleared her throat. "I sure wish you'd dump that creep."

"Mike is not a creep." Mom's nose crinkled as she scrutinized Star. "Don't you want me to be happy?"

Star groaned. "I don't see how you can be happy with a guy like Mike."

"What's wrong with him?"

"For one thing, whenever he comes over here, he just makes himself right at home. Either heads to the kitchen and helps himself to whatever he wants or expects you to wait on him hand and foot. It irritates me when he starts hollering, 'Hey, Nancy, would you get me a beer?'" Star lowered the pitch of her voice to imitate Mike. " 'Oh, Nancy, my shoulders are all knotted up. Could you rub 'em for me, huh?' "

Mom opened her mouth as if to defend her man, but Star cut her off.

"Oh, and don't forget how Mr. Wonderful flops on the couch to watch TV. The guy acts like he owns the place." Star frowned deeply. "And he's always tellin' me what to do, like I'm a little kid and he's my dad."

Mom shook her head. "Oh, come on, Beatrice; it's not that bad."

"Yeah it is."

"Mike asked me to marry him."

"What?" Star gasped, as her mouth dropped open. "I hope you told him no."

Mom sank into a chair at the table. "I didn't say no, but I didn't say yes either. Just said I'd give it some thought and let him know in a few weeks."

Star took a seat, too, and clutched her mother's arm. "If you marry

Mike, I'll have to move out, because I won't stay in the same house with another crummy stepfather!"

"I'll admit Wes wasn't a good husband or stepfather, but Mike's different. He's kind, easygoing, and the restaurant he manages here in Goshen pays him real well."

"Yeah, I know all that, but I still don't like the guy, and I hope you'll think this through and say no."

"Whether I marry Mike or not is my decision, Beatrice, not yours."

Star clenched her fingers until her nails bit into her skin. "Why do I have to keep reminding you, Mom? I go by Star now, not Beatrice. You know how much I hate that name."

"I realize that, but your father insisted on naming you Beatrice after his mother."

"Well, it's a dumb name, and he was a jerk if he liked it." Star leaned forward with her elbows on the table. "Tell me about my dad."

"A few weeks after you were born, he decided that he didn't want to be a father, so he took off down the road and never came back." Mom blinked her eyes rapidly. "I've told you all this before."

"Yeah, but you've never told me much about him. I want to know everything—what he looked like, what he did for a living, where you two met, that kind of stuff."

Mom pushed her chair away from the table and stood. "That's all in the past, and I'd just as soon forget it. Right now I'm going to my room to change out of my waitress uniform, because Mike will be coming here for supper soon."

"Figured as much, and it's all the more reason for me to be gone." Star leaped out of her chair, picked up her guitar, which she'd set in the corner, and headed out the door. *Mom might think Mike's a great catch, but I'm sure he's just like all the other men in her life—nothing but a loser!*

Mishawaka

"Where are the kids?" Stuart asked when he entered the living room where Pam sat in front of her sewing machine near the window. "On a nice day like this, I figured they'd be outside playing."

"Devin's over at his friend Ricky's, and Sherry's upstairs, sick in bed."

Stuart's eyebrows shot up. "What's wrong with her? She wasn't sick when I left for work this morning."

"I got a call from her school shortly after noon saying she was running a fever and had vomited during recess, so I went right over and picked her up."

"How's she doing now?" he asked.

"About the same. I've been checking her temperature regularly, but it hasn't gone down yet."

"That's not good. How come you didn't call me at work?"

"I didn't want to worry you. Besides, there was nothing you could do."

"Did you at least call our pediatrician?"

Pam could hear the irritation in Stuart's voice. Well, she was irritated, too. Didn't he think she was capable enough to take care of their daughter or smart enough to know when to call the doctor? How was she supposed to have any confidence in herself when all he did was put her down or question her intelligence?

"Of course I called Dr. Norton," she snapped. "I'm not stupid, you know."

"Never said you were. Just wanted to be sure our little girl gets well."

Pam folded her arms stiffly, feeling more defensive. "I want that, too, Stuart. Despite what you may think, I am a good mother."

Stuart's eyes flashed angrily. "Give me a break, Pam. I never said you weren't a good mother. Just like always, you're putting words in my mouth."

She blew out her breath in a lingering sigh. "This conversation is getting us nowhere."

"It would be if you'd tell me what Dr. Norton had to say. Or were you even able to get past the receptionist so you could speak with the doctor directly?"

"I wasn't able to talk to her at first, but she did return my call."

"And?"

"She said Sherry's symptoms sound like the flu that's been going around and asked me to let her know if the fever spikes or if Sherry's stomach doesn't settle down soon. If it's the twenty-four-hour flu bug, then I'm sure she'll feel better by tomorrow."

"I hope so." Stuart shifted his weight from one foot to the other. "Uh, I hope you don't expect me to watch the kids tomorrow if Sherry's still sick."

"Well, you did say you'd stay with them while I go to the quilting class."

"Yeah, I know, but that was before Sherry got sick. You know I don't do well with the kids when they're sick. For that matter, they don't do so good with me, either. It's you they want when they're not feeling well."

"Maybe you could take the quilt class in my place," Pam suggested.

His eyes widened. "Huh?"

"If one of us doesn't go, we won't know the next step in making the wall hanging, and I don't want to get behind."

"Then why don't you just quit the class?" he asked.

She shook her head determinedly. "No way! I paid good money to take that class, and I really do want to learn how to quilt. Please, Stuart, say you'll go in my place."

"Huh-uh. I don't think so."

"It's pretty ridiculous and selfish that you don't want to go there alone, but yet you won't stay with the kids either." Pam's chin trembled. "Don't you care about anyone but yourself?"

" 'Course I do."

"Then prove it."

Stuart sat mulling things over then finally nodded. "I may be crazy, but all right, I'll go. Maybe it won't be so bad this week."

Elkhart

"Sleep well, precious one," Paul whispered as he placed Sophia in her crib and bent to give her forehead a kiss. "Pleasant dreams."

Sophia looked up at him through half-closed eyelids and smiled.

Paul's heart clenched. He had to admit he was a bit overprotective of his daughter, but she was all he had left of Lorinda. His baby girl had her mother's dimpled smile, and oh, so many things about Sophia reminded him of Lorinda.

He tiptoed quietly from the room and made his way down the hall, swallowing past the lump in his throat. Today would have been Lorinda's twenty-fifth birthday. If she were still alive, they'd have celebrated the occasion with some of their family. Paul would've bought a bouquet of yellow roses, Lorinda's favorite flower. And Maria probably would have fixed enchiladas and baked a carrot cake with cream cheese frosting— also Lorinda's favorite. They'd have laughed and played games, and if Lorinda's folks had been able to come, they would have shared humorous stories from Lorinda's childhood. But it wasn't meant to be. Lorinda was spending her birthday in heaven instead of here with her family.

Paul ambled into the living room and sank onto the sofa. So many memories—so many regrets. If he'd just seen that truck coming, maybe he could have avoided the accident. Of course, as Paul's priest had told him on more than one occasion, the trucker, who'd only sustained minor injuries, had admitted that he'd run the red light, so if anyone was to blame, it was him.

Then why does Carmen blame me? Paul wondered. *Is she angry because I followed my family when they moved to Indiana? Does she think if we hadn't left California, Lorinda would still be alive? Well, accidents happen there, too—probably even more than here because it's so heavily populated.*

Paul had tried talking to Carmen on the day of Lorinda's funeral, but she'd barely said more than a few words in response, and those she had spoken were hurtful: *"Lorinda would still be here now if it weren't for you."*

Paul leaned forward and let his head fall into his open palms. If Carmen hated him, that was one thing, but did she have to take it out on Sophia? By not keeping in contact, she was cutting herself off from her only niece. And that meant, short of a miracle, Sophia would never get to know her mother's sister. Where was the fairness in that?

Of course, many things in life weren't fair. Look at all the problems some of his second-grade students had gone through with their families this past year. Little Ronnie Anderson's folks had ended their ten-year marriage in an ugly divorce; Anna Freeman had lost her grandma to cancer; and Miguel Garcia had been diagnosed with leukemia. Life was hard, and many things weren't fair, but Paul knew he must keep the faith and trust God to help him through each day. Sophia needed him even more than he needed her. Together they would take one day at a time, and Paul would remember to be thankful for all of God's blessings.

CHAPTER 17

Shipshewana

Emma was surprised when her students showed up for class on Saturday morning and Stuart was alone.

"Where's your wife?" Ruby Lee asked as they all took seats around Emma's sewing table.

"Our daughter came down with the flu, so Pam stayed home to take care of her," Stuart said. "I'm here to learn what I can so Pam doesn't fall behind."

Emma wasn't sure if Stuart's distraught look was because he was worried about his daughter or irritated that he had to come to class. During the first two classes, it had been obvious that he'd felt coerced into coming, and he hadn't shown much interest in learning to make a quilted wall hanging at all.

"It's too bad about your daughter and also Pam missing the class," Emma said.

Ruby Lee clucked her tongue noisily. "I missed many events when my boys were young and came down sick, but then that's just a part of being a mother."

"If Sophia got sick, I'd stay home with her," Paul interjected, "even though I'd probably have to rely on my sister for help, because I'm sure I'd be a basket case if my little girl became ill."

Star folded her arms and frowned. "Nobody ever cared when I got sick—except for one time when I was visiting Grandma and came down with a bad cold. She fussed over me like I was someone special. Even served me breakfast in bed. It felt nice to be taken care of that way and to feel like I meant somethin' to somebody."

Emma's heart went out to Star. She'd obviously had a rough childhood, and with the exception of her grandmother, the poor girl probably hadn't felt much love at all.

"Are you sayin' your ma didn't take care of you when you got sick?" Jan questioned.

Star lifted her shoulders in a brief shrug. "Mom took me to the doctor whenever I was really sick, but when she was at work and I had a cold or the flu, I pretty much had to fend for myself."

"You mean she left you at home alone?" Paul asked with a look of disbelief.

"Yep."

His forehead wrinkled deeply. "I would never leave my little girl alone! What was your mother thinking?"

Star tipped her head and looked at Paul as though he were a complete idiot. "She didn't leave me alone when I was a baby. I went to day care back then. She didn't start leaving me alone till I was in school and old enough to manage on my own while she was at work."

How crazy is this? Star thought. *Now I'm defending my mom? Guess there's something to the saying that a person can talk bad about someone in their family, but no one else had better do it.*

Emma came around behind the table and placed her hands on Star's shoulders. "I'm sorry you had to be alone when you were sick. I'm sure you must have been lonely and scared."

"Yeah, well, I appreciate your sympathy and all, but it won't change the past. Now can we forget all this doom and gloom and get on with our lesson?"

Emma, taken aback by the young woman's abruptness, quickly took a seat on the other side of the table. "Before we begin, I'd like to see how each of you did on your quilting projects this week."

The students placed their unfinished wall hangings on the table, and Emma looked them over. She was disappointed to see that very little work had been done to Pam's and nothing at all on Stuart's.

As though sensing her disappointment, Stuart said, "Pam did a little more sewing on her project before Sherry got sick."

"What about you, man?" Jan spoke up. "Doesn't look like you've done a thing since last Saturday."

Emma tensed, thinking Stuart might lash out at Jan, but she was surprised when he lowered his gaze to the table, removed his ball cap, and mumbled, "I didn't do anything to it 'cause I wasn't planning to come back to the class again."

Emma nodded slowly. "I had a feeling that might be the case."

"It's not that I have anything against you people," Stuart was quick to say. "I just don't feel comfortable about using a needle and thread. Besides, with the way Pam's talked about our problems, I figured you all probably think I'm a terrible husband."

No one said anything. Then Emma finally spoke. "Marriage is about loving the other person enough to do some things just for them—even things you don't want to do."

"Guess you're right." Stuart pulled his fingers through the top of his hair, making it stand nearly straight up. "So maybe I'll change my mind and stick it out through the whole six weeks. Then I'll see if Pam keeps her end of the bargain and goes fishing with me."

"I wouldn't count on that," Jan spoke up. "Most of the women I've ever known say they'll do one thing and end up doing just the opposite."

"Men are no better," Star interjected. "All my mom's *wonderful* boyfriends have been losers—promising this, promising that, and never keeping their word on anything."

Emma figured the conversation was becoming too negative and might lead to a disagreement, so she suggested that everyone take turns using the battery-operated sewing machines so they could get more of their pattern pieces sewn together.

While they worked, Emma was surprised to see how much more easygoing and relaxed Stuart seemed to be. He even cracked a few jokes.

"I may not be so good at sewing," he said, "but there's one thing I know I can do better than anyone else."

"What's that?" Ruby Lee questioned.

"I can read my own handwriting."

Ruby Lee chuckled; Paul grinned; Star rolled her eyes; and Jan just shook his head.

Stuart held up the few pieces he'd managed to sew. "Now look at this mess. Good grief, it takes too many pieces of this little material to make up each point of the star, and to make things worse, I can't even sew a straight seam!"

"You'll get a feel for it," Emma said. "It just takes practice."

Stuart placed his material on the table and pointed out the window. "Those cows I see in that pasture across the way remind me of a story someone told me at the sporting goods store the other day."

"What was it?" Paul asked.

"Well, a guy and a gal were walkin' along a country road, and when they came to a bunch of cows, the guy said, 'Would you just look at that cow and the bull rubbing noses?' He glanced over at his girlfriend and smiled. 'That sight makes me want to do the same.' The girlfriend looked that fellow right in the eye and said, 'If you're not afraid of the bull, then go right ahead.'"

Stuart's joke brought a smile to everyone lips, including Jan's.

Emma wondered if perhaps Stuart felt freer to express himself when his wife wasn't with him. If so, it was a shame, because God never intended for married couples to put each other down or argue about petty things.

Ruby Lee had a hard time keeping her mind on the straight line she was trying to make while using Emma's battery-operated sewing machine. Gene was having a meeting with the church board this morning, and she couldn't help but worry about how things were going. Would they listen to what he had to say or insist on having their own way? She knew that earlier this week Gene had talked to each of the board members individually and hoped he'd been able to make them see that he wasn't trying to get the church into debt. He just wanted to see the congregation take a step of faith so it could grow and reach out to more people in the area.

Resolving to put her concerns aside, Ruby Lee looked over at Emma and said, "How are things with your goat? Maggie, is it?"

Emma nodded.

"Is she still getting out of her pen?"

"Not since my son-in-law fixed the latch on the gate. But then, knowing that sneaky little goat, she might just find a way to open it."

"Boy, I can sure relate to that," Jan said with a grunt. "My German shepherd, Brutus, has turned into the neighborhood thief, so I had to build him a dog pen. He's managed to dig his way out of it a couple of times, but I fixed that by diggin' a small trench all the way around the pen and then puttin' some wire fencing in the ground."

"That was good thinking," Star said, giving Jan a thumbs-up.

"Yeah, but it didn't solve the problem, 'cause the other day Brutus got out again." Jan's forehead creased, but the stress lines disappeared under his biker's bandanna. "Since I didn't see no sign of a hole anywhere, I'm guessin' he had to have climbed over the top."

"My folks used to have a dog that did that," Stuart spoke up. "Dad put some wire fencing over the top of the dog pen, and that solved the problem."

"Guess I might hafta do that if Brutus keeps gettin' out. Sure can't have him runnin' all over the neighborhood stealin' other people's things. I just don't have the time to be chasin' all over the place, tryin' to find out who the items belong to that Brutus keeps takin'. If he doesn't quit it, I'm either gonna be the laughin'stock of the whole neighborhood, or no one will be speakin' to me." Chuckling, he added, "Guess there's a positive side to all of this though."

"What's that?" Paul asked.

"I'm actually gettin' to meet some of my neighbors when I go around lookin' for the owner of the things Brutus has taken."

That comment got a good laugh from everyone.

"I heard about a cat that was a kleptomaniac," Ruby Lee said. "After talking to an expert on the subject, the people were told that the cat was probably bored and needed more attention. I guess the cat stole more than a hundred items before the owners finally figured out what to do about the problem."

"Lack of attention could be why your dog's getting out of his pen," Star said. "I visited a website once when I was doin' a research paper for twelfth-grade English. The whole thing was about pets that escape from their pen and run off. Some animal psychologist came up with the idea that when a dog does that, it's also in need of more attention."

Jan nodded as he popped a few of his knuckles. "I've been pretty busy with work lately, and so I haven't spent much time with Brutus. Guess I'll need to take more time out for him and see if it makes a difference. Maybe it'd be a good idea if I take him with me when I make my rounds through the neighborhood tryin' to return all of the things he's taken."

"I've always wanted a dog," Star said wistfully. "But Mom and I have moved around so much it just never worked out for me to get one. I may get a dog when I have a place of my own someday though."

"Another reason you don't want your dog running all over the place, Jan, is to keep him from getting out on the road where he might get hit by a car," Emma said. "That's why I asked my son-in-law to fix the gate on the goat pen. Maggie's a bad one, but I would hate to see anything happen to her."

"That's right," Paul interjected. "On my way here this morning, I saw a German shepherd lying dead in the road. Apparently someone hit the poor dog and then fled the scene, because I didn't see anyone standing around or even a car parked near the shoulder of the road."

"What'd the dog look like?" Jan asked, concern showing clearly on his face.

"Traffic was almost at a standstill, and from what I could tell when I passed the animal, it was black and tan."

Jan's eyebrows shot up. "That sounds like my Brutus. Where exactly did you see the dog?"

"He was on the main road coming into Shipshewana, near the 5 and 20 Country Kitchen," Paul replied.

"That's not far from my place!" Jan leaped out of his chair then turned to Emma. "Sorry, but I've gotta go." Leaving his quilt project on the table, he rushed out the door.

"That poor man sure looked upset," Emma said. "I hope his dog is all right."

Ruby Lee nodded. "Some people's pets are very important to them—almost like children. When my boys were six years old and their cat died, they insisted their dad do a little burial service in our backyard."

"Did he do it?" Star asked.

Ruby Lee nodded. "The boys carried on so much that Gene could hardly say no."

"My kids have been after me to get them a dog, but pets are a lot of work, and I'm not sure they're ready for the responsibility." Stuart's stomach growled, and he covered it with his hands, probably hoping to quiet the noise. "Oops. . .sorry about that. Pam was busy caring for Sherry this morning, and she didn't have time to fix me anything for breakfast. So I just grabbed a cup of coffee and headed out the door."

"Why didn't you fix yourself something to eat? You look capable enough to me," Star said, looking thoroughly disgusted with Stuart.

Stuart shrugged. "Never thought about it 'cause Pam has always made my breakfast."

"Well, there's a first time for everything. Maybe you oughta help your wife out once in a while," Star muttered.

"I do plenty of things to help out."

"Uh, let's take a break, and I'll bring out a treat. Then we can continue working on the wall hangings after that," Emma said with a cheerful smile.

Ruby Lee was quite sure that Emma felt the tension between Star and Stuart. If she had to guess, she'd say that Star was probably angry with someone who'd treated her mother poorly.

"A treat sounds good to me," Stuart agreed. "Have you got any more of those tasty doughnuts you served us last week?"

Emma shook her head. "No, but I do have an angel cream pie I baked yesterday, and there's a pot of coffee on the stove. I'll head out to the kitchen to get them right now."

"I'll go with you." Star left her seat and followed Emma out of the room, leaving Ruby Lee alone with the men.

"Sure hope I get the hang of sewing," Stuart said, motioning to the little he'd done on his wall hanging. "I feel like I'm all thumbs." He held up his hands. "Sore thumbs at that, from getting stuck with the pins so many times. No wonder I've seen women use those little thimble contraptions to cover their fingers."

"I've pricked my finger a few times, too," Paul said with a chuckle. "Makes me appreciate all the sewing my wife used to do."

Ruby Lee was about to comment when her cell phone rang. It was a number she didn't recognize, so she was tempted to let the call go into voice mail. But something told her to answer, as it might be important.

"Hello," Ruby Lee said.

"Is this Mrs. Williams?"

"Yes."

"My name is Joan Hastings. I'm a nurse at the hospital in Goshen, and I'm calling to let you know that your husband's here in the emergency room."

"Oh, can I speak to him?" Ruby Lee asked, thinking Gene must be with one of their parishioners who'd been hurt or had become ill.

"He can't talk to you at the moment," the nurse replied. "He's being examined by one of our doctors."

Ruby Lee's heart started to pound. Gene was in the emergency room being examined by a doctor? Something terrible must have happened. "W–was he in an accident? Is he seriously hurt?"

"He's having trouble breathing and complained of feeling dizzy when he first came in. We've run some tests to see if it's his heart, and—"

"I'll be right there!" Hands shaking, Ruby Lee ended the call and turned to face Paul and Stuart. "W–would you please let Emma know that I had to go? My husband's been taken to the emergency room." Without waiting for either man's reply, she gathered up her sewing and rushed out the door.

CHAPTER 18

Mishawaka

Pam glanced at the clock on the kitchen wall. It was eleven o'clock, which meant the quilting class would be over in an hour.

She opened the refrigerator and poured herself a glass of iced tea, wondering how Stuart was doing. She hated to see him go alone but knew her place was at home, taking care of the kids. Although Sherry was feeling a little better this morning, she wasn't well enough to leave with a sitter. Poor little thing hadn't been able to keep anything down until early this morning when Pam had given her some ginger tea and a small piece of toast.

A niggle of guilt settled over Pam as she remembered that she hadn't fixed Stuart any breakfast—although once in a while, he should be able to manage on his own. After all, he had to have known she was busy taking care of Sherry, and he wasn't completely helpless in the kitchen—just lazy and too dependent on her.

Pam glanced out the window to see what Devin was up to. She

didn't see him jumping on the trampoline, but then she remembered he'd said something about playing in the tree house. Stuart had built it last summer so that he and Devin could climb up there once in a while and have a little father-son time. Trouble was Devin was the only one who used it. Pam had seen Stuart go into the tree house just once, and that was right after he'd built it.

If he didn't spend so much time in front of the TV watching sports, he might take more of an interest in the kids, Pam fumed. *Doesn't he realize how quickly they're growing? Soon they'll be grown and moved out on their own, and then it'll be impossible to get back those wasted years when he should have been doing more things with his family.*

Knowing she needed to focus on something positive, and confident that Sherry was still sleeping, Pam decided to take her iced tea outside on the porch where she could enjoy the breeze that had come up a short time ago.

Stepping outside and taking a seat in one of the wicker chairs, Pam glanced toward the pink and purple petunias she'd planted in her flower garden last week. They were so beautiful and added just the right splash of color to the area where she'd put them.

Pam's thoughts halted when she heard a whimpering noise. Glancing up at the tree house in the maple tree, she realized it must be Devin. She set down her glass and hurried across the yard.

"Devin," she called. "Are you okay?"

More whimpering followed by some sniffles.

Heart pounding, she climbed the ladder to the tree house where she found her son huddled in one corner, tears rolling down his flushed cheeks.

"What's wrong, Devin?" she asked, kneeling on the wooden floor beside him. "Are you hurt?"

He shook his head. "I–I'm scared 'cause Daddy might leave and never come back."

"Now why would you think that?"

"My friend Andy's dad left, and Andy never sees him no more." Devin sniffed and swiped his hand over his damp cheeks. "If Daddy left, I'd really be sad."

Pam slipped her arm around Devin's shoulders and drew him close. "Your daddy's not going to move out of our house."

"Are—are you sure?"

"Yes, I'm very sure," Pam said with a nod, although secretly she'd been worried about that very thing.

Shipshewana

"What did you say this is called?" Star asked when Emma placed the pie on the table and asked her to cut it into even pieces.

"Angel cream pie," Emma replied. "My grandmother used to make it, and she gave me the recipe when I got married."

"Speaking of grandmothers—you sort of remind me of my grandma. Not in the way you look, but the way you treat people. Your kindness and sense of humor make me think of her, too."

Emma smiled. Even though Star was wearing that black sweatshirt again, it was good to see that the hood wasn't on her head today. The young woman had a pretty face, and it was nice to see her tender expression when she spoke of her grandmother—although Emma still didn't understand why Star had purple streaks in her hair, wore a nose ring, and had a tattoo on her neck. But then, there were many things she didn't understand—especially when it came to some Englishers. Even so, Emma knew God had created everyone, and that each person was special to Him.

"I miss my grandma so much." Star's eyes suddenly filled with tears. "She always did nice things for me. Not like my mom, who only thinks of herself."

"What about your father? Where is he?" Emma questioned, wondering how any mother could only think of herself. It wasn't the Amish way to be selfish like that.

"Beats me. I've never met him. He ran out on us when I was a baby, and Mom ended up marrying some loser when I was eight years old." Star's forehead creased as she frowned. "His name was Wes Morgan, and he was really mean to Mom."

"Was he mean to you as well?"

"Not really. He pretty much ignored me. Wes died a few years after they were married, when he stepped out into traffic and got hit by a car. Mom and I have been on our own ever since."

"I'm sorry," Emma said, gently touching Star's arm.

"Yeah, it hasn't been easy, but I'm glad Wes is out of the picture." Star wrinkled her nose. "Now Mom's thinkin' of marrying this guy named Mike."

"I take it you don't care much for Mike?"

"Nope. Don't like him at all. He hangs out at our place all the time, expects Mom to wait on him, and tries to tell me how I should live." Star motioned to the pie. "All the pieces are cut now. Is there anything else you want me to do?" she asked, abruptly changing the subject.

Emma handed Star a serving tray. "You can put the pie on this, along with some plates and forks." She gathered up five plates and forks, which she then handed to Star. "Before you take these out to the others, I want you to know that you're welcome to come by here anytime if you should ever need to talk."

Star blinked a couple of times and stared at Emma with a look of disbelief. "Really? You wouldn't mind?"

"Not at all. I'm a good listener, and perhaps I may be able to offer you some advice."

"Thanks. I might take you up on that offer sometime." Wearing a smile on her face, Star picked up the tray and headed into the next room. Emma followed with another tray that held the coffee and mugs.

When Emma entered her sewing room, she was surprised to see only Paul and Stuart sitting at the table. "Where's Ruby Lee?" she asked.

"She got a phone call saying her husband had been taken to the emergency room, so she had to leave," Paul explained.

"I'm sorry to hear that," Emma said, feeling concern. "I certainly hope Ruby Lee's husband will be okay."

Goshen

When Ruby Lee entered the room where Gene had been examined, she found him sitting on the edge of the table buttoning his shirt.

"What happened?" she asked, rushing to his side, wanting to help with the buttons.

He waved his hand. "Don't look so worried; I'm not going to die. The doctor said I had an anxiety attack, but I'm feeling much better."

"What brought that on?" she asked. "Did something happen during the board meeting to upset you?"

"Yeah. The subject of adding on to the church came up again, and we ended up in an explosive meeting. I think all the bickering got to me, because my chest tightened up and I felt woozy and like I couldn't breathe."

Ruby Lee clutched his arm. "This whole mess with the church isn't good for your health. Surely you can see that. How much longer do you intend to put yourself through this, Gene?"

"I'm fine. There's nothing to worry about."

"You might be fine now, but what about the next time? You could end up really having a heart attack if you keep subjecting yourself to all this conflict with the board members. Won't you reconsider and look for another church? And what about me? I don't know what I would do if I lost you—especially over something like this."

He shook his head. "I've told you before, God called me to shepherd this flock, and until He releases me from that call, I'm staying put."

"What about the plans you have for adding on to the church? Are you going to keep fighting for it or let the idea go by the wayside?"

"I don't know. I'm trusting God to give me further direction, and I feel confident that everything will work out as it should—for our church building, our congregation, and for us, Ruby Lee."

I wish I had your optimism, she thought. *If I believed for one minute that it would do any good, I'd speak to each of the board members right now and give them a piece of my mind!*

Shipshewana

By the time Jan turned onto the road his house was on, he was out of breath from peddling his bike so hard. After he'd left Emma's, he'd gone to the intersection where Paul had seen the dead dog, needing to know if it was Brutus who'd been hit by a car. But the only sign of the accident was a large bloodstain on the pavement. The body of the dog was gone. He could hardly look at the crimson spot without imagining his faithful pet lying there lifeless. It had been all he could do to call the Humane Society and ask if they had his dog. He'd been told that a German shepherd had been killed and brought in earlier today, but since there were no tags or license to identify the dog's owner, they'd already disposed of the body.

It's just as well that I didn't see the dog's remains, Jan thought. *If it was Brutus, I don't think I coulda stood seein' him lyin' there, dead.*

Another thought popped into his head. *Maybe I'll find Brutus at home, safe in his pen, and then all my worries will have been for nothin'.*

Even though Jan hardly ever prayed, he found himself thinking, *Please, Lord, don't let my dog be dead.*

Anxious to see if Brutus was there, Jan didn't bother to stop at the mailbox. Instead, he pedaled quickly up the driveway and halted the bike, letting it fall in front of the dog pen. It was empty. No Brutus in sight.

"Brutus, where are you boy?" Jan called, hoping against hope that the dog might be somewhere on the property or at least close by. This was one time he wished Brutus was roaming the neighborhood, looking for something he could carry off and bring home.

Still no response to Jan's call.

Jan clapped, hollered the dog's name several more times, and gave a shrill whistle. Nothing. Not a whimper or a bark.

"Oh man," he moaned. "Brutus is dead, and it's all my fault. If I'd only done somethin' right away to keep him in his pen, this wouldn't have happened. Now it's too late, and I've lost my best friend."

Jan tried his best not to get choked up, wondering what his friend Terry would think if he stopped by and saw him blubbering like a baby. But Jan couldn't seem to help himself. That four-legged animal had gotten inside his heart, and he was miserable without him.

Jan looked up and noticed his cranky neighbor, Selma, peeking around the curtain in her kitchen window. Did she know Brutus was gone? When she found out he was dead, she'd probably be glad. He wished that he'd had the smarts to get a license and some ID tags for Brutus. At least then the Humane Society could have called and let him know when the dog was brought in.

Jan felt so miserable he was tempted to go in the house and drown his sorrows in a few beers. But what good would that do? It wouldn't bring Brutus back, and it would only dull the pain for a little while. No, he was better off without the beer and may as well face this thing head-on. It wasn't like the dog's death had been the only disappointment he'd ever had to face. Jan had faced a lot of disappointments along the way.

CHAPTER 19

When Emma woke up on Sunday morning, it was all she could do to get out of bed. She'd been extremely tired when she went to sleep last night and felt a strange tingling sensation along part of her waist. This morning her symptoms had increased, and her ears were ringing, too. She figured the fatigue could be from working too hard and not getting enough sleep, but she didn't like the constant irritation bothering her stomach. Maybe she hadn't gotten all the soap out when she'd washed clothes the other day. Could she be having an allergic reaction?

Maybe I shouldn't go to church today, Emma told herself as she ambled out to the kitchen. *Might be best if I stay home and rest—just in case I'm coming down with something contagious. But I'll need to let Mary know.*

Emma filled the teakettle with water and set it on stove, and while the water heated, she got dressed. She'd just set her head covering in place when she heard the teakettle whistle.

Returning to the kitchen, she poured the water into a ceramic teapot, dropped a tea bag in, and went out the back door.

When Emma entered Mary's yard, she was greeted by her fourteen-year-old grandson, Stephen, who was leading one of their buggy horses out of the barn.

"Guder mariye, Grossmammi," he said cheerfully. "Are you comin' over to our house for *friehschtick*?"

Emma shook her head. "No breakfast this morning. I just need to speak to your mamm."

Stephen pointed to the house. "She's probably in the kitchen. Would you tell her I'll be in as soon as I get Dan hitched to the buggy?"

"Jah, I sure will." Emma, feeling even wearier than before, stepped onto the back porch. When she entered the kitchen, she found her two young granddaughters, Lisa and Sharon, setting the table, while Mary stood at the counter cracking hard-boiled eggs.

"Guder mariye, Mom," Mary said, turning to smile at Emma. "Will you be joining us for frieschtick?"

Emma shook her head. "I'm not feeling like myself this morning, so I'm just going to have a cup of tea and stretch out on the sofa."

"Are you *grank*?" Mary's dark eyes revealed the depth of her concern.

"I'm not sure if I'm sick or not. Just feel really tired, and my skin feels kind of prickly right here." Emma touched the left side of her stomach.

"Have you checked for any kind of a rash?" Mary questioned.

"Jah, but I didn't see anything. Why do you ask?"

"I'm wondering if you might be coming down with shingles again. It seems to me when you had them before you mentioned your skin felt prickly at first."

Emma frowned. She'd come down with shingles a week after Ivan died and had been absolutely miserable. "I do hope it's not shingles again. I sure don't have time for that right now."

"Nobody has time to be grank, Grossmammi," Lisa spoke up. "But when it happens, there ain't much you can do about it."

"Isn't," Mary corrected. She looked back at Emma. "If you're not feeling well, would you like me to come over to your house and fix you something to eat before we leave for church?"

Emma shook her head. "I'll be fine with the tea, and maybe I'll have a piece of toast."

"All right then, but I'll be over to check on you sometime after we get home," Mary said.

"Stop by if you must, but I'm sure I'll be fine." Emma patted the top of Lisa's head and then turned toward the door.

Lingering on Mary's porch to take in the quiet of the morning, Emma leaned her head on the railing post and breathed in the heavy scent of lilacs that had been blooming along the fence for the last week. Overhead in the trees, the red-winged blackbirds sang, *Jubile-e-e! Jubile-e-e!* Pausing to enjoy peaceful moments like this could make up for any day that had started out wrong.

Emma's weariness increased, so she didn't linger long. Approaching her own back porch, she'd just made it to the first step when a wave of dizziness caught her off-balance. She quickly grabbed for the railing, thankful that she was able to keep from falling over.

Please, just let me get into my house.

The wooden boards creaked beneath her feet as she took each step slowly, inching her way up, still wavering. At the door, she closed her eyes for a minute, steadying herself and breathing deeply. Relieved when the dizziness started to fade, she was able to enter the house.

When Emma stepped into the kitchen, she checked the teapot. The tea was plenty well steeped, so she poured herself a cup, fixed a piece of toast, and took a seat at the table. Then she bowed her head for silent prayer.

The Amish Quilting Tradition

In the plain culture of both the Old Order Amish and Mennonite women, a quilt shows love, much the same as a favorite food is carefully prepared as a display of affection. Quilt patterns are a reflection of daily living and often resemble things found in nature or on the farm, like stars and fences. Quilting displays a woman's ability as a seamstress, and she may show her quilts for the admiration of others without intimidation. Her quilts reflect her personality, as does a well-kept home or garden. In a culture that does not encourage prideful self exhibition, quilting becomes one way a woman can express artistic skills in a useful way that benefits others more than herself.

But quilting in the traditional sense didn't become evident in the Amish culture until the 1870s. At first, the attention focused on stitches to hold layers of fabric together. Often called whole cloth quilting, the style allowed women to use very elaborate feather or scroll designs that often weren't visible unless one was close to the quilt. Later, the piecing of different fabrics and colors came into use and became more detailed, even as the decorative quilt stitching became less intricate. At first the fabrics used were solid and dark, much like the plain choice of clothing, but later they added pastels and whites.

The Amish create their quilts not for art, but for functionality. Still, by the 1970s, modern urban dwellers were becoming fascinated by the beauty of Amish fabric work. Soon it became acceptable for Amish women to use their sewing skills to sell their work and contribute to the family income.

At a very young age, girls are taught the basics of sewing quilt patches. Quilting techniques are shared from generation to generation, and quilts are often passed down to children and grandchildren. Many women find time to quilt during long winter evenings. It's a relaxing pastime that is also very worthwhile and useful. Often, women will get together for an all-day quilting bee, which is also a time of fellowship and sharing.

Photo of a Bars quilt from the International Quilt Study and Museum in Lincoln, Nebraska. This quilt was probably made in Pennsylvania around 1900.

❧ Emma's Quilt Collection ❧

Photo of a One Patch quilt taken in Arthur, Illinois by Richard Brunstetter. This quilt uses ties to bind it instead of quilted stitches.

Emma Yoder's sewing room is a welcoming place with many windows letting in the natural light that is very helpful while sewing. Her husband, Ivan, added the room onto the house after most of their children were grown and out of the home. If she let her guard down, Emma could easily feel pride in this room's beauty and function and in the love it represents.

Emma has a large collection of quilts. Many she has made, but several came from her mother and other relatives. She does try to use them all in various ways, but some she considers just too special to do more than display occasionally on her quilt rack in an area away from direct sunlight.

Weaver Fever is one of her most favorite quilts. The piecing looks complicated, but with a good bit of planning up front, the design comes together with ease. Her Weaver Fever quilt was made while her mother was still living. Emma worked on it with her mother and sister. The hours of time spent together talking while they stitched (both by machine and hand) are represented in the quilt. It is a treasure that warms Emma's heart each time she looks at it on the guest room bed where it usually resides.

One Patch is another favorite that, in its simplicity, brings joy to Emma's heart. It was the pattern she used to teach her daughter Mary to piece together a quilt. They worked on the project together when Mary was just eight years old and opted to use ties to hold the fabric layers together instead of quilted stitches. Emma still has the quilt that covered Mary's childhood bed for many years. Eventually, she will see that Mary takes it home with her.

Photo of a Weaver Fever quilt in Wanda E. Brunstetter's collection taken by Richard Brunstetter.

❧ The Double Wedding Ring ❧

A quilt given to young couples when they get married commonly is thought to have a long cultural history. But historians generally agree that the Double Wedding Ring pattern first appeared in the 1920s and became popular during the Depression era.

The Double Wedding Ring has a light, airy feel because of the large open spaces inside the connecting rings. The design is made of several wedged pieces—often various scraps from bigger sewing projects—joined together to create an arch. The centers are usually done in a lighter contrasting color of fabric to help accent the rings. Often this pattern is done without an outer border, so that the rings create a scalloped edge to the finished quilt.

The double wedding ring marriage ceremony also rose in popularity around the same time as the quilt pattern. American jewelers started marketing the idea of a wedding band for the husband in the late 1800s, but the practice didn't come into widespread popularity until the World War II era.

The ring—or unbroken circle—symbolizes eternal, never-ending love. So the Double Wedding Ring quilt, with the rich meaning associated with it, naturally became a popular gift at weddings.

Pam Johnston was especially drawn to this quilt pattern and wished someone had given her and her husband, Stuart, a quilt like that when they got married. Perhaps in her mind, such a gift would have served as a blessing over their marriage bed and brought a better sense of unity to their years together.

Photo of a Double Wedding Ring quilt taken in Arthur, Illinois by Richard Brunstetter.

❦ The Star ❦

There are several variations of star-patterned quilts, the Mariner's Compass and the Lone Star being among the oldest documented. Star Stephens thought the Lone Star pattern fit her perpetual feelings of being alone and unloved. She recalled seeing the easy-to-recognize pattern among quilts in her grandmother's collection, though she didn't know if it was one her grandmother had actually stitched.

The Lone Star is one of the most dramatic of the star patterns, in which a large star bursts from the center of the quilt in a radiating placement of colors. The typical Lone Star has six or eight points comprised of many diamond-shaped pieces.

Star pattern quilts are quite popular among the Amish. Many of the earliest Lone Star (also called Bethlehem Star) quilts were found in Pennsylvania. Stars on a quilt may suggest the quilter's respect for God's creation. Many of the star patterns among the Amish have backgrounds of dark colors, making a lighter colored star stand out like a beacon against a night sky.

Photo of a Lone Star quilt in Wanda E. Brunstetter's collection taken by Richard Brunstetter.

❦ The Log Cabin ❦

A block pattern with a long history (as seen in wood inlays on chopping blocks or the weave of reeds in baskets), the Log Cabin pattern is well loved and well recognized.

Building off a small center square, strips, or logs, of material are added one by one to build a square. Depending on fabric choices and how the squares are joined together, the Log Cabin pattern can be the foundation of numerous overall quilt designs.

Upon meeting Jan Sweet, Emma assumed a strong and manly biker-type would enjoy the outdoors and things like camping, so she had him study the Log Cabin pattern. When done in shades of brown that graduate from light to dark, the pattern can have a very rugged and masculine appeal.

Photo of the Log Cabin pattern from the International Quilt Study and Museum in Lincoln, Nebraska. This quilt was possibly made in Holmes County, Ohio.

❦ The Dahlia ❧

Ruby Lee Williams is a gardener who enjoys tending and arranging flowers. Naturally, she was drawn to Emma's Dahlia quilt. She could imagine using this quilt in one of her new home's many window seats to cuddle up in as she enjoyed the view of her neatly manicured flowerbeds.

The Dahlia, also known as Star Flower, is a variation of a star design. The basic pieced block uses the eight-point Star or Sawtooth Star pattern. The Dahlia design has a unique quality, in that it uses petals of fabric created apart from the main quilt block and appliquéd on later. The bulk of each petal is gathered at the center of the flower creating an extra three-dimensional effect.

Photo of the Dahlia quilt in Wanda E. Brunstetter's collection taken by Richard Brunstetter.

❦ The Tumbling Baby Block ❧

The Baby Block pattern, also known as Tumbling Block, resonated with Paul Ramirez because his wife had started making a baby quilt similar to that pattern before she died. In the Tumbling Baby Block, a single diamond shape and varied placement of colors creates an optical illusion of stars, hexagons, diamonds, and cubes. In order to achieve the illusion of stacked cubes or boxes, three fabrics in various intensities of colors must be used. The darker color is always in one position in the hexagon, the medium color in another, and the lighter color in the third position, generally reflective of how light and shadow would fall on a cube. The Tumbling Baby Block is first pieced into hexagons and then the hexagons are added to each other in succession. Joining diamonds and hexagons is generally not for the beginning quilter, but modern patterns using simplified techniques have made this design much more easily achieved.

Photo of the Tumbling Block quilt in Wanda E. Brunstetter's collection taken by Richard Brunstetter.

✌ Emma's Quilt Class Pattern ✍

After the joys and trials of teaching her first quilting class, Emma decided to create a simple wall hanging pattern that a beginner could do. Without a doubt, she was inspired by Star and Jan as she combined Log Cabin quilt blocks with an Eight Point Star layout. She used sashing to frame the pieces, which ended up representing the new way Emma had of looking through the window of souls she encounters in life. The finished small quilt measures 35" square. Read all directions before starting.

Materials (solid 100% cotton fabric is recommended):
- ⅛ yard or less of 3 shades of blue, from light to dark, and 2 shades of green, light and medium
- Scrap of bright yellow at least 8" x 2"
- ½ yard of dark green
- ½ yard of red
- 1 ½ yards of black

Instructions:
- From the yellow, cut four 1.5" squares and one 2"square
- From the light blue, cut four 1.5" squares and four rectangles 1.5" x 2.5"
- From the light green, cut four rectangles 1.5" x 2.5" and four rectangles 1.5" x 3.5"
- From the medium blue, cut four rectangles 1.5" x 3.5" and four rectangles 1.5" x 4.5"
- From the medium green, cut four rectangles 1.5" x 4.5" and four rectangles 1.5" x 5.5"
- From the dark blue, cut four rectangles 1.5" x 5.5" and four rectangles 1.5" x 6.5"
- From the dark green, cut four rectangles 1.5" x 6.5", four rectangles 1.5"x 7.5", and eight 8.5" squares
- From the black, cut four 7.5" squares and four 8.5" squares
- From the red, cut four strips 2" x 15"

(Tip: before cutting, you may want to wash and dry your fabric. Then iron it using a spray starch. Starch will give the fabric body and keep it from moving or stretching as you sew. As you start your cuts, be sure to cut along the straight grain of the fabric.)

- Sewing is done with a ¼ inch seam allowance.

1. Log Cabin Blocks

To build the Log Cabin blocks, start by sewing a 1.5" square of yellow to a 1.5" square of light blue. Press seams to the dark side, away from the center square. To the long side, add a 1.5" x 2.5" rectangle (or log) of the light blue. Press seams to the dark side. (Continue pressing seams after each "log" is added.) Along the side where the short end of the 1.5" x 2.5" log and the yellow center square are joined, sew a 1.5" x 2.5" log of the light green. Along the side that has three fabric pieces join a 1.5" x 2.5" log of the light green. Keep laying the logs in this manner, referring to the drawing for help. The last piece you will add is the dark green 1.5" x 7.5" log. Your Log Cabin block should finish at 7.5" square. Square up and trim if necessary to get the 7.5" measurement. Make four Log Cabin blocks as described.

2. Half-Square Triangle Blocks

Take each of your black 8.5" squares and pair them with a dark green 8.5" square. Using a ruler, draw a line from one point to another, diagonally down the middle of the square. Measure ¼ inch from the line and draw another line. Turn the fabric and draw another line ¼ inch from the center line. Sew down both outer lines, stopping ¼ inch from the edge of the fabric. Cut down the center line and press each section open by ironing to the black side. Using a square ruler, measure and trim each half square triangle block to 7.5". You will have eight half-square triangle blocks when done.

3. Four Composite Blocks

Take a Log Cabin block and sew it to a half-square triangle block so that the greens meet. Be sure the 90 degree angle of the triangle block meets the Log Cabin block at the point where the green logs make a 90 degree angle. Join a black 7.5" square to the (color) side of a triangle block, then join that to the Log Cabin section. Refer to the diagram. Press seams to the dark side. You will now have a large composite block made up of one Log Cabin, two half-square triangles, and one black square. Create four of these groupings. They should measure 15" square. If not, square them up with a square ruler and rotary cutter, trimming away any excess.

4. Adding the Inner Sashing

Join two of your large blocks together with a strip of red sashing along the sides of the Log Cabin blocks (refer to the diagram for placement). Press seams. Join the other two blocks in the same manner. Press seams. Take the remaining 2" inch yellow block and piece the center sashing with a red strip, yellow block, red strip. Press seams to the dark side. The finished length of this center sashing should match the long sides of your two joined blocks. Sew the pieced sash to join the two double block pieces into one large four-block piece.

5. Attach Borders

Add a 2" border to the top and bottom using the red material. Press seams. Add the 2" border to the sides. Press. Use the remaining black material for backing and binding. You can quilt this in the ditch along your main seams, or you can find an instructor like Emma to teach you various quilting techniques.

Finished size will be 35" square, unless yours turned out like Emma's sample. She tried the pattern out by having her twelve-year-old granddaughter work on it. The Log Cabin blocks were a bit challenging on the sewing machine for the girl. After squaring up her blocks and trimming, her final quilt top was a bit smaller but still a pleasing project.

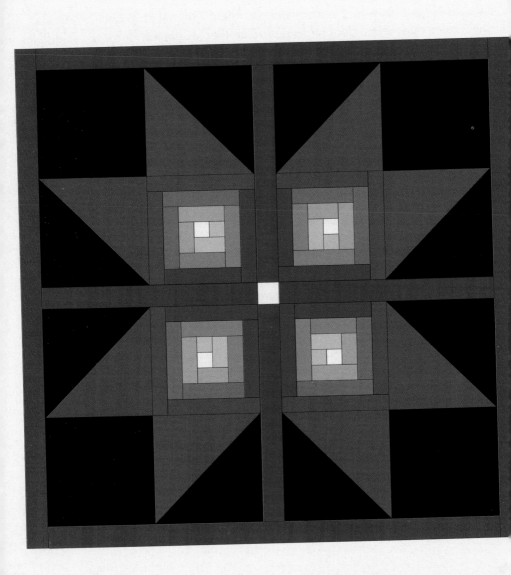

When she finished eating, she put the dishes in the sink and took the rest of her tea to the living room.

Emma yawned. Unable to keep her eyes open, she removed her head covering, stretched out on the sofa, and closed her eyes. The gentle breeze blowing softly through her open living room window, the smell of fresh air, and the melody of birds singing outside in the maple tree at the corner of her yard were all she needed to lull her into a deep slumber. The last thing she remembered hearing was the distant sound of her goats in some unknown conversation with each other out in their pen.

Sometime later, Emma was awakened by a knock on the door. Still half-asleep and thinking it was probably Mary or someone from her family, she called, "Come in!"

Emma was surprised when Lamar stepped into the room.

She sat up quickly, smoothing the wrinkles in her dress and setting her head covering in place. "Ach, I didn't expect it was you."

"Sorry if I startled you," he said. "I spoke to Mary after church, and she said you'd stayed home because you weren't feeling well."

"I'm just a little under the weather. I don't think it's anything serious."

"You look *mied*," he said with a look of concern. "Have you been doing too much lately?"

Emma's spine stiffened as her defenses rose. "I have not been doing too much, and I'm feeling less tired after taking a nap."

"I'm worried about you, Emma."

"Well, you needn't be. I'm fine."

Lamar shifted his weight a few times as though uncertain of what to say next. "Well, uh. . .guess I'll be going."

"I appreciate you stopping by," Emma said, knowing she couldn't be rude.

Lamar was almost to the door when he turned back around. "If there's anything I can do for you, please let me know."

She gave a brief nod.

When Lamar went out the door, Emma leaned her head against the back of the sofa and moaned. *Won't that man ever take the hint? I am not interested in a relationship with him, and I don't want him to do anything but leave me alone.*

Goshen

As Ruby Lee stood at the back of the church with Gene, greeting people as they filed out of the sanctuary, a knot formed in the pit of her stomach. Gene had preached a meaningful sermon this morning, and yet not one person had even uttered an *amen*. Normally their church was a lively place where people often shouted *amen* and *hallelujah*. Not today, however. You could have heard a feather fall all the way from heaven the entire time Gene had been preaching. Was it his topic—stepping out in faith—or was it the fact that there had been so much gossip circulating about their pastor wanting to get the church into debt?

Whatever the case, Ruby Lee couldn't help but notice that some of the congregation had slipped out the side door rather than going through the line to greet their pastor and his wife. This only confirmed to Ruby Lee that she and Gene ought to leave this church, because she was quite sure that's what most folks wanted them to do.

Why couldn't Gene see that, too? Did he enjoy going through all this misery with no end in sight? Did he think the Lord would bless him for his diligence and playing the role of martyr? Ruby Lee knew that if Gene was going to stay here, then she had to as well because her place was at her husband's side. She was glad their boys were away at college and couldn't see how their father was being treated. She was sure it would have hurt them as much as it did her, and they probably would have been more vocal about it than she had been. It surprised her even more that only a short time ago these same church people who were now ignoring them and saying hurtful things about them had been their good friends. Or at least she'd thought they had been.

Drawing in a quick breath and plastering a smile on her face, Ruby Lee reached for the next person's hand. "Good morning, Mrs. Dooley. May God bless you, and I hope you have a good week."

Mishawaka

Pam tiptoed down the stairs. She'd just checked on Sherry and found her sleeping peacefully upstairs in her room. After Sherry had finished eating a little oatmeal for breakfast, she'd climbed back into bed with her favorite stuffed animal and fallen asleep. So far no one else in the family had gotten sick, and Pam hoped it stayed that way. Stuart thought maybe they should have moved Sherry to the spare bedroom next to theirs, but Pam had decided to sleep in Devin's room, which was across the hall from Sherry's, while Devin slept in the guest room downstairs.

Feeling the need for a little time to herself, Pam went to the living room, grabbed a book she'd been wanting to read, and curled up on the couch. Stuart and Devin were in the yard playing catch, so the house was peaceful and quiet.

Pam had only been reading a few minutes when Stuart entered the room and bent to nuzzle her cheek.

"Stop it. I'm busy right now," she mumbled.

"Doesn't look like you're busy to me. Looks like you've got your nose in a book."

"That's right, and it's the first minute I've really had to myself since Sherry got sick on Friday, so if you don't mind—"

Stuart flopped onto the other end of the couch. "How's our little gal doing?" he asked, lifting one of Pam's feet and starting to rub it.

"Better. She kept the oatmeal down that I gave her earlier."

"That's good to hear. Unless she has a relapse, you should be able to go to the quilt class this Saturday."

"Yes, but I wish you were going with me."

"I'm considering it."

Her eyebrows lifted. "Really?"

He gave a nod. "I felt more relaxed there yesterday than I did the week before."

"How come?"

He cleared his throat a couple of times. "Well, it was nice to have the chance to just be myself."

"What are you saying—that you couldn't be yourself when I was there?"

"Yep, that's pretty much the way it was."

Pam clenched her fingers tightly around the book, irritated with his answer. "Why can't you be yourself when I'm there?"

"Because I'm not comfortable with you telling everyone our problems and trying to make it look like I'm responsible for everything that's gone wrong in our marriage."

"I don't do that."

"Yes you do, and it makes me feel awkward and stupid."

"Fine then, I won't say a word about anything at the next quilt class. Will that make you happy?"

"Yeah, sure. . .like that's ever gonna happen." He picked up her other foot and began rubbing it, probably hoping it might soothe her tension, as it had when he'd rubbed her feet many times before.

Pam's irritation mounted, barely appreciating the foot massage, which at any other time would have been so relaxing that she'd have fallen asleep.

"I could keep quiet throughout the whole class if I wanted to."

"Great. I'll go with you next week, and then we'll see."

She set the book aside and gave a nod. "It's a deal!"

Stuart pushed her feet aside and stood. "Now that I'll have to see in order to believe."

Pam wrinkled her nose and caught herself just in time before sticking out her tongue.

After Stuart left the room, she bolted upright. "Oh, great. What did I agree to now? Can I really keep quiet throughout the whole class?"

CHAPTER 20

Shipshewana

On Monday morning, Emma still wasn't feeling well, but she forced herself to get out of bed, fix breakfast, and do a few chores. She really needed to get some laundry done, but she wasn't sure she had the energy for it.

Emma stepped into her sewing room, took a seat in the rocking chair, and leaned her head back, feeling ever so drowsy. It had been a long time since she'd felt so fatigued. She was almost at the point of dozing off when she heard the back door open. A few seconds later, Mary entered the room. "I came over to see how you're doing," she said.

Emma sighed. "Not as well as I'd like to be. I'm still awfully tired, and I haven't even washed my clothes yet."

"I'll do it, Mom."

Emma shook her head. "You have enough of your own work to do."

"My laundry is already out on the line, and I really don't mind helping you."

"Oh, all right. You can wash the clothes, but I'm going to help you hang them on the line." Emma didn't know why it was so hard for her to accept Mary's help. She never thought twice about helping others, yet when it came to being on the receiving end, she usually wanted to do things on her own. Even so, she appreciated her daughter. In fact, all her children would make any parent feel grateful. No matter how busy they were, they never hesitated to drop what they were doing if help was needed elsewhere. Emma just didn't want to become a burden.

Mary smiled. "If you're feeling up to helping, that's fine with me."

Emma followed Mary to the basement and took a seat on a folding chair while Mary filled the gas-powered wringer-washer with water.

"It was nice of Lamar to stop by and check on you yesterday," Mary said as she put some towels into the washer. "When I spoke to him after church, he seemed concerned about you not being there."

Emma rubbed a spot on the front of her dress where some tea must have dripped.

"Lamar seems to be a very nice man," Mary continued. "I also think he's lonely."

Emma folded her hands and began to twiddle her thumbs. She didn't care for the way this conversation was going. "If he's lonely, then he needs to find something to occupy his time. Keeping busy has helped me not to be so lonely since your daed died."

"From what I can tell, Lamar keeps plenty busy with the hickory rocking chairs he makes. Besides, staying busy is no guarantee that a person won't be lonely."

"I suppose you're right." Despite Emma's activities in her yard and with her quilting projects, she still felt lonely at times—especially in the evenings, which was when she and Ivan used to sit out on the porch or in the living room to relax and visit after a long day. Oh, how she missed those special times.

"I think Lamar would probably like to find another wife," Mary said.

Emma clenched her fingers into a tight ball. "Jah, well, that's fine. It's just not going to be me."

—————

Star had just gotten off work, and instead of going straight home, she decided to drive over to Shipshewana to see Emma. She wanted to talk to her more about Mom's new man friend—tell her what happened yesterday when Mike came over. She was still upset and needed someone to share her feelings with, and it sure couldn't be Mom. Had Mom taken Star's side yesterday when Mike jumped her about wearing dark-colored clothes and too much eye makeup? No! Had Mom told Mike to get his shoes off the couch when he'd sprawled out to watch TV for the day? Of course not! Mom pretty much let Mike do whatever he wanted, even though they weren't married.

"And I hope they never are," Star mumbled as she started her car's engine.

As she pulled out from Walmart, she began to sing the lyrics to one of the songs she'd been working on. "Never gonna be the princess, holding tight to Daddy's neck; never gonna be the apple of his eye. Never gonna walk the aisle hand in hand; a sweet vignette. Never gonna answer all the whys."

Tears pricked the back of Star's eyes, and she blinked to keep them from spilling over. No point giving in to self-pity, because it wouldn't change a thing. If Mom ended up marrying Mike, there wasn't anything Star could do about it. She just needed to take one day at a time and try to focus on other things. Maybe someday one of her songs would be discovered and she'd become a real star; then she wouldn't need anyone—not even Mom.

Star continued to sing as she drove toward Shipshewana. When she pulled into Emma's yard sometime later, she saw Emma and a younger woman hanging clothes on the line.

Seeing that Emma wasn't alone, Star was hesitant about getting out of the car. But when Emma looked her way and waved, she knew she couldn't turn around and leave. That would be rude. So Star turned off her car's engine, stepped out, and headed across the yard.

When she reached the clothesline, Emma smiled and said, "What a nice surprise. What brings you by here this Monday morning?"

Feeling suddenly shy and more than a bit uncomfortable due to the other woman's curious expression, Star dropped her gaze to the ground and mumbled, "Just got off work."

"I didn't realize you worked in Shipshewana," Emma said.

"I don't. I work at the Walmart in Goshen." Star dragged the toe of her sneaker along a clump of grass. "Thought maybe it would be a good time to visit with you awhile, but I can see that you're busy right now."

"I'm not too busy to talk." Emma placed her hand on Star's arm. "Besides, you just drove probably half an hour to get here, and I surely can't send you away."

Emma's gentle touch felt warm and comforting. It made Star think of Grandma again, but she wasn't sure how to respond. She really did need to talk to Emma but didn't want to do it in front of the other woman.

"Oh, silly me," Emma said. "I don't believe you've met my daughter. Star, this is Mary. She lives next door and came over to help me with the laundry."

"We did meet briefly on the first day of your quilting class, but we weren't introduced." Mary held out her hand. "It's nice to meet you, Star."

Star, feeling a little more relaxed, shook Mary's hand. "Yeah, I remember now. Nice to meet you, too."

"What kind of work do you do at Walmart?" Emma asked as she hung one of her plain blue dresses on the line.

"I stock shelves in the wee hours of the morning."

"That must be nice in some ways," Mary said, "because it gives you the rest of the day to do other things."

"Yeah." Star bent down and picked up a wet towel from the wicker basket. "This looks like fun. Think I'll help, if you don't mind."

Emma laughed. "We don't mind at all, but I'm surprised you would think hanging out the laundry is fun."

"Well, fun might not be the best word for it," Star said, "but it's different. With the exception of the time we've spent living in my grandma's house, Mom and I have always washed and dried our clothes at the Laundromat." Star pointed to a sheet flapping in the breeze. "Do you hang things out when the weather is nice and then use the dryer when it's raining or snowing?"

Emma shook her head. "Oh no. We don't have automatic clothes dryers, but if we did, I'd really miss the fresh scent that clings to the sheets. For me, it's almost like sleeping in the outdoors when I cover up at night and smell the earth's sweet fragrance on my bedding."

"Oh that's right. I forgot you don't use electricity in your homes. So what do you do about washing your clothes? Do you have to wash 'em in a big round tub with a washboard?"

"Some of the washing machines we use in this community are run with a generator, but Mom's machine is run by a gas-powered motor that's set up outside, and the drive shaft is run into the washing area," Mary explained.

"Oh, I see." Star couldn't imagine living without the benefit of electricity and doing without all the modern conveniences. She did remember, though, how good the sheets smelled when she'd stayed at Grandma's house a few times before Grandma had become so ill.

That must be what Emma meant about the fresh earthy scent. Grandma probably hung her clothes out to dry sometimes. Funny how I'd forgotten that little memory of Grandma's sheets until Emma spoke of it.

They visited about other things until all the clothes were hung, and then Mary said she needed to do some things at her home, so she bid them good-bye.

"Would you like to take a seat on the porch?" Emma asked. "All that bending and stretching left me feeling rather worn out."

Star nodded. "Then I guess we should both have a seat, because I'm kinda tired, too."

As they walked to the porch, Star couldn't help but notice Emma's slow-moving gait. "Are you feeling all right today?" she asked, reaching out to steady Emma as they took seats on the porch swing.

"I've been feeling rather drained for the last few days. Just don't quite feel like myself." Emma smiled, although the usual sparkle in her blue eyes wasn't there. "I stayed home from church yesterday to rest, but I guess it didn't help because I don't have much energy this morning either."

"Maybe I oughta go so you can take a nap." Star started to rise, but Emma shook her head and motioned for her to sit back down.

"There's no need for you to rush off. I can rest right here while we visit."

"Okay, if you're sure." Star seated herself again and tucked a lock of hair behind her ear as a breeze lifted it from her shoulder. It was warm out today, and she was wearing jeans and a black tank top instead of her usual hooded sweatshirt. She was glad the job of stocking shelves at Walmart didn't require that she wear a uniform. She wouldn't feel comfortable dressed in one of those.

"How was your weekend?" Emma asked.

Star shrugged. "Could have been better. At least Sunday sure could have."

"What happened?"

Star began telling Emma how Mike had acted—controlling the TV remote, telling Star how she should dress, and complaining because he thought she wore too much eye makeup and too many rings on her fingers. He'd also griped about the small gold hoop in her nose, saying it looked ridiculous.

"I finally left the house and went for a walk just to get away from him. Don't know what I'm gonna do if Mom marries that guy." Star pursed her lips. "Mom's so gullible when it comes to men, and I'm not sure she's making a right decision where Mike is concerned. Fact is, she's made many poor choices and hasn't always been honest with me about things either. It really makes me mad."

"People are human, Star, and sometimes due to circumstances or just plain immaturity, they make poor choices." Emma sighed. "I made some poor choices myself when I was a young woman during my courting days."

Star tipped her head. "Courting? Is that the same thing as dating?"

"Well, I believe it's a little different," Emma said. "Courting is done with the intention of discovering if you want to be with the person forever. Dating is not as serious. At least that's how I understand it."

"Well, dating or courting, I can't imagine a nice lady like you making poor choices."

"I did though. When I was seventeen, I chose the wrong boyfriend."

Emma stared into the yard as though remembering the past. "His name was Eli Raber, and he had a wild side to him. Eli liked to drink, smoke, and run around. He also had a bright red car he kept hidden behind his daddy's barn."

Star leaned forward, listening intently as Emma went on to tell that Eli had it in his mind to leave the Amish faith and wanted Emma to join him.

"I almost did, too," Emma admitted. "Had it not been for Ivan coming along when he did, I might have run off with Eli and gotten into who knows what kind of trouble." She smiled, and some of that sparkle returned to her eyes. "Ivan was so kind and polite. He had good morals and was a dependable worker—helping his father in his harness shop. It didn't take me long at all to realize I'd found a good man."

"Hmm. . . I see."

"Does your mother love Mike?" Emma asked.

"I guess so. At least she says she does."

"Is he in love with her?"

"Supposedly, but then who knows? He could just be putting on an act to impress her."

"Does he have a steady job?"

"Yeah. He manages a restaurant in Goshen, and from the gifts he brings Mom, I'm guessin' he makes pretty good money."

"And is this man kind to your mother?"

"He seems to be—so far, anyway. According to Mom, Mike doesn't drink, smoke, or do drugs either."

"Then perhaps marrying him is what your mother needs."

"Maybe so, but it's sure not what I need."

"What do you need, Star?"

Star drew in a deep breath, and when she released it, her bangs lifted up from her forehead. "I need someone who won't look down their nose at me and criticize everything I say or do. I need someone who'll be my friend. I need someone who'll care about me the way Grandma did."

Emma placed her hand gently on Star's arm. "I care about you."

"Even though I dress weird and say things in a different way than you do?"

Emma chuckled and motioned to her head covering. "Some people probably think I dress weird, too."

Still not quite comfortable talking about her life, Star pointed to the pretty flower arrangement in the corner of Emma's yard. "That's an unusual flowerpot. Did you get it at the Shipshewana flea market?"

Emma explained that one morning, rather than throwing her husband's old work boots out, she'd planted carnations in them. "It's a beautiful reminder of how hard Ivan worked to provide for me and our family," she said. "I have the other boot in another nature garden out back, where I can see it when I'm looking out the kitchen window. I planted petunias in that one."

Emma went on to tell Star that the rock in the front yard where the boot sat had been found by her husband while they'd been walking through the woods together one afternoon during their courting days.

Emma paused for a minute, and Star looked at her intently, thirsty to hear more.

"After Ivan and I got married, we lived on a farm, where we worked hard and soon became busy raising our children," Emma continued. "No matter how busy things got, one thing we remembered to do was to make time for having fun." She chuckled. "I can still recall a little joke I played on Ivan one time that had us all laughing."

"What was it?"

"On his forty-ninth birthday, instead of throwing the newspaper away after he'd finished reading it, I hid the paper for a whole year. Then the following year on his birthday, I replaced the current newspaper with the one from the year before. It was hard to keep from laughing as I sat across from Ivan at the breakfast table, slyly watching as I finished my cup of coffee and he read the paper."

"Did he catch on?" Star asked.

"He never noticed it was year-old news until he was almost done reading the entire paper." Emma giggled as she touched her cheeks. "You should have seen Ivan's expression when he commented about the articles sounding like news that had happened a year ago. And, oh my... I laughed so hard, I thought I was going to pop the seams in my dress."

"How'd he take it when he realized it was an old newspaper?"

"He actually took it quite well. Even laughed about it and told the rest of our family how I'd fooled him real good on his fiftieth birthday."

Star smiled and leaned back in her chair, noticing the laugh lines that had formed around Emma's eyes. Something about being with Emma made Star feel good. She hadn't felt this relaxed or lighthearted in years.

"You know, Star," Emma said, "those are the kinds of joys, even though they're simple, that help to keep a person grounded."

Star was quiet for a moment, thinking how wonderful it must be to have such happiness being with another person. "I like you, Emma Yoder. Yeah, I like you a lot."

Emma slipped her arm around Star's waist and gave her a hug. "I like you, too."

CHAPTER 21

"Y ou look like you've eaten a bowl of sour pickles for breakfast," Terry said when Jan climbed into his truck that morning. "Are you dreadin' going to work that much?"

"It's not the work I dread; it's the comin' home."

"Since when have you ever dreaded that?"

"Since my dog was killed."

Terry's eyes widened. "Brutus is dead?"

Jan nodded soberly.

"Oh man, how'd that happen?"

"He got out of his pen and was hit by a car."

"But I thought you fixed the pen so he couldn't get out."

"I thought that, too, but I guess he must've climbed the fence and gone out over the top."

"I'm real sorry to hear that. Did you bury him out back?"

Jan shook his head. "It didn't happen here. Paul—one of the guys who attends the quiltin' class on Saturdays—said he saw a dead dog on his way to Emma's that looked just like Brutus. It was over by the 5 and 20 Country Kitchen."

"Did you see the dog?"

"Nope. By the time I got there, the body was gone. Figured someone from Animal Control had probably hauled it off." Jan nearly choked on the words. "And I was right, 'cause when I called the Humane Society, they said a dead German shepherd had been brought in."

"How do you know it was Brutus? Did they identify him by his tags?"

"Didn't have any. I stupidly let the dog run around without a collar and never even bothered to get him a license or an ID tag. The description of the dog was the same, though, and when I came home on Saturday, Brutus wasn't in his pen or anywhere in the yard." Just talking about losing the dog made Jan feel sick. He'd been struggling with his emotions the entire weekend.

"That don't actually prove the dead dog was Brutus."

"Maybe not, but since Brutus didn't come back, it's pretty clear to me that it had to be him."

"Guess you're probably right," Terry said as he pulled out of Jan's driveway.

As they headed down the road, a thought popped into Jan's head. "Say, would you mind makin' a quick stop before we head on over to LaGrange to start our next roofin' job?"

"Sure. Where do you want me to stop?"

"At the Amish woman's home who teaches the quiltin' classes. She lives a short ways from here."

"Why do you wanna go there?" Terry asked.

"When I found out about the dog that had been hit, I left Emma's in such a hurry I forgot and left my quiltin' project on her table. If I don't pick it up, I won't be able to work on it this week."

"I still don't get why you're takin' that class, but to each his own, I guess."

"You got that right." Jan frowned when Terry lit up a cigarette. "Thought you'd given up that nasty habit."

"I've been tryin' to, but when I get stressed-out I need a smoke."

"What's got you feelin' stressed?"

"My folks." Terry groaned. "After being married thirty-five years, they're talkin' about splittin' up."

"That's too bad, man. Now you know why I've never gotten married. Too many complications, and it seems like there ain't much commitment anymore."

"Yeah, but I know some couples who've made it work."

"Guess that's true. Emma Yoder's a widow, and I'll bet you anything she and her husband had a good marriage. Even with him gone, her face lights up like a jar of lightnin' bugs whenever she mentions his name."

"Yeah, well I hope my folks get their act together soon, 'cause I sure don't wanna see 'em go their separate ways. They've been married too many years to throw in the towel."

"Maybe they oughta see a marriage counselor. That's what the couple takin' our class is doin'; although I ain't sure it's done 'em much good." Jan bumped Terry's arm. "Turn right here. That's Emma's house up ahead."

When they pulled into Emma's yard, Jan was surprised to see Star sitting on the front porch by herself. What was even more surprising was that she wasn't wearing her black hooded sweatshirt.

"You wanna come up to the house and meet Emma and Star?" Jan asked, turning to Terry.

"Naw, you go ahead."

"Okay. I'll just be gone long enough to get what I left." Jan hopped out of the truck and hurried across the yard.

"I'm surprised to see you here this mornin'," he said to Star as he stepped onto the porch.

"Came to talk to Emma awhile." She smiled. At least he thought it was a smile. Her lips were curved slightly upwards. "I'm surprised to see you here, too."

"I'm on my way to work, but I wanted to come by and get the quiltin' project I left when I ran outta here on Saturday."

"So what'd you find out? Was it your dog that had been hit?" she asked.

"It must have been, 'cause when I got home Brutus wasn't in his pen, and there ain't been no sign of him since."

"That's too bad." Star's somber-looking face let Jan know that she felt his pain. He figured behind that defiant attitude lay a heart of compassion. Out of all of Emma's other students, Star was the one who seemed the most real. Probably didn't have a phony bone in her body. Jan kind of liked her because she had spunk. Didn't care what anyone thought of her either. Too bad she wasn't a couple of years older, or he might consider asking her out. 'Course, he'd known a few other guys who'd dated younger women, but then he wasn't really looking to get serious about anyone again. Right now with all the roofing jobs he had lined up for the summer, he had enough to occupy his time.

"Did you check at the Humane Society to see if the dog had been taken there?" Star asked.

He nodded, unwilling to admit that he hadn't bothered to get Brutus any form of identification.

"So, where's Emma?" he asked, quickly changing the subject before he ended up blubbering about how much he missed Brutus.

Star motioned to the door. "She went to the kitchen to get us some iced tea."

"Guess I'll go inside and ask about my stuff, and then I need to be on my way."

"Before you go, you might like to know that you weren't the only one who left the class early the other day," Star said.

"Oh?"

"Yeah, Ruby Lee got a call from the hospital, sayin' her husband had been taken there."

"That's too bad. What was wrong with him?"

Star shrugged. "I'm not sure. Ruby Lee took off like a shot after she got the call. Hopefully it wasn't serious and she'll be back for the class this Saturday."

Jan couldn't help but notice the look of concern on Star's face. It was refreshing to meet a young woman who cared about people. He looked forward to getting to know her better in the coming weeks—maybe some of the others in the class as well. It seemed that joining their little quilting club was one of the few things he'd done right lately, rather than adding to the list of bad decisions he'd made.

Carrying two glasses of iced tea, Emma left the kitchen. She was just passing through her sewing room when she nearly collided with Jan.

"Oh my! You startled me. I—I didn't realize you were here."

"I'm on my way to work and decided to stop by and get my wall hangin'," he explained, looking a bit embarrassed. "I left here in such a hurry on Saturday I forgot to take it with me."

"Yes, I was sorry about that," Emma said, noticing the look of sadness in Jan's eyes. "Did you find out whether it was your dog that had been hit?"

Jan nodded soberly. "I'm sure it must've been Brutus."

"You must miss him very much."

"Yeah, I sure do, but it's my own stupid fault. Shoulda made sure his pen was secure all the way around and over the top, 'cause I'm convinced that must be how he got out."

"Blaming yourself will not bring the dog back, and it won't help you feel any better about losing him, either," Emma said gently.

"I know that." Jan hung his head. "Guess it's a good thing I'm not tryin' to raise any kids, 'cause I'd probably bumble that, too."

Emma set the glasses of iced tea on the sewing table and impulsively reached out to touch Jan's arm. "I'm really sorry for your loss."

"Thanks. I appreciate that."

"You know, Jan, a lot of accidents have happened within my Amish community, and even within my own family unit." Emma paused a moment to gather her thoughts. "One time when I was a little girl, one of my friends drowned in her uncle's pond."

Jan's eyes widened. "That's a shame."

She gave a nod. "It was a shock to everyone, and at first Elsie's parents blamed themselves for not keeping a close enough watch on her."

"I can understand that."

"They weren't the only ones who blamed themselves. Elsie's uncle Toby blamed himself because he should have put a fence up around the pond."

Jan gave a nod. "Guess they were all to blame then, huh?"

Emma shrugged. "I'm not sure if anyone was really to blame, except for my friend, who knew she couldn't swim and shouldn't have gone anywhere near that pond. The point is, blaming didn't bring Elsie back, and until her folks and her uncle came to accept Elsie's death and moved on, there was no healing for any of them."

"But they did finally accept it. Is that what you're sayin'?"

Emma nodded. "They still grieved and missed Elsie, of course, but when they stopped blaming themselves and accepted her death, knowing she was in a better place with God, then healing began in their hearts."

"But Brutus is a dog. He wouldn't have gone to heaven. Right?"

Emma turned her hands palm up. "Only God and those who are with Him right now know whether there are animals in heaven or not." She smiled up at Jan and gave his arm another gentle pat. "The main thing to remember is that your dog isn't suffering, and if you focus on the good memories you have of him, it'll help to heal the pain you feel so intensely right now."

Jan, his eyes now glassy with tears, smiled and said, "Thank you, Emma. I'm sure glad I stopped by here today, and I look forward to seein' you on Saturday for another quiltin' lesson."

Emma nodded. She hoped, Lord willing, that she'd be up to teaching the class.

CHAPTER 22

Elkhart

For the last couple of days, Paul had been trying to reach Carmen, but here it was Wednesday, and she hadn't returned any of his calls.

Should I try again before I leave for school? he wondered, glancing at the phone. *Guess there's not much point. Carmen obviously doesn't want to talk to me, or she would have responded to at least one of my calls.*

Paul didn't know why it bothered him so much that Carmen had cut them out of her life. It wasn't as if she was Sophia's only aunt. It just hurt to know that she blamed him for Lorinda's death and didn't care enough about Sophia to come for a visit—or at least keep in contact with them.

He glanced at Sophia sitting in her high chair, patiently waiting to be fed. Not only would his precious little girl never know her mother, but it looked as if she wouldn't know her aunt Carmen either.

Paul had spoken to Lorinda's mother last night, asking about the trip they were planning to make to Indiana sometime this summer. When he'd mentioned that he hoped Carmen might come with them, Ramona had dismissed it lightly, saying Carmen had just started a new job and wouldn't be able to take time off for any trips this year. While that might be true enough, it didn't excuse Carmen for refusing to answer his calls.

Carmen was five years younger than Lorinda and had always been very independent. She'd gone to college right out of high school, and after she'd graduated and landed a job as a reporter for one of the Los Angeles newspapers, she'd rented an apartment several miles from her folks. Ramona had suggested that Carmen live at home for a while so she could save her money for other things, but Carmen wouldn't hear of it. She wanted to be out on her own. Carmen's career seemed to come first, and as far as Paul knew, Carmen didn't have a serious boyfriend.

Oh well. . .it's none of my business what Carmen does. I just wish she'd open the lines of communication with me again, Paul thought as he took a seat beside Sophia to feed her a bowl of cooked cereal.

Sophia looked up at him and grinned. "Pa-pa-pa."

Paul leaned over and kissed her soft cheek. "That's right little one, and you can always count on me."

Goshen

After Gene left to make a hospital call on one of their parishioners, Ruby Lee had felt the need for some fresh air and sunshine, so she'd left the house right after breakfast and headed for the Pumpkinvine Nature Trail.

As she walked briskly along trying to clear her head, she spotted a clump of violets growing along the edge of the path. Seeing the flowers caused Ruby Lee to think about her friend Annette, whose favorite flowers were violets. She'd e-mailed and called Annette several more times, but no response. Was Annette mad at her? Could she have said or done something that may have ruined their friendship? It didn't make any sense. Even though Ruby Lee had originally decided to keep her frustrations to herself, she desperately needed to talk to someone about the church's problems and the way Gene had been responding to them. She'd hoped Annette might offer some sympathy and understanding— maybe even give her a suggestion or two. If Annette lived closer, Ruby Lee would pay her a visit, but a trip to Nashville wasn't possible right now. Ruby Lee had commitments at church, not to mention finishing the quilt class she'd enrolled in.

Refusing to give in to self-pity, which seemed to be right at the surface these days, Ruby Lee picked up the pace and hurried on.

Concentrating on the soothing motion of Rock Run Creek, which ran beside the trail, and the gentle breeze whispering through the canopy of trees overhead, she tried to relax. She had only gone a short ways when she spotted a young, dark-haired woman with a ponytail, who was dressed in a pair of black shorts and a matching tank top, running along the trail in the opposite direction. As the woman approached, Ruby Lee realized it was Star; although she almost didn't recognize her without that usual black sweatshirt.

"Hey, sister! I'm surprised to see you here on the Pumpkinvine Trail," Ruby Lee called. It felt good to see a familiar face—someone who wasn't likely to judge.

"Hi, how's it going? How's your husband doing?" Star asked.

"He's fine. We were worried at first that it might be his heart, but everything checked out okay." Ruby Lee chose not to mention that the doctor had told Gene he'd had an anxiety attack. Star would probably want to know why, and Ruby Lee didn't feel like talking about it—at least not with her.

"Do you come here often?" Ruby Lee asked as Star turned and

started walking in the same direction as her.

"Once or twice a week." Star picked up a stone and threw it in the water. "Or whenever I need to run and take out my frustrations. It's great here, isn't it?"

"Yes, it really is a beautiful place. I come here frequently, and for the same reason as you," Ruby Lee admitted. "Only I don't run."

Star stared at Ruby Lee, as though in disbelief. "I can't imagine you having any frustrations."

Ruby Lee blinked her eyes. "What makes you think that?"

"You're always so happy-go-lucky during our quilting classes—like you don't have a care in the world. Except for last Saturday when you got the call about your husband, that is. I could tell you were pretty upset."

"Well, we all have our share of troubles, so there's bound to be times when we're upset and need to do something to help relieve our stress."

"That's for sure."

"I wonder how Jan is doing," Ruby Lee said, quickly changing the subject. "He seemed really upset on Saturday when Paul told him about seeing that dead dog on his way to Emma's."

"I saw Jan on Monday," Star said. "I dropped by Emma's to talk to her about some things I've been dealing with at home, and while I was there, Jan stopped by to pick up his quilting project."

"Did he say anything about his dog?"

"Yep. Said when he got home Brutus wasn't in his pen, so he's almost sure it was his dog that was hit."

"That's a shame."

"Yeah. Poor guy called the Humane Society, and they said they'd disposed of the dog's body, so Jan couldn't even go there to see whether it was Brutus or not. Jan tried to hide it, but I could tell he was taking it pretty hard." Star's expression was one of compassion, causing Ruby Lee to see a different side of the young woman.

As they continued to walk, they talked about Emma and how sweet and kindhearted she seemed to be.

"Emma's full of good advice, too," Star said. "Even shared with me some things about her past."

"Is that so?"

"Yeah, but I guess it's not my place to be blabbin' any of the things she told me."

"No, you're right. When someone confides in us about something, it's best not to tell anyone else."

"So what do you think of Stuart and Pam?" Star asked, taking their conversation in a little different direction.

"Well, it's really not my place to say, but I believe they're both very unhappy in their marriage," Ruby Lee replied.

"I got that impression right off the bat. Think they'll finish taking Emma's classes?"

"I don't know. I guess we'll have to wait and see how it goes." Ruby Lee motioned to a nearby bench. "Shall we take a seat?"

They sat quietly for a while, watching the squirrels run back and forth across the path. Then Ruby Lee asked Star a few questions about herself and was surprised to learn that the young woman not only sang and played the guitar, but had composed a few songs.

"Why don't you sing something you've written for me?" Ruby Lee asked.

Star's dark eyes widened. "Here? Now?"

"I wish you would."

"But none of my songs are completed yet. I just have a few lines written on each of them," Star said.

"That's all right. I'd like to hear some of the lyrics you've come up with."

"Well, okay." In a hesitant voice, Star began to sing. "Can't seem to look behind the right door; maybe that's 'cause I don't know exactly what I'm looking for. . . ." As she continued into the chorus, her tone grew stronger. "It's hard to breathe. . . . It's hard to sleep. . . . It's hard to know who you are when you're a lost and falling star."

When Star finished the song, she turned to Ruby Lee and said, "It's not much, but at least it's a beginning to something that I hope I'll be able to complete."

"Oh, I'm sure you will, and Star, you certainly have a lovely voice," Ruby Lee said truthfully. "The words to your song were well written, but my only concern is that they evoke a message of sadness and hopelessness. Is that the way you really feel?"

Star nodded solemnly. "Nothin' ever goes right for me, and I—I feel kinda lost, like I don't know what purpose I serve here on earth."

Ruby Lee placed her hand over Star's, unable to speak around the lump in her throat. Here was a young woman without hope, and Ruby Lee, a pastor's wife and professing Christian, couldn't think of a thing to say but, "I'm sorry, Star."

"That's just how it is—life stinks!" Star leaped to her feet. "Guess I'd better finish my run and head for home. Mom's probably havin' a hissy fit wondering why I'm so late gettin' home from work this morning. See you on Saturday, Ruby Lee." She turned and sprinted in the opposite direction, leaving Ruby Lee alone on the bench, feeling even worse than when she'd left home. Oh, how she wished she had shared the love of Jesus with Star right then. She'd seen Star's need and how quickly she covered up her emotions, and yet she'd missed the perfect opportunity to tell the confused young woman about God's love. Was it because she felt so hopeless and sad herself? Truth was, Ruby Lee really needed someone to encourage her today, but Star, not even knowing Ruby Lee's need, hadn't been able to do that. Worse yet, Ruby Lee hadn't met Star's real need either.

Shipshewana

Emma cringed as she directed her horse and buggy toward the health food store. Every move she made and every bump in the road made the lesions on her stomach rub against her clothes and hurt like the dickens. While Emma was getting dressed that morning, she'd discovered several painful blisters and realized she had in fact developed another case of shingles. She'd immediately gone to the phone shack to call her naturopathic doctor but was unable to get an appointment until tomorrow. So she'd decided to head to the health food store near the Shipshewana Flea Market to find a remedy that might help with her painful symptoms. If her blisters continued to hurt like this, she wondered how she could teach the quilting class on Saturday. She would have asked Mary to take over for her, but Mary and her family had left this morning for Sullivan, Illinois, to attend the wedding of Brian's cousin, and they wouldn't be back until Saturday evening.

When Emma arrived at the health food store, she guided her horse up to the hitching rail and gritted her teeth as she climbed down. Just the slightest movement caused pain, making her wish she'd asked someone else to make the trip for her. Emma really wished she could be home in bed.

When she entered the store, she headed for the aisle full of herbal preparations, where she found some pills labeled as help for the pain and itching of shingles. She also discovered a bottle of aromatic oils to dab on the blisters.

"Need some help?"

Emma jumped at the sound of a man's deep voice. Surprised, she turned and saw Lamar beside her. "I...uh...came here to get something that might help with shingles' pain."

Lamar's eyebrows furrowed. "For you, Emma?"

She nodded slowly. "The eruptions came out this morning. Now I know why I haven't felt well the last few days."

"I had a case of shingles a few years ago," Lamar said. "My doctor gave me a B-12 shot."

"Did it help?"

"I believe so. He also gave me a shot to help prevent any nerve pain."

"I couldn't get in to see my doctor today, but I'll go there in the morning." Emma motioned to the bottles on the shelf. "In the meantime, I think I'll use one of these." She sighed deeply. "I hope I'm feeling better by Saturday. I can't imagine trying to teach my quilt class feeling like I do right now."

"I'd be happy to fill in for you," Lamar offered.

Emma tipped her head back and looked up at him in surprise. "Oh, I doubt you'd know what to do."

"You're wrong about that." Lamar smiled. "My wife used to run a quilt shop, and I helped out there. In fact, I even designed some rather unusual quilt patterns for her to make."

Emma's mouth fell open. "Are you serious?"

"Sure am."

"I appreciate the offer, but I think I'll be able to teach the class." At least she hoped she could, because despite what Lamar said about having helped his wife, she couldn't imagine how things would go if he tried to teach the class in her place. But when Saturday came, if she felt like she did now, as much as it would sadden her, she'd have to cancel the class.

CHAPTER 23

Mishawaka

When Stuart entered the kitchen on Friday morning, he found Pam sitting at the table drinking a cup of coffee.

"Where are the kids?" he asked after he'd poured himself some coffee and joined her at the table.

"They're still in bed. I figured I'd let them sleep awhile so I can have some quiet time to myself."

"Guess you won't get much of that once school's out for the summer."

"No, I sure won't."

Stuart blew on his coffee and took a sip. "Since tomorrow's Saturday and I have the day off, why don't you get together with one of your friends? You can go shopping all morning and then out to lunch while I keep an eye on the kids."

Pam shook her head. "Tomorrow's the quilting class, remember?"

He snapped his fingers. "Oh yeah, that's right. I almost forgot."

"It sounds to me like you did forget," she said, scowling at him.

He shrugged. "Okay, so maybe I did. There's no big deal in that, is there?"

"Well, that all depends."

"On what?"

"On whether you just conveniently forgot."

"I didn't conveniently forget. Things have been busier than usual at work this week, and my brain's tired; that's all."

"Are you sure you didn't suggest I go shopping with a friend so you wouldn't have to go to the quilting class with me?"

"No, that's not how it was."

"Would you rather go without me again?"

Stuart's irritation mounted. "Are you trying to put words in my mouth?"

"No, I just thought—"

Knowing that if he didn't get out of there immediately he'd start yelling, Stuart pushed away from the table. "I've gotta go or I'll be late for work."

"But you haven't had your breakfast yet."

He gestured to the table. "I don't see anything waiting for me. . . unless it's invisible."

Tears welled in her eyes. "You don't have to be sarcastic. I was waiting to start breakfast until you'd had your coffee."

"Well, I don't want any breakfast!" Stuart hauled his coffee cup to the sink and rushed out the back door, slamming it behind him. It seemed like every time he tried to have a conversation with Pam, they ended up in an argument. He was tired of it, and her turning on the tears didn't help. He was sure she did it just to make him feel like a heel, and it wasn't going to work this time. If things were ever going to be better between them, Pam needed to get off his back and quit antagonizing him all the time.

Shipshewana

After Jan ate a quick breakfast, he went out to the garage to get some tools for the roof he planned to strip today. Terry would be here to pick him up soon, and then they could be on their way.

When Jan entered the garage, his gaze came to rest on his motorcycle, parked beside his truck. Oh how he wished he could ride it right now. Just head on down the road and leave all his troubles behind. But he knew he couldn't do that. He had a responsibility to complete a roofing job, not to mention the quilting classes he'd paid good money for and really did want to finish. Besides, if he rode the Harley and got stopped by the police, he'd probably have his license permanently suspended. No, he could hold out for a couple more months until he got his license back. No sense taking any foolish chances on his bike. He'd done that already, and just look what it had cost him.

Jan ambled across the room and took a seat on the cycle. Gripping the handlebars and closing his eyes, he let his mind wander for a bit, wondering just where his life was going. With the exception of work and riding his motorcycle, he really didn't have much purpose—not like he would if he were a married man raising a family. But he'd given up on that idea several years ago, convincing himself that he was better off alone. Besides, he figured living a quiet, boring life was better than a life full of complications. Had he been wrong about that? Should he have taken a chance on love again? Was it too late for that now?

Brutus sure kept me on my toes, he thought, redirecting his thoughts. *At least the dog gave me a reason to come home every night.*

Jan wondered if he should get another dog to take Brutus's place. Maybe a pup he could train from the get-go would be better than a full-grown dog with bad habits, like stealing and escaping from his pen.

But do I really want to go through that puppy stage? he wondered. *All the chewin' and numerous trips outside till it's housebroken. On the other hand, puppies are cute and have that milky-sweet breath. Guess I'll have to think on it a bit more before I jump into anything I might later regret.*

Woof! Woof!

Jan's eyes snapped open. Had he been so deep in thought that he was hearing things, or was that a dog barking outside the garage?

Woof! Woof! Woof!

Jan leaped off the bike and jerked open the garage door.

Brutus, tail wagging like a windshield wiper at full speed, bounded up to Jan with a toy football in his mouth, which he promptly dropped at Jan's feet. Then he sat down in front of Jan, tail still wagging, as if waiting for some sort of praise at the gift he'd just delivered.

Jan, unable to stop the flow of tears, squatted on the ground and let the dog lick his face. He'd never been one to show much affection, but he couldn't resist giving Brutus a gigantic bear hug.

"Where have you been all this time, boy? I thought you were dead." Relief flooded Jan's soul, and he nearly choked on the words as he tenderly scratched the fur on his dog's neck and then behind his ears. "I don't know whether to scold you or feed you a juicy steak dinner."

The dog whimpered, and then he nuzzled Jan's hand with his nose and leaned in for more attention.

Other than some mud caked on his paws, Brutus looked to be in fairly good condition. Jan figured someone must have taken the dog in—maybe some family with a kid, which would explain the toy football at least.

Jan was really stoked to know that Brutus wasn't dead, but he knew the dog could end up that way if he didn't get him secured in his pen while he was at work during the day. He planned to get him a collar, a license, and an ID tag, too. No way was he going to ruin a happy ending by being so careless again. So after Jan had given Brutus some food and water, he put him in the garage while he went to work covering the top of the dog pen with chicken wire. He'd just finished the last section when Terry's truck pulled in.

"Hey, man, isn't that a little like lockin' the barn door after the horse has escaped?" Terry called after he'd stepped out of the truck and headed toward the dog pen.

"Good news! I was wrong about Brutus. He showed up this mornin', and he's in my garage right now." Jan gave Terry a wide smile. "Now ain't that a kick?"

"Oh man, that's really great. Where was he all this time? Do you know?"

Jan shook his head and stepped out of the pen, appreciative that his good friend was truly happy for him. "I think when he got out he must've been roamin' around lookin' for more things to steal and some family probably took him in. Maybe that's why he couldn't come home all these days."

"What makes you think that?"

Jan explained about the good condition Brutus was in and how he'd come home with a kid's toy in his mouth. "And now that I've made his pen escape-proof, I'm sure it won't happen again. Talk about learnin' a good lesson." Jan pointed to the sky. "I think Someone up there must be lookin' out for me."

Terry thumped Jan's back. "I'm sure glad Brutus is back home again, 'cause you've been pretty hard to work with these last several days."

Jan shrugged his broad shoulders. "What can I say? I missed my dog. Never thought I would, but boy, I sure did!"

Terry gave Jan's back another good thump. "Well, if you'd get yourself a wife, you wouldn't need a dog."

"Like I've told you before, I'll go out on a date now and then, but I ain't gettin' seriously involved with any woman. Havin' a dog is trouble enough."

———•———

Goshen

Ruby Lee took a seat in front of their computer and logged into her e-mail, hoping she might find something from Annette.

A sense of relief washed over her when she discovered an e-mail with Annette's address in the sender's box. It was titled "Letting You Know."

Ruby Lee brought the message up and soon realized it had been sent from Annette's daughter, Kayla:

Dear Ruby Lee:

It's with regret and great sadness that I'm writing to let you know my mother passed away two weeks ago.

Ruby Lee gasped. "What? Wait a minute! No, this just can't be!" Tears sprang to her eyes as she continued to read Kayla's message:

Mom's cancer came back, but she didn't go to the doctor or tell anyone until it was too late. We've all been in shock—especially Dad. He's so depressed, he can barely cope. Someone in the family should have let you know sooner, but we couldn't find Mom's address book, and I just got into her e-mails today and discovered several you had sent to her. I apologize for letting you know this way.

Sincerely,

Kayla.

P.S. Please pray for our family—especially my dad.

Ruby Lee's head swam with swirling emotions—anger, shock, and grief—because Annette hadn't let her know that the cancer had returned and she was just now learning that her friend was dead.

"This just can't be true! Girlfriend, I would have been there for you if I'd known," she wailed. Hadn't Annette wanted her support? Ruby Lee couldn't imagine going through such a terrible ordeal all alone. And now her friend was gone? It was too much to take in.

Tears streamed down Ruby Lee's face. Trying to get a grip on what she'd just learned, she closed her eyes in continued disbelief. *My problems are nothing compared to what Annette must have gone through. Oh how I wish she'd responded to my phone calls and e-mails. If I'd only known, I would have dropped everything and gone to Nashville to be with her.*

Ruby Lee let her head fall forward into her outstretched palms and sobbed. "Dear Lord, where were You through all of this? Why'd You let my best friend die? If only I could have been there for her."

As quickly as she said the words, Ruby Lee felt remorse. "Guess I should have tried harder to get ahold of you, Annette. Oh, I'm so very sorry." The tears continued to flow as she tried to sort out this unwelcome news.

Shipshewana

For the last few days, Emma had spent much of her time on the sofa with an ice bag pressed against her stomach. Of all the things she'd been doing to help with the pain and itching of the blisters, the cold compress seemed to help the most. She'd seen her naturopathic doctor on Thursday, and he'd given her a B-12 shot and some lysine capsules. Those things had helped some, but she was still quite miserable— although not as bad as she had been the first time she'd come down with shingles.

As much as Emma hated to do it, she knew she had to call her quilting students and cancel tomorrow's class because she was in too much pain to teach them right now.

Gritting her teeth in determination, Emma stepped out the door. She was halfway to the phone shack when a horse and buggy pulled into the yard. A few seconds later, Lamar stepped down.

"Wie geht's?" he asked, walking toward her.

"Not so good," Emma admitted. "I was just heading out to call my quilting students and let them know I won't be able to teach the class tomorrow." She sighed. "Hopefully by next week I'll feel well enough, but I'm in too much pain to do it this week."

Lamar's usual smile turned into a frown. "I told you the other day that I'd teach the class for you. Are you too full of *hochmut* to accept my help?"

She planted both hands against her hips and winced as a jolt of pain shot through her left side. "I am not full of pride! I just wasn't sure you knew enough about quilting to take over my class."

"I know a lot more than you think, and since you're in no shape to teach the class yourself, you ought to at least let me try."

Emma contemplated his offer a few seconds and finally nodded because, really, what other choice did she have? She just hoped it didn't prove to be a mistake.

CHAPTER 24

Star was surprised when she pulled her car into Emma's yard on Saturday morning and saw a horse and buggy parked at the hitching rail. Had Emma invited one of her friends to join them today, or had someone from her Amish community dropped by for a visit? If that was the case, Star was sure whomever was here would leave as soon as Emma started teaching the class.

Just as Star got out of the car, Paul's van pulled in, followed by Ruby Lee in her vehicle. A few minutes later, Stuart's SUV came up the driveway. This time Pam was with him.

They all started walking toward the house, and Jan pedaled up on his bicycle. He must have seen the horse and buggy, too, because he turned his head in that direction.

"Look out!" Paul shouted just before Jan's bike crashed into the fence. Jan, unable to keep the bike upright, landed on the ground with a thud!

"I'm okay. Nothin's broken. I'm just fine," he said, after he'd stood and dusted himself off. Jan's red face let Star know he was a bit embarrassed. She couldn't blame him. She'd be embarrassed, too, if she'd done what he did.

He squinted as he studied his bike and then took a look at the fence. "Seems like they're both okay, too."

Star stepped up to Jan. "How's it going?" She knew that, having just lost his dog, he must still feel depressed.

He grinned. "It's all good! Brutus ain't dead after all! He came home yesterday mornin'."

"That's great news." Star was pleased to see the smile on Jan's face. "I'm sure you were really glad about that."

"You got that right," Jan said with a nod. "And I covered the top of Brutus's pen with heavy chicken wire so he won't get out again when I'm gone. Like I told my friend Terry, I've learned a good lesson from this."

Everyone else said they were happy for Jan, too—everyone but Ruby Lee and Pam. Ruby Lee, though silent, did give Jan's arm a little pat, but Pam said nothing at all. Star wasn't surprised. From the first moment she'd met Pam, she'd thought her to be quite high and mighty and into herself. People like that were hard to take. People like Pam needed to learn a lesson in humility.

Star hadn't cared much for Stuart at first, either, but at least he didn't dress and act like he was better than anyone else, and he'd been a lot easier to talk to last week when Pam wasn't with him. Too bad the snooty woman hadn't stayed home again today.

"Guess we'd better get into the house," Paul said, knocking on the door. "Don't want to keep Emma waiting."

A few seconds later, the door opened, and they were greeted by a pleasant-looking Amish man with gray hair and a long, full beard to match. He introduced himself as Emma's friend, Lamar Miller. Star realized then that he was the man who'd brought the doughnuts by Emma's, because Emma had mentioned his name.

When Star and the others followed Lamar into the sewing room, she glanced around. "Where's Emma?"

"She came down with shingles earlier this week and isn't feeling up to teaching the class today." Lamar's sober expression showed that he was truly sorry about that.

"That's too bad. Emma said she was feeling tired when I visited her the other day, so that must have been the reason for it." Thinking Emma's illness meant the class had been canceled, Star turned toward the door.

"You don't have to leave. I'll be teaching the class today," Lamar announced.

"Oh?" Star whirled around. "What qualifies you to teach the class?"

Lamar's cheeks reddened. "I used to work with my wife in her quilt shop. Believe me, I know what I'm doing."

Star, a little unsure, looked at Jan. When he gave her a smile and a nod, she pulled out a chair at the table and took a seat. Everyone else did the same.

With the dubious expressions she saw from the others, Star was sure she wasn't the only one in the room who thought it was a little strange that this Amish man could be capable of teaching a quilt class. But it was only fair to give him the benefit of the doubt.

She glanced over at Pam, who still hadn't said a word since she and Stuart arrived, which was strange, since all the other times Pam had been here, she'd had plenty to say. Star figured Pam and Stuart may have had a fight on their way here and weren't speaking. Well, that suited Star just fine because the less snooty Pam had to say, the better it would be for everyone. It wouldn't hurt her to sit and listen for once, instead of yammering away at Stuart so she could hear herself talk or make a point.

"From what Emma has told me, I understand that each of you has been working on a wall hanging," Lamar said, redirecting Star's thoughts. "Now, I'm going to start by showing you a couple of patterns I designed myself, and then I'll let you get to work on your projects."

"You've designed some quilts?" Ruby Lee asked, eyebrows lifted.

A wide smile stretched across his face. "I've always been somewhat of an artist, and as I said, when my wife opened a quilt shop, I helped her sometimes. It didn't take long before I was designing some new patterns." Lamar reached into a large cardboard box set on one end of the table and withdrew a quilted wall hanging made from white and three shades of blue material. "I call this one Goose Feathers on the Loose." He grinned. "Makes me think of the time one of our geese was chasing the dog. She flapped her wings so hard that she left a trail of feathers."

Laughter, as well as oohs and aahs came from everyone but Pam and Ruby Lee. They both, however, let their fingers trail over the design of feather-like stitches.

"Here's another one I created," Lamar said, removing from the box a quilted pillow top in various shades of brown, designed to resemble some type of bird tracks. "This one I call Pheasant Trail, because some of the menfolk in my family like to hunt."

"Those are both really great," Stuart said. "You're sure talented, Lamar."

Star nodded in agreement. "I'll say!"

"Thank you," Lamar said, blushing slightly. "It gives me pleasure to make nice things."

"So, is designin' quilts what you do for a living?" Jan asked.

"No, it's just a hobby. My real craft is making hickory rocking chairs, and I'm only doing that part-time these days."

"Well, you certainly could design quilt patterns full-time," Paul said, "because these are really unique."

Lamar gave a slight nod in response, and then he asked everyone to bring their wall hangings out and lay them on the table so he could see what they'd done.

They all did as he asked—everyone but Ruby Lee. She just sat, staring out the window as though occupied with her own thoughts at the moment. She'd been so pleasant and talkative when Star had met her on the Pumpkinvine Trail the other day. Something was definitely wrong with her today.

"Mine doesn't look so good," Stuart mumbled. "Some of my stitches are crooked, and some look like they're only half-stitched 'cause the sewing machine kept skipping or something. My wife said I didn't have the tension set right, but even after she fixed it for me, things weren't much better." He pointed to the few pieces he'd sewn onto his wall hanging. "The thread broke on me a couple of times, too."

"Some people who are first learning to sew end up having to take a lot of their stitches out," Lamar said. "You just have to watch and see that your stitches are straight, and that the tension is set right when you thread your needle and put the bobbin in place. We'll work on the projects for a while, and then I'll serve you some doughnuts that I bought fresh at the bakery this morning."

"That sounds good to me, so I'll keep trying," Stuart said. "But I'm still not sure I can sew a straight stitch." He motioned to Pam's quilted project. "Hers looks pretty good, though, wouldn't you say?"

"Yes, it's coming along real well," Lamar said after he'd inspected the pieces Pam had stitched onto her wall hanging.

Pam smiled but didn't say a word.

"What's up with you today?" Star asked. "Do you have a sore throat or laryngitis?"

Pam reached into her purse, pulled out a notebook and pen, and wrote a short message. *"My throat's fine. I promised Stuart I wouldn't say anything today."*

Star looked over at Stuart and frowned. "You asked your wife not to talk to anyone?"

His face turned red as he shook his head. "I didn't mean she couldn't say anything at all. I just meant I didn't want her talking about our problems or putting me down." He nudged Pam's arm. "Say something so they know you can talk."

Pam glared at him. "You're so stupid."

Star laughed. She just couldn't help herself. She looked over at Jan, and then he started laughing, too. Paul, Lamar, and Ruby Lee weren't laughing, and of course neither was Stuart. He looked downright miffed.

"No, you're stupid, Pam," Stuart mumbled.

"Would you two please stop?" Ruby Lee's hand trembled as she pointed first at Stuart, and then Pam. "You need to appreciate each other and stop quarreling all the time. Have you ever stopped to think about how things would be if something happened to one of you? Worse yet, what if one of you died, leaving the other alone?"

"That's right," Paul chimed in. "Once your mate is gone, it's too late to make amends for anything you may have said or done that was hurtful. I'm so thankful for all the good times my wife and I had together before she died. Lorinda and I didn't have the perfect marriage, but we had a good one, and we loved each other very much. You need to remember that things can change in a blink," he added, looking right at Stuart.

Stuart lowered his gaze and gave a little grunt.

"Do you have any idea how I felt when my wife died?" Paul continued. "It was like a part of me had died, and to make things worse, my wife's sister blamed me for the accident. She's made no contact with me since Lorinda's funeral—not even to see how Sophia, her only niece, is doing."

Paul's pained expression let Star know how much his sister-in-law's accusation and avoidance had hurt him. "What makes her think the accident was your fault?" she questioned.

"She said I should have been paying closer attention, and thinks if I'd seen the truck coming, I could have somehow gotten our car out of his way." A muscle on the side of Paul's cheek quivered. "I've spoken to my priest about this, and he says Carmen needed someone to blame."

"People often like to blame others for the bad things that happen to them," Lamar interjected. "I believe it's our human nature."

Paul nodded. "Sometimes people blame themselves. One thing I've learned through all this, though, is that life's too short to hold grudges or play the blame game. Good communication and a loving relationship with your family—that's what's really important."

"I'm a widower, too," Lamar said, "and my wife, Margaret, and I always tried to keep the lines of communication open. I'm thankful for the happy years we had together, which has left me with lots of good memories. Other than my children reminding me of what our love created, the memories I have of my wife are all I have left to hold on to."

Pam frowned and folded her arms, as though refusing to budge. "Well, if Stuart took more interest in me, it would be easier to make our marriage work."

Ruby Lee sucked in her breath as tears welled in her dark eyes and dribbled onto her flushed cheeks.

"Are you okay?" Star asked, touching Ruby Lee's arm. "Are you upset about something today?"

Ruby Lee gave a slow nod.

"Would you like to talk about it?" Pam asked. "Tell us what you're feeling right now?"

Ruby emitted a soft little sob and covered her mouth. "I—I can't go on like this. My faith is wavering, and I. . .I'm almost beginning to doubt that God is real." She sniffed deeply. "If. . .if He's truly the heavenly Father, then I don't think He cares about His people."

The room got deathly quiet. Star couldn't believe what Ruby Lee had just said. She'd thought the happy-go-lucky woman was strong in her beliefs. Up until now, she'd never let on that her faith in God had faltered. For Star to think God might not exist was one thing, but Ruby Lee was a pastor's wife. As far as Star was concerned, Ruby Lee had no right to be saying such things.

No one said anything at first; then Paul spoke up. "I suspect you're speaking out of frustration, Ruby Lee. Please tell us what's wrong. Is it your husband? Is he ill?"

"No, he's fine—at least physically." Between sniffles and sobs, Ruby Lee shared with the class about the problems they'd been having at her husband's church because he wanted to add on to the building. Then, after wiping her nose on the tissue Pam had handed her, Ruby Lee told how her friend had passed away two weeks ago, and she'd just found out about it the other day. "So much drama! I. . .I can't take this anymore," she said tearfully. "I used to be able to pray and feel some peace, but lately there just are no peaceful feelings for me."

I had no idea poor Ruby Lee's been going through so much, Star thought. *Sure wish she woulda said somethin' to me about all this the other day.* She glanced at Pam and noticed that even her eyes were glassy with tears.

Maybe the prissy woman did care about someone other than herself.

Rising to her feet and looking at Lamar, Ruby Lee said in a quivering voice, "I–I'm sorry, but I can't stay. I made a mistake coming here today." She grabbed up her quilting project and rushed out the door.

CHAPTER 25

Emma yawned and stretched her arms over her head. She didn't know how long she'd been asleep, but it seemed like she'd been lying on her bed for a good long while. The ice bag that had been pressed against her stomach when she first lay down was now warm, so she assumed that several hours must have passed.

She reached for her reading glasses lying on the table beside her bed and slipped them on after she sat up. Looking at the alarm clock, she realized it was half past noon.

Emma removed her glasses and ambled over to the window. There were no cars in the driveway, so she figured all her quilting students must have gone home. Lamar probably had too, since she didn't see any sign of his horse and buggy.

Emma redid her hair into a bun at the back of her head and put her head covering in place. Smoothing the wrinkles in her dark green dress, she made her way to the kitchen. When she stepped inside, she opened her mouth in surprise. Lamar stood in front of the stove, stirring something that smelled delicious.

At her sharp intake of air, he turned from the stove. "Oh good, you're up."

Leaning on the counter for support, all Emma could do was squeak, "Y–you're still here?"

He smiled and nodded. "Figured when you woke up you'd be hungry, so when I found some leftover soup in the refrigerator, I decided to heat it up for your lunch. Oh, and I added some canned peas and carrots that I found in your cupboard," he added with a sheepish grin. "Hope that's okay with you."

Emma gave a slow nod. "When I looked out my bedroom window, I didn't see your horse and buggy, so I figured you'd gone home."

"Nope. I put Ebony in the corral and moved my buggy to the back of your shed where it's in the shade." Lamar turned back to the stove and gave the kettle of soup a few more stirs. "I think it's about ready, so if you'll take a seat at the table, I'll dish you up a bowl."

Emma, unsure of what to say, stood staring at the back of Lamar's head. She wasn't used to having someone take over in her kitchen like this, and she sure hadn't expected Lamar to fix her lunch.

As though sensing her discomfort, he looked over his shoulder and said, "As soon as I serve up your soup, I'll be on my way."

Not wishing to be rude, Emma smiled and said, "Why don't you stay and join me? Unless you have other plans, that is."

"Nope. I have no plans at all for lunch." Lamar smacked his lips. "This sure smells good. Can't guarantee what it would taste like if I'd made it from scratch, though." He chuckled and went on to tell Emma about some of the blunders he'd made in the kitchen since his wife died.

"I may know how to craft a sturdy hickory rocking chair and design a quilt pattern, but I still don't know my way around the kitchen that well," he said. "One day I spent almost an hour searching for some salt I'd bought, only to find that I'd put it in the refrigerator by mistake." He shrugged his shoulders. "Finally decided to quit worrying about things so much and just do the best I can, because one thing I've discovered is that a day of worry is more exhausting than a week's worth of work."

Emma nodded. "That's true enough."

Lamar ladled some soup into two bowls, and Emma set out a basket of crackers and a glass of water for each of them.

Once they were seated, they bowed their heads for silent prayer. When they were both finished, Emma picked up her spoon and was about to take a bite of soup when Lamar said, "It's pretty hot. Better give it a few minutes to cool."

Emma set her spoon down and ate a few crackers instead, since she really was quite hungry and didn't want Lamar to hear her stomach growling.

"How are you feeling?"

"How'd it go today?"

They'd both spoken at the same time; so Emma motioned to Lamar and said, "Sorry; you go first."

"How are you feeling?" he asked. "Are your shingles blisters still causing you a lot of pain?"

"Jah, but I'm feeling a bit better than I did yesterday, so that's a good sign." Emma's throat felt dry, so she reached for her glass of water and took a drink. "How'd things go with the quilt class today?"

In response to Emma's question, Lamar's forehead wrinkled. "I think I did okay with the lesson, but that group of people you're teaching are sure a bunch of half-stitched quilters."

"What do you mean?"

"They've all got problems, Emma, and with the exception of Pam, none of 'em can sew all that well."

"I know they have problems, but then who doesn't?"

"True."

Emma went on to explain that some of her students had opened up to her, and she'd been trying not only to teach them to quilt, but to help with their problems at home.

"From what I can tell, they've got plenty of those." Lamar took a bite of his soup. "It's cool enough to eat now," he announced.

Emma began eating, too, and as they ate, they talked more about the people in her class.

"That couple—the Johnstons—seem to be having trouble with their marriage," Lamar said.

Emma nodded. "They're seeing a counselor who suggested they do more things together."

"Is that why they're taking the quilt class?"

"Jah, and hopefully it'll help bring them closer."

"Even Paul, who seems to be fairly stable, opened up to the class and told how painful it is that his sister-in-law blames him for his wife's death."

Emma frowned. "How can that be? From what Paul's said, his wife was killed when a truck slammed into the side of their car."

"That's right, but I guess Paul's sister-in-law thinks he could have done something to prevent the accident."

"That's *lecherich*," Emma said with a shake of her head.

"It may be ridiculous, but as I told Paul today, some people have to find someone to blame when things don't go as they'd like."

"Unfortunately, that's true. Some even blame God for all their troubles."

"What about the big fellow with the girl's name tattooed on his arm? Why's he taking the class?" Lamar asked, moving their conversation in a little different direction.

Emma explained about Jan's probation officer suggesting he find something creative to do, and then she told him the reasons the others had given for taking quilting lessons.

"Ruby Lee had some problems today," Lamar said, frowning.

"With her quilting project?"

He shook his head. "She shared with the class that her best friend had died two weeks ago, and she'd just found out about it."

"Oh, that's a shame."

"Jah, and she also mentioned that they've been having problems in their church, and it's affected her faith in God."

"What kind of problems?"

Emma listened intently as Lamar repeated all that Ruby Lee had shared with the class. "She ended up leaving early, and I felt bad because I wasn't sure what to say in order to help with her distress."

"It's okay, Lamar. You don't know those people very well." Emma pursed her lips. "As soon as I'm done eating, I'm going out to the phone shack and give Ruby Lee a call. I just hope I'm up to teaching the class next week, because if anyone else shares their problems, I really want to be there for them."

"I can understand that."

"Changing the subject," Emma said, "Sometime I'd like to see those quilt designs you've created."

Lamar smiled and pushed back his chair. "No problem there. I brought two of 'em with me today to show to your class."

He left the kitchen and returned a few minutes later with a cardboard box, which he placed on the counter. "This one I call Pheasant Trail," he said, holding up a quilted pillow slip.

"Ach! That's beautiful," Emma said, amazed at not only the design of what looked like a trail made by a bird, but also the pretty shades of brown material that had been used.

"This one I call Goose Feathers on the Loose," Lamar said, reaching into the box again and retrieving a wall hanging done up in white and a few shades of blue. Emma thought it was even prettier than the other.

"That feather design is beautiful. You certainly are creative," she said. "I never imagined you had the ability to do that."

Lamar's thick eyebrows furrowed. "What are you sayin', Emma—that I'm *dumm?*"

"No, no, of course you're not dumb. I just meant. . ." She paused and fanned her face, which suddenly felt very warm. "I'm just surprised, that's all, because I've never known a man who has the kind of talent you have or enjoys working with quilts."

Lamar's frown was replaced with a smile. "I think your students were a bit surprised as well," he, said with a twinkle in his eyes.

"I'm sorry that I doubted your ability to teach the class. You obviously know quite a bit about quilts."

"At least from the designing end of things, I do," he said with a nod. "Of course, working with my wife in her quilt shop, I learned a lot about making quilts, too."

Emma leaned closer to the table and started eating her soup. She wondered what other things she didn't know about Lamar.

Goshen

Soon after Star got home from the quilt class, she decided to work in her grandma's flower beds. They were getting overgrown with weeds, and it didn't look like Mom was going to tackle them anytime soon. When

Mom wasn't working, she was busy entertaining know-it-all Mike, with whom she was spending the day. He'd come by for Mom right after breakfast, saying he wanted to take her shopping at the mall in South Bend, and then they would see a show and go out to dinner after that. Why they couldn't have gone to the mall in Goshen, Star couldn't figure out, but at least with Mom and Mike being in South Bend, it was better than him hanging around here all day. Now Star would have the run of the house.

Star had just finished pulling weeds in one flower bed and had moved over to start on another when their nineteen-year-old neighbor boy, Matt Simpson, came out of his house and sauntered into Grandma's yard.

Oh great, Star thought. *Here comes Mr. Pimple Face, who can't even grow a beard.*

"What are you up to?" he asked, kneeling beside Star on the grass.

"I'm weeding the flower beds. What's it look like?"

"Hmm. . ."

"I'd appreciate it if you'd move back, 'cause you're invading my space."

"Hey, don't mind me. I'm just tryin' to be friendly," he said, moving back just a bit.

Star stabbed her shovel into the ground and pulled up a weed. *Maybe if I ignore him, he'll go away.*

"Say, what are you doin' for supper this evening?" Matt asked.

Star kept digging and pulling at more weeds, hoping he'd take the hint and leave.

"Hello. Uh. . .did you hear what I said?"

"I heard you all right, and quit winking at me."

"I wasn't. The sun was in my eyes, and I was squinting, not winking." He leaned closer again. "What are you doin' for supper?"

"I really don't know. I'll probably fix a sandwich or something."

"I thought maybe you'd like to go out for a burger and fries."

"With you?"

"Yeah."

She glared at him. "Get lost, creep. I wouldn't give the time of day to someone like you."

His blue eyes flashed angrily, and he pushed some of his auburn hair out of his eyes. "What's that supposed to mean?"

"It means, no. I'm not interested."

"Why not?"

"Because you're a loser, and losers are nothing but trouble. I ought to know; I had a loser for a dad and another loser for a stepdad." She grimaced. "Losers are losers; that's all they'll ever be."

Matt frowned. "Sorry about your loser dads, but it's no reason for you to compare me with them, 'cause I'm not a loser!"

"Oh, yeah? Then how come you're still living at home, sponging off your folks, and won't look for a job?"

"Who told you that?"

She shrugged. "Let's just say it's common knowledge."

"For your information, I do have a job."

"Oh really? Doin' what?"

"I have a paper route now, and I've got enough money in my wallet to take us both out for a burger and fries. A milkshake, too, if you want it."

She grunted. "Give me a break. I'm not goin' anywhere with you!"

Matt wrinkled his freckled nose. "That suits me just fine, 'cause unless you were willing to wear something sensible on our date, I wasn't plannin' to take you out anyways."

"I wear what I feel good in, and if you don't like it, that's just too bad."

"Why do you have to be so mean? Are you tryin' to hurt me so I'll leave you alone?"

She gave a nod. "That's what I do best. . .I push people away—especially losers like you."

Looking more than a little hurt, Matt stood and shuffled out of the yard. "You know," he yelled over before going into his house, "I knew your grandma, and I can't believe you're even related to her! And you know what else? You're nothin' like her, even if you are pullin' weeds in her garden the way she used to like to do!" With that, he stormed into his house and slammed the door.

Star flinched. She knew she'd been hard on Matt, but if she'd given the poor sap even a hint of niceness, he might have thought he had a chance with her. "Like that'll ever happen. If I was gonna go out with someone, it would be with a guy like Jan, who at least has a decent-paying job and likes some of the same things as me. Not that he'd be interested in someone as young as I am." She stabbed the shovel into the dirt again. "But if he did ask me out, I'd probably say yes."

CHAPTER 26

Shipshewana

Shortly before noon on Wednesday of the following week, Emma stepped outside and headed for the phone shack to check her messages. She hoped she might hear something from Ruby Lee. She'd tried calling her on Saturday and then again on Monday. Both of those times, though, she had to leave a message on Ruby Lee's answering machine. Could Ruby Lee be out of town, or was she avoiding talking to Emma?

I wish I'd been able to teach my class on Saturday, Emma thought as she approached the phone shack. *Maybe I could have said something to help Ruby Lee when she shared her troubles with the others.*

Emma was almost to the shack when the door opened suddenly and Mary stepped out. "Ach, Mom, I didn't know you were out here!" Mary said, jumping back, her eyes going wide.

"I came to make a phone call," Emma replied. "Sorry if I startled you."

"No problem. I'm done with the phone now." Mary moved aside. "How are you feeling, Mom? Are you still in a lot of pain?"

Emma shook her head. "I'm doing better every day. I don't think this bout with shingles is quite as bad as the first time I had them."

"I'm glad to hear that."

"I plan on teaching my quilt class this Saturday," Emma said. "I appreciated Lamar's help last week, but I don't want to impose on him again."

Mary smiled. "I know I've said this before, but I think Lamar is really a very nice man, and I also wanted to tell you that—"

"I'd better get my phone call made," Emma said, quickly changing the subject. She wasn't in the mood to hear more of her daughter's thoughts about Lamar, because she had a hunch that Mary wanted to see her get married again. Why, she couldn't imagine. Didn't Mary realize that no one could ever take Ivan's place in Emma's heart? For that matter, could Mary so easily accept a stepfather? Maybe she thought if Emma married Lamar, then the family wouldn't have to help her so much.

All the more reason for me to show them that I can be independent, Emma thought.

"Would you like to come over to my house for lunch after you're finished with your phone call?" Mary asked.

"I appreciate the offer, but I'd better pass. I have some chicken noodle soup simmering on the stove, and after I eat, I'm going to take a nap. I want to make sure I get plenty of rest between now and Saturday."

"That's probably a good idea."

Mary gave Emma a gentle hug, said good-bye, and headed for home.

Emma stepped into the phone shack and dialed Ruby Lee's number. Again, no one answered, and Emma had to leave another message.

"Hello, Ruby Lee, it's me, Emma Yoder. I've been trying to get in touch with you," she said. "I hope you'll be at the quilting class on Saturday. In the meantime, if you'd like to talk, please give me a call."

When Emma left the phone shack, she stopped at the goat pen and watched Maggie and the other goats frolic awhile. She was glad Maggie couldn't get out and make a pest of herself any longer. It had just made more work for Emma whenever the goat messed things up in her yard.

After Emma arrived back at the house, she discovered that a tear in her front screen door had been fixed. She figured Mary's husband must have done it, maybe while she was taking a nap earlier in the week. Emma had been so out of it lately, she hadn't noticed much of anything.

She paused to run her fingers over the spot where the tear had been and noticed what a fine repair job it was. She'd have to thank Brian for his thoughtful gesture right away.

Emma entered her house and went to the kitchen to check on the soup. Seeing that it was thoroughly heated, she turned off the stove and headed for Mary's house.

"Did you change your mind about joining me for lunch?" Mary asked when Emma entered her kitchen a few minutes later.

"No, I just came over to tell Brian thanks for fixing the tear in my screen door."

Mary shook her head, "Brian's still at work, and no, Mom, it wasn't him. Lamar fixed the tear in your screen."

"How do you know that?" Emma asked, raising her brows.

"Because I saw him do it."

"And you never said anything about it to me?"

"I was going to mention it when I spoke to you a bit ago, but you said you were in a hurry to make a call, so I decided it could wait."

"Oh, I see." Emma was thankful the screen had been fixed, but she wished it had been Brian who'd done it and not Lamar. Now she felt obligated to repay him in some way, because he'd done three nice things for her in one week.

Goshen

Since Mom was working at the restaurant and Star had gotten off work earlier this morning, Star had the house to herself again. That was fine with her. She was thankful Grandma had left this old house to Mom, because it was a place she could just relax and be herself. When Star was alone, she could sing and play her guitar without Mom telling her to tone it down. She could work on writing more songs without any negative comments. This morning, however, Star had decided to go through some of Grandma's things that she'd found in the attic.

As she sat on the floor in the dusty, dimly lit room looking through a box of pictures she'd found in an old trunk, tears sprang to her eyes. She'd never seen any of these photos before, and it was hard seeing pictures of herself when she was a girl, sitting on Grandma's lap. Those had been happy days, though, when Star felt loved and secure. But seeing the pictures made her miss Grandma even more.

If only I could feel that kind of love from Mom, she thought. *But then, under the circumstances I guess she did the best by me that she could. It couldn't have been easy raising a child alone. Maybe that's why Mom married Wes. She was hoping to give me a father.*

Anger boiled in Star's chest. *That creep was anything but a father to me, and he sure wasn't the kind of husband Mom or any other woman needed. He should have been put in jail for all the times he hit Mom. But no, Mom had either been too afraid of him to file a report, or maybe she was just plain stupid and liked to be smacked around. Who knows? Maybe Mom thought Wes was the best she could do and didn't realize that she deserved better.*

Star swiped at the tears dripping onto her cheeks. The past was in the past, and it didn't make sense to cry over what couldn't be changed. At least they were rid of Wes now, and even though she didn't care for

Mike, she had to admit, he was a better choice for Mom than the wife abuser. Even so, Star hoped Mom wouldn't marry Mike, because then Star would feel forced to move out of Grandma's house—the only place that had ever truly felt like home.

Bringing her troubling thoughts to a halt, Star reached into the trunk and pulled out a few more photos, stopping when she came to a picture of Mom holding a baby in her arms. Star knew the baby was her, because she'd seen other baby pictures of herself. But part of this picture had been ripped away. Could there have been someone else in the photo? Had Mom, or maybe Grandma, torn the picture like that?

Was my Dad in the other half of this picture? Star wondered. *Should I show this to Mom and ask her about it or keep it to myself?* Knowing Mom and the way she avoided the subject of Star's real dad, Star figured if she showed the picture and started asking a bunch of questions, Mom would get real mad. However, if it was her dad, then Star really wanted to know, because she'd always wondered what he looked like and whether she resembled him or not. Maybe Mom had some other pictures of him hidden away somewhere that Star didn't know about.

Star started to put the picture back in the trunk but changed her mind. She'd keep it in her wallet for now—until she decided whether to mention it to Mom or not.

CHAPTER 27

Mishawaka

While Pam prepared supper on Friday evening, tears welled in her eyes as she reflected on the things Ruby Lee had said during the last quilt class, things about appreciating each other and not quarreling all the time. She could still hear the tone of almost desperation in Ruby Lee's voice when she'd said, *"Have you ever stopped to think about how things would be if something happened to one of you? Worse yet, what if one of you died, leaving the other alone?"*

Maybe I don't appreciate Stuart enough, Pam thought as she reached for some garlic powder to sprinkle on the ground beef patties Stuart would soon be putting on the grill. *Maybe it would help if I try to be a little nicer to him and show more appreciation for the good things he does.* That was one of the things their counselor had suggested, only Pam hadn't put it into practice. But then, neither had Stuart.

"Daddy wants to know if the patties are ready," Devin said, dashing into the kitchen at full speed and nearly running into the table. He was still in high gear, since today had been the last day of school and the kids' summer vacation had officially begun.

Pam dabbed at her eyes so Devin wouldn't see her tears. "Slow down, son. You know you're not supposed to run in the house."

"Sorry," the boy mumbled, "but Daddy said I should hurry 'cause the barbecue's ready and he don't wanna waste the gas."

"Yes, the patties are ready, and I'll take them out to him right now." Pam picked up the platter and headed out the back door, hoping her eyes weren't too red from crying. She found Stuart on the patio, fiddling with the control knob on their gas barbecue.

"Here you go," she said sweetly, handing him the platter.

"Thanks." Stuart put the patties on the grill and then stood off to one side where he could keep a watch on things. "What else did you fix to go with the burgers?" he asked.

"I made macaroni salad, and we'll have chips, dip, pickles, and olives. Oh, and I baked some chocolate cupcakes for dessert."

"Sounds good." He offered her a crooked grin.

Pam's heart skipped a beat. He hadn't looked at her that sweetly in a long time.

Maybe there was some hope for their marriage, after all.

She leaned close to his ear and whispered, "I appreciate your help fixing supper tonight."

"No problem. I'm glad to help out. And you know how much I enjoy barbecuing. Besides, it's a nice way to celebrate the kids' last day of school." Stuart slipped his arm around Pam's waist and pulled her close. It felt nice to have him show her some attention.

They stood like that for several minutes, until Stuart had to flip the burgers. "You know, I've been thinking it might be fun if I took Devin on a camping trip this summer. . .just the two of us. It would give us some father-son time, and I can teach him how to fish."

"Why can't we do something as a family?" she asked. "Something we'd all like to do."

He quirked an eyebrow. "Such as?"

"We could take the kids to the Fun Spot amusement park. Or better yet, why don't we make a trip to Disney World in Florida?"

Stuart shook his head. "A trip like that would take too long. I've only got a few days of vacation time left this year—just long enough for a few camping trips."

Irritation welled in Pam's soul. "Camping! Camping! Camping! Is that all you ever think about? Don't you want to do anything Sherry and I might enjoy?" She clenched her fingers so tightly that her nails dug into her palms. "Don't you love me, Stuart?"

"You oughta know I love you, but I enjoy being in the woods, and since you don't like to camp, I thought I'd take Devin." He paused long enough to flip the burgers again. "Can't you and Sherry do something together? You know—some little mother-daughter thing like shopping or going to a movie?"

She shook her head. "I want us to do something as a family."

"Then go camping with us."

"I don't like camping—especially in a tent. Worse than that, I don't like being at home while you run off and do whatever you like with no consideration for what I might want to do."

He frowned. "I'm taking that stupid quilt class, aren't I? I'm doing it because I love you and want to make you happy."

"The class is not stupid!"

His eyes narrowed. "I just said I love you, and all you heard was my comment about the class being stupid?"

"You didn't think it was stupid when you went two weeks ago

without me. Why was that, Stuart?" Pam's voice rose higher with each word she spoke. "And why did you enjoy the class when you went alone but hate it when I was with you?"

"Lower your voice," he said. "The kids or the neighbors might hear you hollering and think there's a problem over here."

"Were you just showing off for Emma and the others in the class, trying to impress them? Or were you trying to make me look bad—like I have all the problems and you're Mr. Nice Guy?" she hissed, not caring in the least who might be listening or what they thought. "And who cares if the neighbors hear us and think there's a problem? There *is* a problem. Don't you get it?"

"I know there's a problem, and no, I wasn't trying to make you look bad. I told you before how it was. Don't you believe me?"

"No, I don't! What I believe is that you'd rather be alone or with other people than spend time with me." She stamped her foot and scowled at him. So much for trying to make things work with Stuart. He was absolutely impossible! "You're just like my father, you know that? He spent more time away from home than he did with me and Mom, and I hated him for it! They made me work hard in school, forcing me to get straight As. And yet when I did, all I got for my hard work was money and some really nice clothes. What I wanted was their unconditional love and to be with them as a family, but Dad never cared about any of that. All he cared about was himself!"

Stuart looked stunned and seemed unable to speak. "You. . .you've never told me any of that before," he finally said. "I always thought you loved your dad, and that everything was perfect in your home when you were growing up."

Pam gulped on a sob. "I did love him, but things were far from perfect. I've never admitted it to anyone before, but now you know."

Stuart reached his hand out to her, but she quickly pulled away. "I've lost my appetite. The rest of the food's on the kitchen table. You and the kids can eat whenever the burgers are done."

"What about you? Aren't you going to eat with us?"

"I'm not hungry. I've got a headache, and I'm going to bed!" Pam whirled around and dashed into the house. Tired of every conversation turning into an argument, she just wanted to be alone.

Goshen

"It's nice to be home, isn't it?" Gene said as he and Ruby Lee entered their house and headed for the kitchen. "I'm sure our own bed will feel really good tonight."

Ruby Lee nodded. Sunday, after another tension-filled church service, Gene had suggested they take a few days off and go somewhere to be alone so they could think and pray about their situation. They couldn't really do that at home—not with the phone ringing at all hours of the day. Even in their new home, people often dropped by unannounced. So Ruby Lee and Gene had booked a room at a lovely bed-and-breakfast outside Middlebury and spent the last four days in solitude. While nothing had been definitely decided, Ruby Lee thought Gene might actually be considering leaving the ministry. If that's the way he chose to go, she'd be relieved. She was tired of trying to help people with their problems, only to be kicked in the teeth. She, and especially Gene, deserved better than that.

"Guess I should check our messages," Gene said. "Unless you'd rather do that."

She shook her head. "You go ahead. I'm going to see what I can throw together for supper." She opened the refrigerator door. "We have plenty of eggs. Does an omelet appeal to you?"

"Sure, that's fine."

When Gene punched the button to replay the messages, Ruby Lee recognized Emma's voice as the caller of the first message, asking if Ruby Lee was okay and saying if she needed to talk, to please give her a call. Following that were a couple of advertising calls, including one from a man who wanted to tune the piano at the church. Two more calls from Emma said pretty much the same as the first one had, but Emma ended the last message by saying she was feeling better and hoped to see Ruby Lee at the quilt class on Saturday.

"Are you going to call her back?" Gene asked. "She sounded eager to talk to you."

"Tomorrow's Saturday, so I'll see her then." Truth was, Ruby Lee had debated about not going to the class tomorrow morning. It would be hard to face the others after her outburst last week. But she wanted to finish her wall hanging and needed help with the next step, so she would swallow her pride and go. After all, it wasn't like she was the only one who'd ever had a display of emotions during one of their classes. Truth be told, it had felt somewhat healing to share her grief and frustration with her newfound friends. Maybe later she would share even more.

CHAPTER 28

Look what Mike bought for me when we were in South Bend the other day," Mom said, holding her left hand out to Star after she'd taken a seat beside her at the breakfast table. "We had to have it resized, so he wasn't able to give it to me till last night."

Star blinked at the flashy ring on her mother's finger, noting how huge the diamond was. "Is it real?"

"Of course it is, silly. Do you really think Mike would give me a fake?"

"So what'd the guy do, rob a bank?" Star nearly gagged, watching Mom wiggle her finger as she stared at the prisms within the diamond catching the light.

"What? No, of course not." Mom smiled widely. "He's been saving up to buy me a really nice engagement ring."

Star wrinkled her nose. "I suppose that means you've decided to marry the creep."

"Mike is not a creep. He's a steady worker and a good man. A much better man than any other I've ever known, and we're planning to be married in September."

"That's just great. Super awesome, in fact. Yeah, this is the best news I've had all year."

"You don't have to be sarcastic about it. Just what have you got against Mike anyway?"

Star held up one finger. "He's bossy." She held up a second finger. "He's opinionated." A third finger came up. "He's a control freak."

Mom flapped her hand. "Oh, he is not. When have you ever seen Mike try to control me?"

"Not you, Mom; although he does expect you to wait on him a lot. It's the TV he really likes to control." Star frowned. "As soon as he comes in the door, he grabs the remote, and on goes the TV. From then on, he's in charge of whatever we watch. Not only that, but he doesn't like anything about me."

"That's not true, Star."

"Oh, isn't it? The last time he came over, didn't you hear how he was on my case about the clothes I wear and the kind of music I listen to?"

"He has a right to his opinion." Mom stuck the end of her finger in her mouth and bit off a hangnail. "You already know how I feel about the way you dress, so you shouldn't be surprised that Mike doesn't care for it either."

Star slapped her hand on the table, just missing her glass of orange juice. "I don't care what he thinks! I don't want another crummy stepfather!"

"He's not going to be a crummy stepfather or a crummy husband either. Despite what you think, Mike is good to me, and—"

"Well, I hope he does better by you than Wes did. 'Course anyone would be better than that wife abuser." Star picked up her glass of juice and took a drink. "What about my real dad? Did he abuse you, too?"

Mom's forehead wrinkled. "Now what made you ask that question?"

"You've never really given me all that much information about him, so for all I know, he could have treated you even worse than Wes."

"I've told you all you need to know about your dad. He didn't abuse me physically, but he was wild and undependable. And being a new father, he proved that when he ran out on us when you were a baby."

Star reached into her jeans' pocket, pulled out her wallet, and removed the picture she'd found in Grandma's attic the other day. "Was it my dad's picture that was ripped away from this?" she asked, handing the photo to Mom.

Mom stared at the photograph in disbelief. With a slow nod, she said in a whisper, "Yes, it was your dad. I tore him out of the picture."

"Why?"

Mom picked up her coffee cup and took a drink before answering. "I. . .I didn't want any reminders of the guy around. The day I tore that picture, I was very angry with him."

"Was he really that bad?"

Tears gathered in the corners of Mom's eyes. "Can't you let this go? I'd rather not talk about it. I just want to focus on my future with Mike."

It was obvious that the subject of Star's real father was a touchy one. Mom had no doubt loved him at one time, and when he'd pulled up stakes and deserted them, it had probably broken her heart. From what Star had seen all these years, whenever the subject of her dad came up, Mom still held a lot of hurt and anger toward him, so maybe it was best if she just dropped the subject. After all, what was the point? If her dad didn't care enough about her and Mom to stick around and support them, then he really wasn't worth knowing.

"Could I have the picture back?" Star asked. "It's a good one of you and me, don't you think?"

"You're right. It is." Mom handed the picture to Star and smiled. "So what are your plans for the day?"

"I'm goin' to Emma Yoder's quilting class. Today will be our fifth lesson, and I'm hoping Emma's well enough to teach the class again because she explains things better than her Amish friend did. Although he was quite an interesting guy and knows something about designing quilt patterns," Star added.

"Well, before you go, there's something else I wanted to say about Mike. I think you should know that—"

"I've gotta go now, Mom, so hold that thought till I get home from Emma's," Star said, glancing at the clock on the far wall. She gulped down the rest of her juice, grabbed her sack with the quilt project in it, and raced out the door. She would deal with Mom marrying Mike when the time came, but she didn't have to like it.

Middlebury

As Stuart and Pam passed through Middlebury on their way to Shipshewana, Pam kept her head turned to the right. Maybe if she pretended to be looking at the scenery they were passing—scenery she'd seen many times before and knew almost by heart—Stuart would stop trying to make conversation. She was still upset with him for wanting to take Devin camping, while she and Sherry sat at home by themselves. Sure, she could probably think of something the two of them could do together, but Pam wanted to do more things as a family. Maybe if she continued to whine about it, Stuart would change his mind. Or maybe if she gave him the cold shoulder long enough, he'd wake up and realize how insensitive he was about her needs.

"When I checked the weather report on the Internet this morning, it said we might be getting some rain next week," Stuart said.

Pam silently focused on the black, box-shaped buggy up ahead. The little Amish girl who sat in the back looked out at Pam and waved. She was so cute that Pam waved back and smiled, despite her gloomy mood.

"Wish it would have rained today." Stuart grunted. "Then I wouldn't mind being cooped up in Emma's house all morning with a bunch of people I'd rather not know."

"That's not what you said after you attended the class without me," Pam mumbled. "You seemed quite interested in what all had been said and done that day. And to be honest, I really don't want to talk about the weather."

"Why do you have to be so critical of everything I say and do?" he questioned.

She gave no response.

"You know, sometimes I wonder why we ever got married. All we seem to do is fight."

"Then I guess we made the biggest mistake of our lives when we tied the knot, huh?"

"Maybe we did, but we loved each other, and I wish we could start over."

"I'd be happy to start over if you agreed to spend more time with me."

"What do you think I'm doing right now?"

"You're only doing it out of obligation. You take no pleasure in being with me, do you?"

A muscle in Stuart's cheek twitched. "Just stop it, Pam. You're putting words in my mouth again, and I'm gettin' sick of it, because we've been through all this before."

"That's a really dumb answer, Stuart."

"Can you give me an example of what a better answer would be? I mean, what exactly is it you want me to say?"

"How about, 'I love you, Pam,' and—"

"I've told you that many times."

She bumped his arm. "I'd appreciate it if you didn't interrupt when I'm talking."

"Sorry," he mumbled. "Go ahead and say what you were going to say, but let me remind you that you're one of the biggest interrupters I know."

Pam turned her head away. "Never mind, Stuart. Like all the other times, this is getting us nowhere."

"Just say what you were gonna say and be done with it!"

"What's the point? You're not going to change your mind about going camping with Devin."

"I don't know why you should begrudge me a little quality time with my son."

"*Our* son, Stuart." Pam placed her hand on her stomach. "I carried him for nine whole months. I've also nursed him back to health whenever he's been sick."

"I realize that. When I referred to Devin as *my* son, it was just a figure of speech."

"Whatever." She stared out her window until another thought popped into her mind. "You know what, Stuart?"

"What?"

"Maybe Sherry and I will do something together—something she'll think is really fun, like going to a baseball game. She likes sitting with you and watching the games on TV. Maybe then you'll realize what it feels like not to join us." Pam really didn't want to take Sherry to a game, but it was the only thing she could think of at the moment that might make Stuart realize how she felt.

"Sure, go ahead," he muttered. "You and Sherry can do whatever you want while Devin and I are camping."

Pam clenched her teeth. She'd be glad when they got to Emma's so she could make conversation with someone sensible—someone like Emma, who seemed to care about everyone's needs.

Shipshewana

Emma hummed softly as she placed needles, thread, scissors, and six small quilting frames on the table in her sewing room. She was glad she felt well enough to teach the class today and looked forward to showing her students how to quilt the patterned pieces they'd already put together. It gave her a sense of satisfaction to teach others the skills she'd learned at a young age. And being able to listen to and offer helpful suggestions about her students' personal problems made the class even more rewarding.

Glancing at the battery-operated clock on the far wall, Emma saw that she had about ten minutes before class started. That should give her just enough time to walk to the end of the driveway and get the mail.

With that decided, Emma hurried out the door. She was almost to the mailbox when a horse and open buggy pulled onto the shoulder of the road. Lamar was in the driver's seat.

"Guder mariye," he said with a friendly wave. "How are you feeling, Emma?"

"I'm doing better," she replied with a nod. "What brings you by here this morning?"

"Just thought I'd stop and see if you were feeling up to teaching your class today." His eyes twinkled when he smiled at her. "If you're not, then I'm more than willing to take over for you again."

Emma bristled. "I told you when you came by yesterday that I'm feeling better and can manage the class on my own."

"I know, but today's another day, and I thought even though you were doing better yesterday, you might not feel up to teaching the class today."

"I'm fine," Emma said a bit too sharply. She didn't know why this man got under her skin so easily. She knew she should appreciate his concern, but at times like now, Lamar seemed overly concerned and almost intrusive. Emma's irritation made no sense, really, because when Ivan was alive, she'd never minded if he'd shown concern for her well-being.

"I'm glad you're feeling better, but since I have no other plans this morning, I'd be happy to at least give you a hand with your class."

Emma shook her head so vigorously that the ribbon ties on her head covering swished around her face. "I appreciate your offer, but I'm sure I can manage fine on my own," she said, pushing the ribbons back under her chin.

"Oh, I see."

Emma couldn't help but notice the look of defeat on Lamar's face. Was it because he was lonely and needed something to do, or did he enjoy quilting so much that he really wanted to help? Either way, she wasn't going to change her mind about this. She saw too much of Lamar as it was, and if she let him help in the class today, he might end up taking over the lesson. Worse yet, he might think she was interested in having more than a casual friendship with him.

Just then, much to Emma's relief, Stuart and Pam's SUV pulled onto the driveway.

Emma gave them a friendly wave; then she turned to Lamar and said, "Some of my students are here now, so I really must go." Without waiting for Lamar's response, Emma grabbed the mail from the box and hurried toward the house.

CHAPTER 29

After all Emma's students arrived, they followed her into the sewing room and took seats around the table.

"It's good to see that you're back, Emma," Paul said warmly.

Everyone nodded in agreement.

"How are you feeling?" Ruby Lee asked.

"I'm doing much better," Emma replied. "Last week I was in a lot of pain and wouldn't have done well if I'd tried to teach the class. I'm sorry I couldn't be here."

"Ah, that's okay. It was nice of your friend Lamar to take over for you," Jan said. "He seemed like a real nice fellow, but we're all glad you're feelin' better and can teach the class today."

"Yes, I appreciated him filling in for me, but I'm also glad to be back." Emma smiled, looking at each one. "I missed all of you."

"We missed you, too," Star said sincerely. It was nice to see that even though she wore the black sweatshirt again, the hood wasn't on her head. Emma also noticed that Star seemed more relaxed around the others than she had when she'd come to the first quilting class.

"Today I want to teach you how to do the quilting stitches on your wall hangings. So if everyone will lay their work on the table, I'll tell you what we'll be doing next."

Once everyone had done as Emma asked, she explained that the process of stitching three layers of material together was called *quilting*.

"But before we begin the actual process, you'll each need to cut a piece of cotton batting approximately two inches larger than your wall hanging on all sides," she said. "The excess batting and backing will then be trimmed even with the quilt top after all the quilting stitches have been completed."

Emma handed some batting to each of her students. "Now, in order to create a smooth, even quilting surface, all three layers of the quilt need to be put in a frame," she continued. "For a larger quilt, you would need a quilting frame that could stretch and hold the entire quilt at one time. But since your wall hangings are much smaller than a full-sized quilt, you can use a frame that's similar to a large embroidery hoop." She held up one of the frames she'd placed on the table earlier.

"That suits me just fine," Jan spoke up. " 'Cause I've done some embroidery work before and know all about usin' a hoop."

Emma smiled. "It's important when using this type of hoop to baste the entire quilt together through all three layers. This will keep the layers evenly stretched while you're quilting. Just be sure you don't quilt over the basting, or it will be hard to remove those stitches later on."

Emma waited patiently until each person had cut out their batting. Then she said, "The next step is to mark out the design you want on your quilt top. However, if you just want your quilting to outline the patches you've sewn, then no marking is necessary. You'll simply need to quilt close to the seam so the patch will be emphasized."

Emma went on to tell them about needle size, saying that it was best to try several different sizes to see which one would be the most comfortable to handle. She also stated that the use of a snuggly fitting thimble worn on the middle finger of the hand used for pushing the quilting needle was necessary, since the needle would have to be pushed through three layers of fabric repeatedly. She demonstrated on one of her own quilt patches, showing how to pull the needle and thread through the material to create the quilting pattern.

"The stitches should be tiny and even," she said. "Oh, and they need to be snug, but not so tight that they'll create any puckering."

Stuart frowned. "That looks way too hard for me. My hands are big, and I don't think I can make tiny stitches or wear that thimble thing you mentioned. It was hard enough sewing the pattern pieces together on the sewing machine."

"For now, rather than worrying about the size of your stitches, just try to concentrate on making straight, even stitches," Emma instructed. "Don't worry when you're doing your best, and remember, I'm here to help you."

"Okay," Stuart mumbled. It was obvious that he still wasn't comfortable using a needle and thread. But at least he was here and trying his best. Emma had to give him credit for that.

"Yeow!" Jan hollered. "My thimble fell off, and I just pricked my finger with the stupid needle! Think I'd do better without the thimble." He stuck his finger in his mouth and grimaced. "That sure does hurt!"

Stuart snickered.

Jan glared at him. "What are you laughin' at, man?"

"I'm not laughing."

"Yeah, you were."

"I wasn't laughing at you."

"I think you were."

Stuart, red-faced and looking guilty said, "I was just thinking that a big tough guy like you with all those tattoos on your arms shouldn't even flinch if he pricks his finger."

Emma held her breath, wondering how Jan would respond.

"Well, what can I say," Jan said. "I may be a big strong man, but I bleed like anyone else."

Emma breathed a sigh of relief.

"I haven't gotten the hang of using the thimble yet either," Paul interjected, looking over at Stuart. "Even though I know it's supposed to help, to me it just gets in the way and feels kind of awkward. You know what I'm saying?"

Stuart nodded and went back to work on his quilting project.

After the first hour had passed, Emma went to the kitchen to get some refreshments. It always seemed like things went better in the class after she'd given her students a snack.

When she returned to the sewing room, she served them coffee, iced tea, and some rhubarb crunch that she'd baked last night before going to bed. As they ate their refreshments, Emma asked each one how their week had gone.

Pam was the first to respond. "It was okay, I guess. Probably would have been better if Stuart and I hadn't argued so much." She cast a quick glance in his direction, and he glared at her.

"Knock it off, Pam. Nobody wants to hear about the problems we're having."

She dropped her gaze to the table and mumbled, "Well, we wouldn't have those problems if we'd both stayed single."

"You've made a good point," he said with a nod.

Emma, feeling the need to intervene, quickly said, "Did you two ever stop to think how your life would be if you hadn't gotten married?"

Neither Pam nor Stuart said anything.

"Think about it," Emma continued. "If you hadn't married each other, you wouldn't have your two precious children."

"I hadn't really thought about it before, but that's true." Stuart looked over at Pam. "That's somethin' to be grateful for, right?"

She gave a slow nod.

"Just remember," Emma said. "It's important for you to work at your marriage if for no other reason than for the sake of your children."

Pam's chin trembled a bit. "Thanks, Emma. You've given us something to think about."

Emma smiled, pleased that they'd made a little progress. She turned to Paul then and asked about his week.

"It went pretty well," he replied. "It was nothing like the stressful one I had previously. I took Sophia shopping for new shoes yesterday afternoon, and I can't believe how big she's getting. Her shoe size actually went up a notch," he added with a proud-father grin. "Plus, she's growing out of her clothes faster than I can buy new ones."

"That's what kids do," Stuart said with a chuckle. "They grow up way too quick. It seems like just yesterday when our two were babies, and now they're both old enough for school."

Paul smiled. "Sophia's saying a few words now, too. She calls me 'Pa-Pa-Pa,' and has even learned the word *no*. It probably won't be too long before she's trying to walk." Paul's face sobered. "Too bad my wife's sister won't be around to see any of Sophia's childhood."

Emma went over to Paul and placed her hands on his shoulders. "I know it must be hard for you to have your sister-in-law cutting you and Sophia out of her life, but just keep praying for her and trusting that someday her eyes will be open to the truth, and she'll make amends."

"I know I need to keep praying," Paul said. "In 1 Thessalonians 5:17, it says we are to pray continually. It's just that sometimes it's hard—especially when we don't see answers to our prayers."

"Oh, God always answers. Sometimes He says yes. Sometimes, it's no. And sometimes He just wants us to be patient and wait." Emma looked at each one in the room. "Prayer is always a good thing, and for me, when I combine quilting and prayer, I can feel the love of God surrounding me."

"I've never believed much in prayer before," Jan spoke up, "but when I thought Brutus was dead, I prayed to God."

"So your prayer was answered then," said Emma.

Jan gave a nod. "Made me wonder if I oughta start goin' to church." His face reddened a bit. " 'Course, I'm not sure how folks would feel about a tattooed biker like me showin' up at their church." He looked at Ruby Lee. "What do you think? Would a guy who's rough around the edges be welcomed in your church?"

"Why certainly," she replied, "but then I'm not sure how much longer Gene and I will be there, and—"

"What do you mean?" Star interrupted. "I thought your husband was the pastor of your church."

"Well, he is. . .right now, at least." Ruby Lee went on to tell the class that she and her husband had taken a few days off and stayed at a B&B near Middlebury where they'd talked things through and prayed about their situation. "It didn't solve the problems we've been faced with at the church," she said, "but it did give us some time alone to reflect and spend some much-needed time in prayer."

Emma took a seat beside Ruby Lee, grateful for the opportunity to speak to her about this. "I'm glad you were able to do that, Ruby

Lee. After talking with Lamar and hearing how things went last week, I knew you must be hurting, so I tried calling you several times. Now I know why you didn't return my calls."

"That's right, and I didn't call when we got home last night because I knew I'd see you today."

"I just wanted to see if there was anything I could do and let you know that I've been praying for you," Emma said, giving Ruby Lee's arm a gentle squeeze.

Ruby Lee smiled. "Thanks, Emma. I appreciate that."

"And you know," Emma added, "God doesn't want us to lose faith in Him or become full of despair. He wants us to trust Him and keep praying as we wait and hope for the best."

"I know," Ruby Lee said quietly. "I'm working hard at trying to do that."

When everyone had finished their refreshments and begun quilting again, Emma turned to Jan and asked, "How'd your week go?"

His face broke into a wide grin. "Pretty good. I've been spendin' more time with Brutus in the evenings, and he seems to be much calmer now. We try to get in a walk around the neighborhood before it gets dark, and I'm actually gettin' to meet more of my neighbors in a positive way now."

"I'm glad your dog came back," Emma said sincerely.

"Yeah, me, too. While he was gone, I really missed the mutt."

"It made me sick to see that dead dog lying by the side of the road and then wondering who it belonged to and if some child would go to bed that night missing his dog," Paul said.

"Yeah," Stuart interjected. "People ought to keep a closer watch on their pets."

Emma turned to Star to check in on her week.

"It was terrible. . .especially this morning when I found out that my mom's definitely gettin' married again—to that guy I don't even like."

"I know you're not happy about this," Emma said, "but do you think your mother's happy?"

Star shrugged. "She seems to be."

"Then maybe you should be happy for her, too," Pam put in.

"I'd like to be, but I can't imagine Mike livin' in the same house with us, criticizing everything I wear, making fun of my songs, and tellin' me what to do all the time."

Emma gave Star's shoulders a reassuring squeeze. "Maybe it won't be as bad as you think."

"Guess we'll have to wait and see how it goes." Star frowned. "If Mike keeps tellin' me what to do and tries to act like he's my dad, then I'll probably end up movin' out on my own."

"I'll be praying for your situation," Emma said.

"Thanks. Like Jan, I've never held much stock in prayer, but I guess it wouldn't hurt to have a few prayers goin' up just in case there is a God and He might actually be listening."

"Oh, there's a God all right," Paul interjected. "He is the One true God, and without my faith in Him, I'd never have made it this far since Lorinda died."

"Same with me after Ivan passed," Emma added. "Psalm 71, verse 3 tells us that God is our rock and our fortress. I'm real thankful for that."

Ruby Lee nodded, and so did Paul, but everyone else remained quiet as they continued to quilt. Emma hoped they were all taking the words of the psalm to heart and that any of her students who didn't know the Lord in a personal way would someday make that decision.

For the rest of the class, things went along fairly well. Then shortly before it was time to go, Paul said, "Oh, I almost forgot. I brought some pictures I took of Sophia the other day. Would anyone like to see them?"

"Of course we would." Ruby Lee smiled. "Who doesn't like to look at baby pictures?"

Paul reached into the sack he'd brought his quilting project in and pulled out a manila envelope. Then he removed two eight-by-ten photos of Sophia and shared them with the class.

"So, you took these pictures of your daughter?" Stuart asked, passing them on to Pam.

Paul smiled. "I sure did, and I was pretty pleased with the way they turned out."

"Well, let me tell you, Paul," Pam said, "these are just as good as the pictures we had professionally done of our kids last Christmas. I think they're amazing."

"Thanks." Paul fairly beamed. "I've been interested in photography since I was eleven years old when my parents gave me a camera for Christmas. I still have that camera, but these days, I use a digital. You know, these new cameras today can almost do the work for you."

"Say, man, you have a real talent there," Jan said after he'd been shown the photos. "If I had skills like that at takin' pictures, I'd be snappin' photos all the time."

Emma couldn't miss the tender look on Jan's face when he studied Sophia's picture. It was too bad he had no wife or children. Emma figured Jan probably liked it that way, because she knew that some folks, like her, preferred to remain single. It wasn't that she liked not being married, for she'd certainly enjoyed the years she and Ivan had together. She just wasn't open to the idea of getting married again.

"I'm sure my parents had no idea the camera they gave me would introduce me to a hobby I enjoy to this day," Paul went on to say.

"Would you like to see some pictures of my twin boys when they were little?" Ruby Lee asked. Before anyone could respond, she had her wallet open and the pictures passed around.

Next, Pam shared some photos of her and Stuart's children, and then Star pulled a picture from her wallet. "Here's one of me when I was a baby," she said, handing it to Pam.

Pam squinted at the picture. "You were a cute baby, and I assume that's your mother holding you on her lap?"

Star nodded.

"What happened there?" Stuart asked, looking over his wife's shoulder. "It looks like someone's picture's been torn out."

"Yeah. My mom ripped it out 'cause it was my dad, and I guess she was really angry with him." Star frowned. "That creep gave me an ugly name, and then before I was even old enough to remember what he looked like, the bum bailed. I used to wish he'd come back so I could get to know him, but maybe it's best that he didn't, 'cause if he didn't care enough about my mom to want to marry her, then he probably didn't care about me."

Everyone in the room became quiet. Even Emma didn't know what to say. No wonder this poor young woman hid behind her dark clothes and seemed so confused about things. She'd never known her father and was obviously deeply troubled about him running out on them when she was a baby. Who could blame her for that? Oh, how she wished there was something she could do to make things better for Star.

"Can I see the picture?" Ruby Lee asked.

Pam handed it to her.

Ruby Lee studied the photo; then she looked over at Star and smiled. "You were a beautiful baby, and you're a lovely young woman now."

"I agree," Emma said, giving Star a tender hug.

Star blinked a couple of times like she was holding back tears. "Thanks. No one's ever said that about me before."

"I'd like to see the photo, too," Jan spoke up. "Whoever that bum of a father of yours was didn't know what he was doin' when he walked out on you."

Ruby Lee handed Jan the photo. He sat several seconds, staring at it with a peculiar expression while shaking his head as though in disbelief. He glanced away then back again, as if to clear his vision. Then he looked over at Star, and in a voice barely above a whisper, he asked, "Is your real name Beatrice Stevens?"

Star nodded, squinting her eyes. "Yeah. How'd you know that?"

Slowly, Jan reached into his back pocket, removed his wallet, and pulled out a picture. "Take a look at this." His hands shook as he handed it to Star, but he didn't make eye contact with her. "It's the same picture you have, only as you can see, in my picture I'm not ripped out."

Star blinked and stared at him as though he'd taken leave of his senses. Everyone else sat without saying a word.

"Bunny was my girlfriend," Jan said, his eyes turning glassy.

"Bunny?" Star repeated.

"Yeah. Bunny was Nancy's nickname. I started callin' her that when we first started dating 'cause her nose twitched whenever she got upset." Jan paused and swiped his hand across his forehead where sweat had beaded up.

Star sat rigid, refusing to look at him.

"Bunny and I met when we both lived in Chicago. We dated awhile and then moved in together. Several months later, I found out she was gonna have a baby, so I asked her to marry me." Jan stopped talking again, and there was a break in his expression. Emma sensed the strong feelings that had swept over him. Drawing in a couple of deep breaths, he continued. "At first, Bunny said she'd have to think about it. Then, as the time got closer to our baby bein' born, she finally agreed to marry me but said she wanted to wait till after the baby came." Jan's voice quavered a bit; then it steadied. "When our little girl was born, we named her Beatrice after my mom."

Star's hands had started shaking now, too, and her voice squeaked as she stood and pointed at Jan. "You. . .you're my dad?"

"It's really a shocker, but yeah, I think I am," Jan said as though hardly believing it himself.

"So you're the mangy cur who walked out on me and my mom!"

He shook his head vigorously. "No, no! That's not how it was. There's something you need to know. I didn't run out on you and your mom. She must have changed her mind about us gettin' married, 'cause without even tellin' me where she was goin', she just took you and split."

Star's eyes narrowed as she glared at him. "You're a liar! Mom would never do something like that."

"No, please listen; I'm not lyin'. I wanted to marry your mom and wanted more than anything for us to be a family. But Bunny had other ideas, and they obviously didn't include me."

Star and Jan seemed oblivious to everyone else in the room. Emma was so shocked by all of this, she simply couldn't think of a thing to say.

"Now you wait just a minute," Star said, her voice high-pitched and intense. "Mom may not have always had her head on straight when it comes to men, and she has been known to lie about a few things, but when it comes to the story she's always told about my dad runnin' off, that's never changed. So I don't think she was lying."

"But you don't understand. I loved Bunny back then, even though she was always headstrong and kinda hard to figure out." Jan left his seat and took a step toward Star. "I probably wasn't the best catch a girl could want, but I had a good payin' job, and there wasn't much I wouldn't have done for you and Bunny. And I want you to know that I did everything I could to find you both. But your mom—well, she did a good job of hidin' from me.

"When I contacted Bunny's mom, even she didn't know where Bunny had gone." Jan drew in a deep breath and released it with a moan. "I can't believe we've been here at Emma's house all these weeks, and I had no clue a'tall that my own flesh-and-blood daughter was right here in front of me. All these years of wonderin', and now, here you are." He seemed to be taking in every detail about Star as though seeing her for the very first time. "You even have the same color eyes as mine, but I can see now that you've got your mother's nose."

Backing up as though to put some distance between them, Star planted both hands on her hips and glared at him. "Stop looking at me that way! Seriously, it's creepy."

Reaching out to touch her arm, he took a step closer, but she backed up even farther. "Don't touch me! I don't want anything to do with you!"

"It must be fate that brought you two together," Pam spoke up, as though trying to calm Star down. Or perhaps she saw this as some kind of happily-ever-after scene she was witnessing. Well, it wasn't. Emma could certainly see that.

"I think it was divine intervention," Emma said, finally finding her voice and walking over to place her hand gently on Star's arm. "It was the good Lord who brought you and your father together."

"Well, I wish He hadn't!" Star pointed at Jan. "You know what? I'm glad you never showed up in my life before, because if you had, I might have hauled off and punched you. I don't believe for one minute that my mom left you." Star grabbed up her things and raced for the door.

"Please, don't go!" Jan called. "I've waited all these years to meet my daughter, and I sure don't wanna lose her now!"

The door slammed behind Star.

Jan groaned and flopped into a chair, letting his head fall forward into the palms of his hands. He sat like that for several minutes; then he lifted his head and turned toward Emma with a look of bewilderment, as though seeking an answer. . .advice. . .anything. The pain on his face was undeniable.

"What was I thinkin'?" he mumbled, shaking his head. "This sure didn't turn out the way I'd imagined it would if I ever found my daughter. No, this went down bad. Yeah, really bad."

CHAPTER 30

I blew it! I really blew it!" Jan slapped his knee and groaned. "I should never have blurted that out like I did. I probably scared the poor kid half to death. Worse than that, she doesn't believe a word I said. I think she hates me."

"Were you telling the truth about not being the one who ran off?" Stuart questioned.

Jan's jaw clenched. "'Course I was tellin' the truth. I'd have no reason to lie about somethin' as important as that!" He scrubbed his hand down the side of his face, fighting the sudden urge to start howling like a baby. "Trouble is, I have no proof. It's Bunny's word against mine."

"Maybe it would help if you spoke to Star's mother yourself," Paul suggested. "You could remind her of how it all happened."

Jan tapped his fingers along the edge of the table. "If I thought for one minute that Bunny would tell the truth, I'd do it. But I have a gut feeling she'd keep on lyin' about all that happened. Besides, I'm pretty sure that after all these years, Bunny probably don't wanna even see the likes of me." He slowly shook his head, feeling worse by the minute. "I've never understood why she hated me so much that she'd just take off with our baby without even tellin' me she was leavin' or where she was goin'. I thought Bunny loved me and wanted to get married, but somethin' must have happened to change her mind." It was all Jan could do to keep his emotions under control.

"I think the best thing you can do is to wait until next week and see what Star has to say then," Ruby Lee said.

"Don't think I can wait that long. Besides, what if Star don't come back? She may never wanna see me again." Jan looked over at Emma with a pleading expression. "Can you help me out here? If you have Star's address, would you tell me what it is?"

Emma shook her head. "I wouldn't feel right about giving you that information without asking her first. And, Jan, I think you really do need to give Star some time to sort things through. Like Ruby Lee said, you can talk to Star again next week. I feel sure she'll be here."

"Maybe Star will talk to her mother, and she'll find out that you were telling the truth," Paul said in a tone of reassurance.

Jan grunted. "Boy, you don't know how bad I'd like to see it go that way, but unless Bunny's had a change of heart, she ain't likely to admit she was wrong."

Emma gave Jan's arm a reassuring pat. "I'll be praying for you this week, and I hope you'll pray, too. Try to remember that God is with us no matter what situation we may face."

Goshen

Star felt so stressed by the time she got to Goshen that her body trembled and she could hardly breathe. She really shouldn't have driven anywhere feeling this upset, but she just wanted to put some distance between her and Jan. She also needed time to calm down before she talked to Mom, so she decided to stop and jog a ways on the Pumpkinvine Trail.

As Star jogged along, her legs threatened to buckle. She still couldn't believe the burly biker was her dad. And as she thought about everything Jan had told her about Mom taking off, her frustration and confusion increased. She didn't know whether to believe him or not. All these weeks she'd seen Jan as a really nice guy—the kind who loved kids and dogs.

Was it all just for show? she wondered. *Or has Jan changed from how he was when he and Mom were dating?* At the moment, Star was angry with both of her parents: Jan for abandoning them when she was a baby, and Mom for refusing to tell Star much about her dad or letting her see any pictures of him. Of course, even if she had seen a picture of Jan from back then, he'd no doubt changed a lot, and she probably wouldn't have recognized him. But if Star's mom had told her his name, she would have figured things out a lot sooner. After all, how many men had a name like Jan Sweet?

Stopping to catch her breath for a minute, Star kicked at a clump of weeds along the edge of the path with the toe of her sneaker and jumped back as a baby rabbit ran into the higher brush.

"Oops. Sorry little fellow. Didn't mean to scare you like that," she murmured, momentarily enjoying the short interruption.

I still can't believe Jan's really my dad, Star thought, as she started running again. *All the times he's been sitting beside me at Emma's, making small talk and acting so friendly as we worked on our quilting projects, and I never had a clue.*

Deciding to pick up the pace, Star panted as she jogged harder. While a trickle of sweat rolled down her forehead and into her eyes, she knew it didn't matter how fast or how hard she ran. The unexpected, shocking news she'd received today was inescapable. She had half a mind to head back to Emma's and give Jan a well-deserved punch. But what good would that do? It wouldn't change the past, but oh, it sure would make her feel better.

Sides aching and gasping for air, Star knew she couldn't run any farther, so she headed back toward her car. She really needed to go home and talk to Mom.

———

When Star entered Grandma's house sometime later, the phone was ringing. She raced across the kitchen and grabbed the receiver. "Hello."

"Star is that you?"

"Yeah, who's this?"

"It's Emma Yoder." She paused. "I was worried about you and wanted to see if you're all right."

"Yeah, I'm fine. Never better," Star mumbled.

"You don't sound fine. The tone of your voice says you're still upset."

Emma's soothing tone caused Star to relax a bit. "I. . .I still can't believe what happened today," she said. "I mean, what are the odds that Jan Sweet would turn out to be my long-lost father?"

"Are you still angry with him?" Emma asked.

"Sure. Why wouldn't I be? He ran out on us, Emma. Big, sweet, lovable Jan ran out on his wife and baby. And I'm supposed to be okay with that?" Star's voice had become shrill, but she couldn't seem to help it. She was still so angry she could spit.

"What did your mother say when you told her about Jan?"

"I haven't told her yet. I just got home from the Pumpkinvine Trail, where I went to try and jog off my frustrations."

Another pause. Then Emma said, "Jan wants to talk to you, Star— and to your mother, too. He was really upset after you left and asked if

I'd give him your address or phone number."

Star grabbed the edge of the counter as fear gripped her like a vise. She wasn't ready to talk to Jan yet. Not until she'd spoken to Mom. "You didn't give it to him, I hope."

"No. I told him I couldn't do that without your permission."

Star breathed a sigh of relief. "Oh good. I appreciate that. Mom would have a hissy fit if Jan showed up out of the blue. I really need to talk to her about all of this first."

"I hope it goes well when you do. Oh, and Star, can I say one more thing?"

"Yeah, sure. What is it, Emma?"

"Don't believe negative thoughts about anyone until you have all the facts."

"Yeah, and I plan to get all the facts, too. I'd better go, Emma. I don't hear the TV in the living room, so I think Mom's probably in her bedroom. I really oughta speak to her now."

"I'll let you go then. Oh, and remember, Star, if you need to talk more about this, just give me a call. Unless I happen to be in the phone shack, you'll get my voice mail. But I'll call you back as soon as I get your message."

"Okay, thanks, Emma. Bye for now."

Star hung up the phone and was about to head for Mom's room when she spotted a note on the kitchen table. She picked it up and read it out loud.

Mike and I are heading to Fort Wayne to see his folks and tell them about our engagement. Since I have next week off from work, and so does Mike, we're planning to stay with his folks until Thursday or Friday. This will give Mike the chance to look at the restaurant he plans to buy there. If it all works out, we'll be moving to Fort Wayne soon after we're married.

I was going to tell you all this at breakfast this morning, but you rushed out of here so fast I didn't get the chance.

There's plenty of food in the fridge, so you shouldn't have to worry about doing any grocery shopping while I'm gone.

I'll see you Thursday evening or sometime Friday.

Love,
Mom

Star's hand shook as she dropped the note to the table. Besides the fact that Mom had taken off without telling her, now she had to wait several days to tell her about Jan. And what if Mom and Mike ended up moving to Fort Wayne? Where would that leave Star? Would they expect her to move there, too? What would happen to Grandma's old house? Would Mom decide to sell it? It wasn't fair. She needed to talk to Mom right now. She needed some answers about Jan.

"Never gonna be the princess, holding tight to my daddy's neck," Star sang as a strangled sob caught in her throat. She paused a minute and swallowed hard. "Never gonna be the apple of his eye. Never gonna walk the aisle hand in hand; a sweet vignette. Never gonna answer all the whys. Ask me what it's like to be connected; ask me why I can't give up control. Ask me how it feels to be protected; ask me who is praying for my soul. Ask me when I knew I'm loved forever. . .never."

CHAPTER 31

Shipshewana

H ey man, how was your weekend?" Terry asked when Jan climbed into Terry's truck on Monday morning.

"It was good in one way but not so good in another," Jan said with a shake of his head. "You're never gonna believe what I have to tell you."

"What do you mean?"

Pausing a bit to get the words out right, Jan moistened his lips and said, "Saturday, I found my daughter."

"Wow, that's really great news, man!" Terry thumped Jan's shoulder. "Where'd you find her?"

"At Emma Yoder's."

Terry's eyebrows shot up. "Your daughter's Amish?"

"Will you listen to what I'm sayin' here? She's not Amish. She's one of the women I've been learnin' to quilt with these past five weeks."

"Huh?"

"That girl I told you about—the one who calls herself Star—I found out toward the end of class last Saturday that she's my daughter, Beatrice."

Terry released a low whistle. "You've gotta be kidding me!"

"No, I'm not kiddin'." Jan went on to explain about the picture Star had shown the class, and how he had one just like it—only his didn't have his picture torn off.

"Now that's really something!" Terry exclaimed. "I mean, what are the odds that the daughter you never thought you'd see again has been right under your nose these last five weeks?"

"When I found out, that same thought went through my head. Pam called it fate, and Emma said it must be divine intervention." Jan sucked in a deep breath. "I'm not sure what I'd call it, but it sure came as a surprise—for both me and Star."

"I'm really happy for you, man." Terry gave Jan's arm another good thump. "You must feel like you're ten feet tall after bein' reunited with your daughter."

"I am glad I finally got to meet her, but unfortunately, she don't feel the same way about meetin' me."

"How come?"

Jan explained the lie Nancy had told their daughter and how Star had reacted when he'd tried to explain what had happened.

"I'm not sure I'll ever see her again," Jan said with a slow shake of his head. "Emma Yoder called me on Saturday evening and said she'd talked to Star. Asked if she could give me Star's phone number and address, but Star said no." He moaned deeply and rubbed the bridge of his nose. "I feel just sick about this, man. I'd given up all hope of ever findin' Beatrice, and now that I have, she don't want nothin' to do with me."

"If you just give her some time to get used to the idea, I'm sure she'll come around."

"Wish I could believe that, but you didn't see Star's face when she lashed out at me and called me a bum." *And I still can't believe I was actually thinkin' of asking her out—my own daughter, for cryin' out loud,* Jan thought. *But then, how was I to know who Star really was? Whew! I'm sure glad I didn't make that mistake.*

"Maybe once Star talks to her mom about it, Nancy will set the record straight," Terry said with a hopeful expression. "Think about it—this is a lot for your daughter to take in—especially in a short time. I'd say it's pretty major."

"I'd like to believe that Bunny will tell Star the truth, but if she hates me as much as I think she does, I doubt she'll admit that it was her who ran out on our relationship and not me. Even after all these years, I suspect I'm still the bad guy. It's probably why she's never once tried to locate me."

Jan tried to imagine what Star must be feeling. After all, her finding out he was her dad and not just some biker dude who'd come to Emma's to learn how to quilt had to have knocked the wind right out of her sails. Did he dare to believe she might come around after she'd had time to think it all through? Did he dare to hope that Bunny might tell their daughter the truth?

"Just take one day at a time and wait to see what tomorrow brings," Terry said. "That's what my folks are doin' in their relationship right now."

"How are your parents gettin' along these days? I've been meanin' to ask about that but keep forgetting," Jan said, glad for the change of subject. It was better if he focused on something else right now, rather than agonizing over Bunny's betrayal and Star's rejection of him.

"They've started seein' a marriage counselor," Terry replied. "It's gonna take some time and a lot of give-and-take on Mom and Dad's part, but I think if they do what the counselor says, they might get their marriage back on track."

"That's good to hear. 'Course, not everyone who goes for counselin' ends up with a happy marriage. Counselin' sure hasn't seemed to help that bickerin' couple who've been takin' the quilting class with me, although it might be that they aren't doin' everything their counselor says."

Terry grunted and pointed out the front window. "I hate to add to your misery this mornin', but I don't think we're gonna get any roofin' done today, 'cause it's started to rain, and it looks like it's gonna be a gully washer!"

Goshen

When Ruby Lee woke up still fighting the headache that had come upon her the day before, she was surprised to see that Gene was already out of bed. He usually slept in on Mondays because it was his day off, but soon after all the trouble at the church started, Gene's sleeping habits had changed. Sometimes Ruby Lee found him up in the middle of the night pacing the floors. Some days he slept at odd hours and for long periods of time.

When is all this going to end? she wondered as she climbed out of bed and padded over to the window. *Will things ever get better? Will Gene and I know peace and a sense of joy again? I feel like such a hypocrite, singing songs of praise during church, smiling, shaking hands, and pretending that my heart's not breaking, when I really wish I didn't have to be there at all.*

Ruby Lee pressed her nose against the window, barely able to see outside due to the rain coming down in torrents.

"This horrible weather sure matches my mood," she mumbled. "So much for working in the garden today."

She turned from the window, slipped into her robe, and stepped into the hall, where the smell of freshly brewed coffee beckoned her to the kitchen. She found Gene sitting at the kitchen table with his Bible open. When she drew closer, he looked up at her and smiled. "Good morning, my love."

"Mornin'," she mumbled as she reached for a mug and poured herself some coffee.

"How are you feeling? Last night you said you had a headache. Is it gone now?"

Ruby Lee winced as she shook her head. Just the slightest movement made the throbbing even worse. "Hopefully it'll be better once I've had some coffee." She seated herself in the chair across from Gene, added a spoonful of sugar to her cup, and gave it a couple of stirs.

"It's a tension headache, isn't it?" he asked.

"Yeah. It came on me yesterday right after church. This horrible weather we're having doesn't help much either."

"Did someone in our congregation say something to upset you?"

"Nothing directly to me, but I heard a couple of the board members' wives talking in the foyer right before the service started." She frowned. "One of them—Mrs. Randall—said she thought the board should ask you to resign."

Gene nodded slowly as his shoulders slumped. "I figure that'll probably happen at the next board meeting, if not before."

"If you know this, then why don't you resign before they ask you to leave?"

His response came slowly. "You know why, Ruby Lee. The Lord Almighty called me to this church to minister to these people—even the difficult ones." He reached across the table and placed his hand over hers. "God doesn't want us to lose faith or give way to despair. He wants us to keep praying and hope for the best, always trusting Him."

"That's pretty much what Emma Yoder told me last Saturday."

"Well, she gave you some good advice."

"But if the people at our church don't want you anymore. . ." Ruby Lee bit her lip to keep from bursting into tears. What was the point in trying to reason with Gene? They'd had this discussion so many times before.

"You know how much I've been praying about our situation and seeking God's will," he said.

All she could do was nod.

"Well, I've finally reached a decision." Gene paused and looked down at his Bible.

Ruby Lee held her breath and waited for him to continue. *Please, Lord. Please let him say we should leave that church full of ungrateful people.*

Gene pointed to the Bible and smiled. "My answer was here all along."

"What is it?"

" 'Fulfill ye my joy, that ye be likeminded, having the same love, being of one accord, of one mind.' Philippians 2:2," Gene read from the Bible. "If the church board is opposed to us borrowing money to add on to the church, then I, as their leader, need to respect that decision and stop pushing them to do what they feel the church can't afford."

"You're giving up your dream of adding on to the church?"

"That's right."

"But if we don't add on, how will the congregation ever grow? I mean, folks can barely find seats in the sanctuary on Sunday mornings now."

He nodded. "That's true, but there are other things we can do."

"Such as?"

"We can have two services or maybe open up a wall and make use of the room that's now being used for storage, which would let us seat more people."

"So you won't resign and look for another church?" she asked, already knowing the answer.

"Nope." Gene's even, white teeth gleamed as he smiled. "I'm stayin' right here for as long as the good Lord tells me to stay."

"What if the board asks you to leave even after you'd told them you're giving up on the building plans?"

"Then I'll abide by their decision."

Ruby Lee released a sigh of resignation. She had a hunch that once Gene met with the board and told them his decision they would probably not ask him to leave. And if that happened, for Gene's sake, she would continue to support his ministry by being the best wife she could be. She would do it because she loved him and knew it was her responsibility.

Quietly, she bowed her head. *Heavenly Father, I truly do know that You exist, and I ask You to forgive me for doubting Your presence and for losing my faith in people. I know You brought Gene and me here for a reason and that You have a definite plan for our lives. Thank You for that plan and for loving me enough to send Your Son, Jesus, to die for my sins. No matter what happens in the days ahead, help me to trust You in all things.*

CHAPTER 32

Shipshewana

Early Wednesday morning, Emma shivered as she stood on the porch and watched the rain come down. It had begun raining on Monday and had continued to rain all day Tuesday. It wasn't just a light rain either. It had come down in torrents, filling the gutters with so much water that they continually overflowed, leaving the flower beds flooded and puddles scattered across the lawn. Along with the rain, strong winds had blown, until at one point, Emma feared some of her windows might break. But the wind had finally subsided. Now if the rain would just let up.

Sure wish I could get out of the house for a while, Emma thought. She would have enjoyed going to the pond and sitting by the tree where Ivan had carved their initials. She always did her best thinking there, and with all that had been on her mind this week, she had plenty to think and pray about. If the rain let up later today, maybe she could still go to the pond. She hoped so anyway, because she didn't like being cooped up in the house for too long.

Emma was relieved when it quit raining shortly after noon. The fresh air felt good, and she was ready to be outside for a while. So she hitched her horse to her open buggy and headed in the direction of the pond to enjoy her and Ivan's special tree.

Emma didn't know why she felt such a strong need to go there today. Could it be because she'd had a dream about Ivan last night and had awakened this morning with him on her mind?

"Oh Lord, I thank You for all the beauty You created," Emma murmured as she looked up at the pretty blue sky. Even the white, puffy clouds that had formed into such unusual shapes were amazing.

The birds sang a chorus of happy tunes from the trees lining the road, and Emma's horse lifted her head as though sniffing the fresh air and enjoying it, too. Even God's creatures were joyous after the rain. Emma loved how clean everything looked and smelled after a good rainfall and didn't mind if a drip now and then splattered on her lap as it fell from the tree branches overhead.

She hardly knew which way to look. A blaze of orange led her onward as she admired a cluster of tiger lilies growing at the edge of the woods. How grateful she was for all God's creation.

A short time later, Emma guided her horse and buggy up the path leading to the pond. She knew it had been raining hard these last few days but hadn't expected to see so much water everywhere. She giggled to herself, watching a family of bluebirds splashing and bathing in one of the puddles. It even appeared as if the pond had grown to be nearly twice its size. Apparently the ground just couldn't soak all that water in.

Searching for an area that wasn't covered with water, Emma finally located a tree where she could secure her horse. Then, carefully stepping around one puddle after another, she made her way down the path leading to her and Ivan's special tree.

As she approached the spot where it had stood so many years, Emma gasped. "Ach, my! What's happened here?" Their beautiful tree had been uprooted, no doubt from all the wind and rain. It lay across the path, surrounded by mud and leaves, no longer a living, growing tree.

Emma stared, feeling sick at heart. *How long has our tree been down?* she asked herself. *If only I'd come to see it sooner; but then how could I have, feeling the way that I did during my bout with shingles?*

It saddened her to know that there would be no more times of coming here to think and pray while she gazed at the initials Ivan had lovingly carved in the trunk of the tree. Emma knew it was silly, but she felt as though she could burst into tears because such a special memory had been taken from her. She wished she were an artist, so by memory she could sketch and preserve that image of what once had been so special to her and Ivan.

Slowly, she walked to the fallen tree, tears clouding her vision as she stared at those precious initials now facing skyward. Running her fingers over the carved-out bark, Emma remembered once again the kindness that had drawn her to Ivan so many years ago. This place that had given them many wonderful yet simple memories would now be missing a piece of their past.

Emma closed her eyes before leaving, trying to keep an image of their initials imprinted in her mind. She knew that once some time had passed, she'd probably come here again, for it was the *place* that held those special memories, not just the *tree*. For now, though, she'd have to let it sink in that their tree would no longer be here, and that this place would be changed forever.

When the weather improved and everything dried out, someone would probably come along and cut up the tree for firewood. *Well, at least it will go to good use, even though our special initials will be gone,* she told herself, trying to remain positive.

Taking one final look, Emma noticed a few wild irises that had been close to where the tree had been uprooted. Because their bulbs were exposed, she decided to take a few home and put them in one of her flower beds. If they survived, her flower garden would hold yet another memory of something dear to her heart.

Swallowing against the lump in her throat while fighting back more tears of despair, Emma turned and slowly made her way up the path. All she wanted to do was go home, where she could occupy her thoughts with the work she needed to do. She knew from experience that keeping busy was the best remedy for self-pity.

Mishawaka

All was quiet that night as Stuart stepped out onto the deck overlooking their backyard. Following the cooler rain they'd had, the weather had turned muggy and warmer than normal—especially for the beginning of June. Summer would soon be upon them, bringing even hotter, humid weather. So this was simply a taste of what was yet to come.

The tall trees surrounding their yard shaded most of the lawn, but from the deck, the leafy branches didn't obscure the beautiful view they had of the sky. How many times had he and Pam talked about sitting out here on a cool autumn evening or a warm spring night, stargazing while sipping from mugs of hot chocolate and eating s'mores. Somehow those plans were always put on the back burner, and they just never got around to doing it.

This was one of those times the stars looked so close—almost reachable. The fireflies were putting on quite a display as well. Their sparkling lights from the land to the sky seemed to mesh and intertwine with the stars.

Too bad Pam isn't out here enjoying all of this with me, he thought with regret. *But no, she'd rather sulk and refuse to talk to me. Don't see how she thinks we're ever gonna fix our marriage problems this way. For someone who complains about not spending enough time together, she has a funny way of showing she wants to be with me. She must not have been listening last Saturday to the things Emma had to say about marriage. Maybe she doesn't care whether we get our marriage back on track or not. Guess I just need to keep pressing ahead and try to focus on something positive.*

As Stuart continued to watch the twinkling display, he reflected on how well this evening had gone with Devin and Sherry. After supper he'd promised them a game of Frisbee, and then as the sun began to set, he and the kids took a walk through the neighborhood while Pam did the dishes. He'd invited her to go with them, but she'd declined. Was it because she was still miffed at him for wanting to take Devin fishing? Well, she ought to get over it and be glad he wanted to spend time with their boy.

Pulling his thoughts back to the walk he and the kids had taken, Stuart thought about the neighborhood they lived in and how it was nice and spacious with plenty of yard space between each of the homes. As he and the kids had meandered down the streets, outside lights from neighbors' homes glowed as if to invite them in. A few "Hi, how are ya's?" were exchanged with those sitting on their porches and at picnic tables. One of their neighbors had waved as he rolled up the hose that had been left in the yard before the storm. Even though most were near-strangers, it was a friendly area. That had been proven to Stuart and Pam many times when there were emergencies in the neighborhood. People would drop whatever they were doing to lend help where needed, and it made them feel secure knowing they could count on others if it became necessary.

When they'd arrived home from their walk, Stuart had thought about roasting marshmallows, but it was near the kids' bedtime. Much to Stuart's surprise, Sherry and Devin had actually cooperated when Pam said it was time for their baths. Their energy level had been kicked up a notch since the end of the school year. But as bedtime approached, he could see that they were slowly unwinding. After kissing him goodnight, the kids had headed upstairs to their rooms. No doubt it wouldn't be long before they'd drift off to sleep with dreams of summer swimming in their heads.

Pulling up a deck chair and taking a seat, Stuart thought how when he'd brought up the subject of camping last week, he hadn't expected Pam would get so upset, and he still couldn't figure out why she didn't like camping in a tent.

Tent camping was the only kind Stuart had ever known, and he thought it was fun when he could rough it for a few days. Every summer when he was a boy, his parents had taken him and his younger brother, Arnie, camping, and they usually went to a different state park each year. What an adventure it had been, and like most kids, he'd always looked forward to their next family camping trip the following year. Stuart's love of camping grew deeper over time, even though one of their trips could have been proclaimed disastrous.

Stuart shook his head and grinned as he remembered that year, arriving at Mohican State Park much later than they'd planned because Dad had taken a wrong turn and gotten them lost. When they'd finally pulled into their campsite, it was close to midnight, so his folks only had time to put in the crucial stakes to keep the tent in place. They'd decided to jury-rig the porch roof on the tent until morning, while Arnie and Stuart quickly gathered wood for the campfire.

Unfortunately, a terrific thunderstorm hit overnight, with high winds, torrential rains, and plenty of lightning to brighten the sky. It wasn't funny then, and they'd all been pretty scared, but afterward it had made a good story, telling everyone how it went unnoticed that the porch roof had filled up with rainwater. During the storm, Mom and Dad had been more worried about the lightning. The pocket of rainwater was too heavy for the weakly extended porch roof to hold, and before daybreak, the overhang collapsed, sending a flood of water through the whole tent.

Stuart chuckled out loud as he remembered the wet awakening they'd all received that morning. Luckily, it was sunny the next day, and they could hang their sleeping bags and wet clothes on a makeshift clothesline to dry.

Oh brother, he couldn't help thinking. *I can only imagine Pam going through something like that. I can almost hear her squealing right now!*

Thinking about Pam, he let his mind drift to something she'd said to him last week. It had shocked him to learn that Pam's childhood wasn't as rosy as he'd thought, and that she'd resented her father. Maybe tomorrow he would attempt to find out more—if she was willing to talk about it.

As Stuart got up and walked over to the porch railing, he caught sight of a falling star and watched as it fizzled out of sight. "Wish Pam had been here to see that," he muttered.

Growing tired, he turned and was about to go into the house to make sure all the lights were out before going to bed when his cell phone rang. He saw on the screen that it was an employee from work and figured he'd better take the call.

———

Having just put the kids to bed and feeling the need for some fresh air, Pam decided to join Stuart on the porch. Maybe if they spent a few minutes alone, enjoying the cool breeze that usually came up on a hot sultry night, they could communicate without ending up in a fight. It was a worth a try, anyway.

Pam had been pleased when Stuart said he wanted to take a walk around the neighborhood with Sherry and Devin. She'd been tempted to join them but figured it would be good if he spent a little time alone with the kids. Besides, she needed an opportunity to reflect on the things Emma had said during their last quilting class. Pam knew she'd been dwelling on the negative and not appreciating all that she had.

Emma was right, Pam thought. *If I hadn't married Stuart, we wouldn't have the pleasure of raising our two very special children.*

Pam was about to open the screen door when she heard Stuart talking to someone. Had one of the neighbors dropped by? It was getting pretty late in the evening for that.

She peeked through the screen and spotted Stuart near the porch railing with his cell phone up to his ear. Curious to know who it was, she stood quietly off to one side, listening.

"Yeah, this isn't good, and I know what needs to be done," Stuart said into the phone. "I'm going to call a lawyer first thing in the morning. I just don't see any other way."

Heart hammering in her chest, Pam moved away from the door and raced down the hall to their room. She knew things hadn't improved much between them and had been worried that Stuart might leave her, but she hadn't expected it would happen so soon—or that she'd have to hear it like this. Would it help if she told Stuart what she'd just heard and pleaded with him to reconsider? Or would it be better not to fight it—just agree to an amicable divorce? After all, even with all the counseling they'd had, their marriage hadn't improved.

"Oh no," she moaned, nearly choking on the sob rising in her throat, "if we go our separate ways, how will it affect the children?"

CHAPTER 33

Goshen

As Star sat at the kitchen table on Friday evening eating a ham sandwich, a sense of irritation welled in her soul. Mom still wasn't home, and she hadn't even bothered to call. Star didn't have the number for Mike's parents either, and since Mom didn't have a cell phone and Star didn't know Mike's cell number, all she could do was sit here.

How could Mom be so inconsiderate? Star tapped her fingers along the edge of the table. *I just wish she'd get here so I can tell her about Jan. I want to hear what she has to say about all of this. Better yet, I can't wait to see her expression when she hears the big news. I'll bet she'll be as shocked as I was to know that her ex—my dad—has been attending Emma's quilting classes with me for the last five weeks.* She shuddered. *And to think, I even had thoughts about what it would be like if he asked me out. Good grief. . . If Jan had been interested in me, I could have ended up dating my own dad!*

Feeling as if she was about to be sick, Star set her sandwich aside and stood. She was just getting ready to clear the table when the back door swung open and Mom and Mike stepped in. *Oh, great! Now I can't say anything to Mom about Jan until Mr. Wonderful leaves.*

"Where have you been, Mom?" Star asked, feeling as though she'd run out of patience. "I was beginning to think you weren't coming home at all."

Mom giggled like a silly schoolgirl and gave Star a hug. "I told you we'd be back on Thursday or Friday."

"Yeah, but I was hoping it would be sooner, because I really needed to talk to you about—"

"Your mom and I were busy all week, looking at some condos and checking on the details for my new restaurant," Mike said, cutting Star off in midsentence.

"Well, you could have at least called," Star muttered, unable to hide her irritation.

"Sorry," Mom said, "but we got so busy I just lost track of time." She looked up at Mike with an adoring smile that made Star feel even sicker. "We're real excited about his new business venture."

"That's right," Mike agreed. "I'll have to make a few renovations to the building I bought, but it should be ready to open for business by early fall—right after your mom and I get back from our honeymoon."

"Where are you going for that?" Star questioned.

Mom's eyes lit up like twinkling lights on a Christmas tree. "Mike's taking me to Hawaii. Now isn't that great?"

Star nodded, finding Mom's chipper tone an annoyance. She knew it wasn't right to feel this way, but it sickened her to see how happy Mom and Mike seemed to be. He stood close to Mom with his arm around her waist and a sappy-looking grin that stretched ear to ear.

"Then after our trip to Hawaii, your mom and I will be moving to Fort Wayne," Mike said.

So Mom would be getting a trip to Hawaii. How nice for her. She'd said many times that she'd always wanted to go there. Star figured she would probably never make it to Hawaii—or for that matter, anyplace else exciting. Well, at least there'd been no mention of her moving to Fort Wayne with Mom and Mike. That much was good. She'd just have to look for an apartment, because Grandma had left this house to Mom, and Mom would probably sell it and use the money to help buy a condo for her and Mike in Fort Wayne. Star would miss this old house when she moved out, but at least she wouldn't have to live with Mike and Mom and watch them gushing all over each other, while Mike, acting as if he were her father, told Star what she could and couldn't do. She'd live on the street in a cardboard box before she'd put up with that!

"Well, Nancy, think I'll head for home now and let you two visit." Mike bent his head and gave Mom a noisy kiss. "See you tomorrow, sweetie."

Star rubbed a tense spot on her neck and looked away in disgust. She hoped Mike was sincere and really did love Mom, but if he turned out to be anything like the other men Mom had been involved with, Star wouldn't be shocked.

"There's somethin' I need to tell you," Star said to Mom after Mike went out the door.

"Can it wait till tomorrow?" Mom yawned and stretched her arms over her head. "It's been a long day, and I'm really tired, so I'd like to take a bath and go to bed."

Star shook her head determinedly. "No, Mom, it can't wait. This is important, and we need to talk now."

"Okay, but let's make it quick. Like I said, I'm really tired." Mom took a seat at the table, and Star did the same.

"I met my dad last Saturday," Star blurted out.

"Hmm...what was that?" Mom asked as she picked at a piece of lint on the front of her blouse.

"I said I met my dad last Saturday."

Mom jerked her head. "Huh? What did you just say?"

Star released an exasperated groan and repeated what she'd said for the third time.

"You. . .you met your dad?"

"Yeah—Jan Sweet."

Mom jumped like she'd been hit by a bolt of lightning. "Oh brother! This is not what I needed to hear today!" She leaned forward and stared at Star, sweat beading on her forehead. "Have you been searching for him behind my back? You found him somehow and set up a meeting last Saturday—is that what happened?"

Star shook her head. "No, we—"

"Well then, how? Where exactly did you meet Jan, and what makes you think he's your dad?"

Star quickly explained how Jan's identity had been revealed last Saturday and ended by saying, "I can't believe I sat there in Emma's sewing room all that time, never knowing my dad was taking the class with me." She groaned and slowly shook her head. "I think Jan and I had some kind of a connection, Mom. Up until last Saturday, when I found out who he was, I liked the guy, and we sort of seemed to be kindred spirits." Star made no mention of her thoughts concerning the possibility of Jan asking her out. She just wanted to forget she'd ever had that silly notion.

"I can't believe Jan's been living so close to us. If I'd had any idea he lived in the area, I never would have moved here to Goshen."

Star tensed. "Are you saying that if you'd known Jan lived in Shipshewana, you wouldn't have come here to help Grandma when she was sick?"

Mom squirmed in her chair. "Well, I. . ."

"Were you that afraid of seeing him again?"

Mom nodded. "I've been afraid all these years that he'd find you."

"Good grief, Mom, was Jan really that bad of a guy? 'Cause if I'm bein' honest here, he sure doesn't seem that way now."

"Well. . .umm. . .he was a biker and much too wild."

"Did Grandma know about Jan?"

"She knew him when we all lived in Chicago, but when she moved to Indiana a few years after Jan and I split up, I don't think she had any further contact with him. And I'm sure she had no idea he lived anywhere near here, because if she had, she would have said so." Mom's cheeks reddened. "Did Jan. . .uh. . .say anything about me?" she asked in a voice pitched higher than normal.

"Yeah, he had plenty to say."

"Such as?"

"He said your nickname was Bunny. In fact, he has it tattooed on his right arm. Is it true, Mom? Did Jan used to call you Bunny?"

Mom gave a slow nod.

"How come you never told me about your nickname? I would think you would have since I changed my name from Beatrice to Star."

"I didn't think it was important, and since Jan was the only one who ever called me Bunny—"

"Jan said he didn't bail out on us," Star said, cutting Mom off. "Said it was you who left and that he'd tried to find us with no success." Star looked her mother right in the eye. "It's not true, is it, Mom? Jan was lying through his teeth about that, right?"

Mom sat staring at the table for the longest time. Then, with tears gathering in the corners of her eyes, she finally whispered, "No, Star, your dad was telling the truth. I lied to you about that. It was me who left, not him."

Star groaned and leaned forward, until her forehead rested on the table. "Why, Mom?" she asked, nearly choking on the words. "Why'd you leave Jan, and how come you lied and told me it was him who'd run out on us?"

"Well, I. . ."

Star lifted her head and could see Mom was visibly shaken. "All these years, I've been thinking what a bum he must have been to leave us like that. And now, after so much time has gone by, you're telling me different? Is lying what you do best?" Star's tone was caustic, but she didn't care. Mom had disappointed her plenty of times in the past but never more than she had right now.

Mom pushed her chair aside and went to the sink for a glass of water. After she drank it, she returned to the table and sank into her chair with a pathetic little squeak. "Jan and I rode with a motorcycle club, but he took it more seriously than I did. He wanted to ride nearly every weekend, which I was okay with at first." Mom swished her hand from side to side, as though hoping to emphasize her point. "Even after I got pregnant with you, I rode with Jan on a few short trips. But once you were born, I realized it was time to settle down and make a home for my baby."

"Jan said he wanted to marry you and make a home for both of us," Star said.

"Puh! That's what he told me, too, but he was wild and free—not the kind of guy who'd ever settle down. At least that's what I thought at the time." Mom drew in a deep breath and released it with a lingering sigh. "Honestly, Star, by the time you were born, I really didn't care about Jan anymore. It had been fun while it lasted, but I was tired of his biker buddies and sick of riding miles and miles on the back of a stupid motorcycle."

Star listened with interest as Mom continued. "Even on the weekends that Jan decided to stay home with me, someone from the gang always hung around our place." She clutched Star's arm. "Don't you see? I just wanted some peace and quiet in my life. I wanted that for you, too, but I didn't think we'd ever have it if I stayed with Jan. So I took off without telling anyone where I was going, not even my mom. I didn't have any contact with her until two years later—once she'd moved from Chicago and I knew Jan was out of the picture."

Star sat for a while, letting everything Mom said sink in. It was a lot to comprehend, and between what both Jan and Mom had told her, she had a lot to think about. "So what was the reason for you letting me think my dad had left us in the lurch?" she asked. "Why couldn't you have just been honest and told me that you'd run away from him?"

A few tears slipped out of Mom's eyes and splashed onto her crimson cheeks. "I. . .I didn't want you to think ill of me for taking you away from your dad."

"Oh, you'd rather that I thought ill of him?"

Mom slowly nodded. "I'm the one who had to raise you, so—"

"*Had* to raise me?" Star's voice rose as she clenched her fingers. "Like it was some heavy burden instead of a joy to raise your daughter? Isn't that how it's supposed to be?"

"I didn't see it as a burden, really. I mean, it was hard being on my own and all, but I loved you and wanted your respect, so I just couldn't tell you that I left your dad."

"Like you've ever really cared about having my respect," Star muttered, feeling even more confused and upset.

"What's that supposed to mean?"

Since Star had started telling Mom the way she felt, she figured she might as well say everything that was on her mind. "It means, with the exception of Grandma, I've never felt loved. You always seemed to care more about whatever boyfriend you were with than you did me."

"That's not true, Star. I worked hard so I could give you everything you needed."

"Giving a person what you think they need is not the same as making them feel loved and good about themselves." Star's knuckles turned white as she clenched her fingers even tighter. "You've never encouraged me to sing or write songs; you've never said I was pretty or smart; and whenever you came home with some creep of a boyfriend, you never cared whether I liked him or not!"

"I. . .I guess you're right about that, and unfortunately, most of them were losers. I just didn't make good decisions." Mom's lips quivered as she spoke. "But I think I've finally found the right one this time. Mike really does care about me, and he wants to give me good things."

"Yeah, *you*, Mom—not me. Mike doesn't want to give me anything but a hard time."

"Oh, come on, Star. You know that's not true."

"Isn't it? All the guy's ever done is criticize my clothes, my music, and anything else he can think of to pick at. Never once has he said anything nice about me."

"I'll speak to Mike about that. If he apologizes, will it make you happy?"

"An apology would be nice if it was heartfelt, but since you and Mike will be movin' to Fort Wayne and I'll be looking for an apartment here, I won't have to be around him much, so I don't really care whether he apologizes or not."

Mom sat quietly, rubbing at a stain on the kitchen table.

"So now I know why you lied about my dad leaving," Star said, moving their conversation back to Jan. "What I don't know is why you refused to let me see pictures of him or even tell me his name."

"I didn't want you to ask any more questions about Jan. Worse yet,

I was worried that you might try to find him."

"Would that have been so terrible? Didn't you think I had the right to know my own dad?"

More tears fell onto Mom's face, and she reached for a napkin to wipe them away. "I. . .I was afraid if you ever met your dad, you might like him better than me. I was afraid he might turn you against me or even try to take you away."

"I've gotten to know Jan fairly well during the last several weeks, and he's always seemed nice to me. Even after he told me about you and him and how you'd split, he didn't really say anything mean about you, although I'm sure he could have." Star paused and drew in a deep breath, hoping it would calm her down a bit. "I see now that Jan was just trying to set me straight about the truth. And then I ended up calling him a liar and a bum who walked out on us! He'll probably never forgive me for that."

"I'm truly sorry, Star, and I hope someday you'll forgive me," Mom said tearfully.

Star, unable to accept her mother's apology, slammed her fist down hard on the table, rattling the salt and pepper shakers. "You know what? This is all so ridiculous—like one of those soap operas you watch on TV. I never got to know my dad, my mom's been lying to me all these years, I called my dad a liar when he told me the truth, and now I'm about to be stuck with another stepdad who I can barely stomach!" Star stood so quickly that her chair toppled over. "You know what's really funny about all this?" she added with a sneer. "All of a sudden you're calling me Star. Are you doing that just to try and win me over, Mom?"

"No, I—"

"Boy, I'll tell ya—my life really stinks!" The walls of the house vibrated as Star fled to her room and slammed the door.

Exhausted from another hard week of roofing, Jan dropped onto his bed and slumped against the pillows. He was thankful for the long hours of work. It kept him too busy to think about the lie Bunny had told Star. But when he closed his eyes, memories of Bunny and how things used to be between them pressed in on him like a stack of roofing shingles.

Jan's mind took him back to the day Bunny had told him she was pregnant. He'd been shocked at first, but after the numbness wore off, he'd actually been excited about the idea of becoming a dad. Being raised an only child, he'd always wished for a brother or sister. Now he'd have a son or daughter to buy toys for, and when the kid was old enough, they could fool around together. He looked forward to holding his baby and going places together as a family. When the kid got older, Jan would teach him to ride a motorcycle, and the three of them would take road trips together. A trip to Disney World or some other amusement park would sure be fun. Jan could only imagine what it would be like to have his own flesh-and-blood child sitting beside him on some crazy amusement ride, where they could laugh and holler like crazy. He figured Bunny would enjoy it, too.

"But none of that ever happened," Jan muttered, as his mind snapped back to the present. Thanks to Bunny running off, he'd been cheated out of knowing and spending time with his daughter all these years. And thanks to Bunny, he was sure that Star hated him.

He moaned. *What should I do about this? If my daughter don't show up at Emma's tomorrow, should I insist that Emma give me Star's address and phone number? Or would it be best if I let all this go and just didn't show up there myself? Maybe it would be better for everyone concerned if I just bowed out of the picture.*

CHAPTER 34

Emma had just finished doing her supper dishes when someone rapped on the back door. Curious to see who it was, she dried her hands on a towel and hurried from the kitchen.

Emma was surprised when she opened the door and discovered Lamar on her porch.

"*Guder owed*, Emma," he said with his usual friendly smile.

"Good evening," Emma replied.

"I have something for you in my *waache*."

"What is it?" she asked, her curiosity piqued as she looked at his wagon.

Lamar crooked his finger. "Come, take a walk with me and see."

Emma stepped off the porch, a little perplexed, and followed Lamar across the yard. When they came to his wagon, he reached into the back and pulled the tarp aside.

Emma gasped when a small wooden table and an image she thought was gone forever came into view, beautifully crafted and preserved for all time.

"See here," Lamar said, pointing to the top of the table. "It's your initials that had been carved in that tree by the pond."

Emma's throat constricted as she struggled with her swirling emotions. "But how? I mean. . . ." She nearly choked and was unable to get the rest of her sentence out.

"I knew about the tree your late husband had carved your initials in because Mary told me. And when you and I met at the pond a few weeks ago, I remembered you saying that you went there sometimes to think and pray."

Emma gave a slow nod. "I was there a few days ago and discovered that the tree had been uprooted by the storm. I figured someone would probably use it for firewood, but it made me feel sad to know that Ivan's and my initials would be destroyed. It was one of the many sweet memories I have of him."

"I understand how that is. When I look at the pretty quilt on my bed that my wife made, it helps to keep her memory alive in here." Lamar placed his hand on his chest.

"So how did this beautiful table come about?" Emma asked.

"Well, you see, when I stopped at the pond a few days ago to see whether it had flooded, I took a walk down the path and discovered that your special tree had been uprooted. Realizing that you'd no doubt miss it, I cut the piece out that had your initials carved in it and made a tabletop from that section. Then I attached it to some table legs I'd already made."

"Danki," Emma said, fighting back tears. "How much do I owe you for this nice table?"

Lamar shook his head. "Not one single penny. I did it to show you how much I care, and seeing your reaction just now is all the payment I need."

"Well, I certainly do appreciate it."

"Shall I take it into the house for you?" he asked.

"Jah, please do."

Lamar lifted the table out of the wagon, and Emma followed him toward the house. She was beginning to see Lamar in a different light, and some of the barriers she'd been hiding behind started to waver. Thinking back, everything about Lamar started coming to light. All he'd ever done was show her kindness, and all she'd ever done was resist it. Maybe if he continued to pursue a relationship with her, she might even consider letting him court her.

"So how'd things go with the quilting class last Saturday?" Lamar asked as they walked through the grass.

"It was interesting, with an unexpected development," she replied.

"How so?"

"Let's get the table into the house, and then I'll tell you all about it while we eat a piece of angel cream pie. How's that sound?"

He grinned at her. "Sounds real good to me."

Mishawaka

"Do you need some help?" Stuart asked when he entered the kitchen and found Pam in front of the sink washing some of their hummingbird feeders. Last year the kids had been fascinated when they'd seen a little hummingbird flitting from one azalea bloom to the next, so this year Pam had purchased a couple of feeders so that Sherry and Devin could watch the hummers up close.

"Guess you can finish washing these." Pam motioned to the feeders that hadn't been washed. "While you're doing that, I'll fill the clean feeders with the fresh nectar I made a while ago."

He smiled. At least she was speaking to him this evening, even if it wasn't in the friendliest tone.

"How'd your day go with the kids?" Stuart asked, hoping to make more conversation.

She gave a noncommittal shrug.

That's just great. He'd tried speaking to Pam yesterday, asking her to share more about her childhood, but she'd refused to discuss it with him. So much for improving their communication skills like their counselor had asked them to do during their last session.

"Did you do anything special today?" Stuart questioned, still trying to get her to open up. He rinsed out the first feeder, set it on the towel Pam had spread on the counter, and waited for her response.

"I finished all the quilting that needed to be done on my wall hanging while the kids played in the sprinkler to get cooled off. It was a scorcher today."

"Yeah, I know." *Good, she's talking again. I think we might be making some progress now.* "I was glad the air-conditioning was working at the store today. When it went out last year during a heat wave, we had a lot of complaints until we got it fixed."

Pam opened the cupboard door and took out a sack of sugar. "Stuart, I need to ask you something."

"What's that?"

"Are you planning to file for divorce?"

His eyebrows rose. "Not this again, Pam. Why are you asking me that?"

"Because I heard you talking on the phone to someone the other night when you were out on the porch, and you mentioned seeing a lawyer."

Stuart rubbed the bridge of his nose, trying to recall the conversation he'd had with his store employee. "Oh, now I remember. Blaine and I were talking about the fact that someone had fallen in the store the other day, and when he said he thought the lady might try to sue, I said I'd be calling our lawyer."

"Really? That's all there was to it?"

"Yeah, Pam. I'm not filing for a divorce, and I hope you're not thinking of doing it either. The kids need both of us, and we have to keep working on our marriage until things improve."

"You're right, and we will," she said with a look of relief.

For the next few minutes, they worked quietly on the feeders. Stuart was just getting ready to ask more about Pam's childhood, but she spoke first.

"What are you going to do about your wall hanging? You've hardly worked on it at all this week, and Emma's going to show us how to put the binding on tomorrow; then we'll be done."

"I'll work on it when I'm finished washing the feeders."

"You'll never get it done on time. There's too much left to do."

"Then I guess it won't get done." *Why does she have to needle me all the time?* Stuart fumed. *Is it really so important that I finish the stupid wall hanging? Just when I said we needed to keep working on our marriage, and she has to start in on me again.*

He grabbed one of the smaller feeders, and in his frustration, gripped it too hard. *Crack!* The glass shattered.

Stuart winced when he saw blood oozing from the ugly gash in his finger. "Oh no! What did I do?"

When he tried to move his finger and couldn't, he realized what had happened. "We've gotta get to ER fast, 'cause I think the tendon in my finger's been cut!"

As Pam turned on the headlights and pulled their SUV out of the hospital parking lot, a feeling of weariness settled over her like a heavy quilt. The day had started out busy as usual, and she'd had no trouble handling that. Over the years she'd become pretty good at doing projects around the house and taking care of the children. But this evening after Stuart cut his finger, it was all she could do to keep her head on straight and think clearly. Now it was catching up to her.

When they'd left the emergency room and stepped outside, she'd been surprised to see that it was already dark. After they'd arrived at the hospital, she'd lost all track of time. With the paperwork that had to be filled out and then waiting for a doctor to look at Stuart's finger to evaluate what needed to be done, every minute seemed to blend into the next. She just wanted to go home and collapse into bed.

It had really shaken Pam up hearing that Stuart had cut a tendon in his finger and would require surgery on it next week. The fact that he'd cut it while helping her clean the hummingbird feeders made her feel guilty—not to mention that she'd been nagging him about not getting his wall hanging done. If she'd only kept her mouth shut, the accident might not have happened.

"Sure hope the kids are doing okay at the Andersons'," Stuart said, breaking into Pam's thoughts.

"They're fine. I called them while you were with the doctor and told Betty we'd be home as soon as we could," Pam said, looking over at Stuart. "Betty said not to worry, because she and Lewis were enjoying Devin and Sherry so much. She even asked if the kids could spend the night."

Stuart nodded. "That's good."

Pam appreciated the Andersons. It was like having a set of grandparents right next door. Devin and Sherry loved spending time with them and vice versa. Whenever the kids found something interesting in the yard, such as a frog or a grasshopper, they would run next door and show Betty and Lewis as if they'd never seen such creatures before. The Andersons' kids were all grown and out of the house, so when the older couple had an opportunity to spend time with Devin and Sherry, they jumped at the chance. Pam hoped when the kids were grown and raising families of their own, that she and Stuart would be good grandparents.

She swallowed around the lump in her throat. *That is, if we're still married by then.*

Even though Stuart had assured her that he wasn't planning to get a divorce, she feared he might if things didn't get better between them.

"I'm sorry I put you through all of this chaos tonight." Stuart reached over with his good hand and patted Pam's shoulder. "I could see how upset you were in the ER."

Pam nodded and sighed, rubbing her temple. "I'm thankful you didn't lose your finger."

"No more thankful than I am. Just wish they could have done the surgery while we were already at the hospital."

"I guess there's a reason they didn't, Stuart. Don't worry though. Like the doctor said, the surgery will be scheduled for next week, and it will be performed as an outpatient procedure. He said the operation should be no more than an hour, so I'm sure you'll do fine." Pam tried to sound reassuring as she pushed the button to roll down her window. She needed some fresh air to help keep her focused until they got home. "Let me know if that's too much air, and I can put the window up a little."

"Thanks, but the night air feels good."

Pam glanced over at Stuart again and noticed that he was looking at the bandage on his finger. "Does it hurt much?"

"Not really." Stuart shook his head. "I thought it would hurt more than this, but I guess it's still numb from the shot they gave me before they put the temporary stitches in." He paused and laid his hand back in his lap. "Can you believe how crowded that ER was? I was beginning to think they'd never get to me."

Pam was about to comment, but the lump in her throat wouldn't let her get the words out. Her resolve was about gone. It hadn't been easy to mask her fear of Stuart's injury in front of Devin and Sherry and then remain positive for Stuart, getting him to the hospital and waiting in the ER, but now her ability to stay strong was slipping from her grasp.

"Pam, are you all right?"

"Oh Stuart!" Once the tears started, she couldn't get them to stop. It was like floodgates opening, and her vision instantly became blurred. She had no choice but to pull over to the side of the road and turn off the engine. Once she did, the sobs came hard, and it was difficult to catch her breath. She put her head in her hands and cried like there was no tomorrow.

Stuart unbuckled his seat belt and touched her shoulder. "Honey, what's the matter?"

Pam was glad Stuart was being patient with her, because it took a while to calm herself enough to speak again. "I was really scared when I saw so much blood coming from your finger. It was all I could do to keep my head and stay calm in front of the kids." She nearly choked on a hiccup. "All I could think of was getting you to the hospital safely." Another hiccup. "Oh Stuart, I don't know what I'd do if anything ever happened to you."

Stuart moved closer, and Pam had never felt more comforted than when he took her in his arms. Careful not to hurt Stuart's injured finger, her arms tightened around his neck, and she started sobbing all over again.

Once she settled down some, she looked at Stuart, her chin quivering. "If. . .if you only knew how good it feels to have you hold me like this." While Stuart gently smoothed a lock of Pam's hair away from her face, she closed her eyes and felt like a little girl again. "I would have given anything to have my daddy hold me like this when I was scared of all those unseen things you imagine when you're little. All I ever wanted was for him to take notice of me and say that he loved me and was proud of my accomplishments. I could be in the same room, watching TV with him, and he wouldn't even notice that I was there. I thought I did everything right—my grades were good in school, and I never gave my parents any trouble. I would have even gone fishing with him if he'd asked me to, but of course, he never did. When I got older—" Pam took a deep breath, and the rest came out in a whisper. "I finally realized one day that my dad was self-centered and didn't really care about me at all." She didn't think she had any more tears left, but now her weeping came out in a soft whimper.

Stuart held on to Pam and rocked her like a baby. She felt comforted, yet her mind swirled with nagging doubts. After opening up to him like this, would it make any difference in the way he treated her? Things were better between them tonight, but how would they be in the morning?

CHAPTER 35

Goshen

On Saturday morning, Star entered the kitchen and found her mother sitting at the table with a cup of coffee and the newspaper.

"How'd you sleep last night?" Mom asked, looking up at Star.

"Not so well." It was all Star could do to even look at Mom this morning, much less answer any questions.

"Me neither. I kept thinking of all the things we talked about last night, and I want you to know that I truly am sorry."

Star poured herself a cup of coffee and stood staring out the window by the sink.

"I've made an important decision."

Star turned around slowly and looked at Mom. "What's that?"

Mom took a drink of her coffee before saying anything. When she set the cup down, she looked at Star and smiled. "I'm going to give you this old house."

"Huh?"

"I'll have no need of it after Mike and I get married, and I'm sure your grandma would have wanted you to have it rather than it being sold to strangers."

"But what about the money you'd get if you sold the house?" Star questioned.

Mom shook her head. "I'll be well taken care of after Mike and I are married, and since your job doesn't pay much, you really can't afford to get an apartment on your own. If you stay here, you'll have all the memories of Grandma around you, not to mention a comfortable place to live and write your songs without interruptions."

A lump formed in Star's throat. She couldn't believe Mom would actually give her Grandma's house. Maybe Mom did feel some love for her after all. "Thank you. I appreciate that," Star said tearfully. "Maybe I'll take some voice lessons and learn how to sing a little better, too."

Mom left her seat at the table and gave Star a hug. "You can if you want to, but I think you already sing quite well."

Star sniffed deeply. "You really mean it?"

"Wouldn't have said so if I didn't."

"Do you think I'll ever make it big in the music world?"

Mom shrugged. "I don't know, but I think you should try."

"Yeah, maybe I will."

"So what are you going to do about today?" Mom asked, abruptly changing the subject.

"What do you mean?"

"Are you going to the last quilting class at Emma Yoder's?"

"Sure. Why wouldn't I go?"

"What if Jan's there? What will you say to him?"

"I had trouble sleeping and was thinking about that most of the night."

"And?"

"Now that I know the truth, the first thing I'm gonna do is apologize to Jan for calling him a liar and a bum."

"Then what?"

"Then I'm hoping we can spend some time together outside of the quilt class—get to know each other better and maybe become good friends."

"That'd be nice. I'll be happy for you if that happens, because, Lord knows, I've kept you hating him long enough." Mom's tone was as sincere as the look on her face, and it gave Star a sense of peace. Now she just hoped Jan would accept her apology.

"There's one more thing, Star." Mom took a sip of coffee before she continued. "I'd like the chance to apologize to Jan. He may not believe me, but I do feel terrible about how all this played out. Years ago, I thought I was doing the right thing, but now I see that all I did was bring on a lot of unnecessary hurt, especially to you. You don't know how much I regret it. Things could have been different, and I see that now. So after you've had some time with Jan and have gotten to know him better, I'd like a chance to make things right. He needs to know that our breakup wasn't all his fault and that I'm truly sorry for taking you and running off like I did."

Star placed her hand on Mom's arm. "I accept your apology, and I. . .I forgive you."

"I know I don't deserve it, but thank you for that."

Feeling somewhat better, Star took a seat at the table. She could hardly wait to get to Emma's and speak to Jan.

Mishawaka

Stuart sneaked a look at his wife as she drove them to Emma's for the last quilting class. He saw the glint in Pam's eyes, as though she was deep in thought. He was content with this moment of quiet, amazed at how quickly things had changed between him and Pam.

They say bad things happen for a reason, he thought, recalling the phrase he'd heard some years ago. Nodding his head, he realized there could be some truth to it. It was hard for Stuart not to grin as he recollected the recent turn of events. He remembered how surprised he'd been by Pam's reaction when the mishap had occurred with the hummingbird feeder. She'd appeared to be subdued on the way to the hospital, concentrating on traffic and getting him to the ER safely.

Wanting to stay alert, Stuart hadn't taken the full amount of his pain medicine this morning, so his finger was thumping like crazy with pain. He could ignore the discomfort, though, as he continued to recall the events of last night.

The trip home from the hospital was when Stuart had gotten a real eye-opener. It was like floodgates opening, and once started, nothing could stop Pam's tears. He still couldn't believe all the frustrations and heartache Pam had kept bottled up about her relationship with her dad. It was as if all the tears she'd held in for years couldn't be held back any longer. If he'd only known all this sooner, he'd have understood her better and realized why she felt the way she did about certain situations. Maybe things would have been different between them and not so combative at every turn.

Stuart knew he and Pam still had a ways to go, but he felt confident that they'd reached a milestone last night. He'd looked at Pam with a sense of awe, just as he was doing now, and realized that she really did love him.

And for himself, despite all their ups and downs, there'd never been any doubt of his love for Pam. He might not have shown it in ways she understood, but he'd always loved her. Never more so than he did right now.

Although Stuart knew how hard it had been for Pam, the fact that she'd finally shared those things about her dad made him feel closer to her than ever before. It was a good dose of reality, coming to terms with how for all these years he'd been putting other things above his wife's needs. He was glad they'd stayed up late last night, talking more about the past and their future. They should have been spending more time over the years really talking and listening to each other, rather than arguing and finding fault.

He remembered hearing Paul say during one of their quilting classes that life goes by in a blink, so from now on, Stuart was determined to make a positive change.

"Never thought I'd hear myself say this, but you know what?" he asked, gently stroking Pam's arm.

"What?"

"Even though my finger hurts this morning, I'm actually happy to be going to our little half-stitched quilting club with you."

Pam smiled. "I'm glad."

"Did you remember to bring the plant you potted for Emma?"

"Yes, I did. Earlier I put it in the back of the SUV so we wouldn't forget to take it to her. I hope Emma likes it," Pam added.

"I'm sure she will. Oh, and I forgot to tell you—the little cooler in the backseat—there's something in there for Emma."

"What is it?" she asked.

"Thought maybe she'd like to try some of the wild berries I picked when I went camping last summer. I took one of the containers from the freezer to give to her. Do you think she'll enjoy the berries—maybe bake something with them?"

"Stuart, that was really thoughtful. I'm sure Emma will appreciate the berries, and since she's always baking something, I'll bet she'll put them to good use." Pam sighed. "You know, today's going to be kind of sad with the classes ending. I've never been good at saying good-bye, and I've grown to know and like Emma so much, it'll be hard to leave her."

"Well, maybe our paths will cross again. Maybe we can stop and visit her when we're in Shipshewana sometime."

"That's a good idea." Pam smiled at Stuart with a look of happiness he hadn't seen in a long time.

The rest of the ride was quiet, but this time, it was more content and peaceful than all the other trips to Emma's had been. Although things weren't perfect between Pam and him, Stuart felt sure they were finally on their way to restoring their marriage.

CHAPTER 36

Shipshewana

Emma stood in the living room, looking happily at her new table and eager to show it to Mary and others in her family. She still couldn't get over Lamar's thoughtfulness in making it for her. Mary had been right—he really was a nice man.

The next time Lamar asks me to go somewhere with him, I should probably accept his invitation, she decided. *Maybe I'll even invite him to join us for supper when I have some of the family over next week.*

Emma's musings halted when she heard a car pull in. She looked out the window, and when she saw that it was Star, she went to the door and opened it.

"Morning," Star said as she stepped onto the porch. "Looks like I'm the first one here."

"That's right. You are. Come in, and we can visit until the others arrive."

Star followed Emma into the house, and when they entered her sewing room, they both took a seat. Emma was pleased to see that Star wasn't wearing her black hooded sweatshirt today. She was dressed in jeans and a white T-shirt, sort of like what Jan usually wore.

"How are you?" Emma asked, hoping Star's anxious appearance didn't mean she'd had a bad week.

"I was pretty stressed-out for most of the week until I talked to my mom—which, by the way, wasn't till she got home last night, because she'd been in Fort Wayne with the guy she plans to marry."

"Did you tell her about Jan and how you'd learned that he was your father?"

"Yeah, and needless to say, she was pretty surprised." Star frowned deeply. "Turns out that Mom lied when she'd said my dad had run out on us shortly after I was born."

"What exactly happened?"

"Mom changed her mind about marrying him. Said she thought he was too wild and had decided that she didn't really love him. So she took off with me and didn't tell Jan or even her mom where she was going."

"Oh my!" Emma couldn't imagine anyone running away like that, but Star's mother was most likely young and very confused back then. And if she thought Jan was too wild, she'd probably done what she felt was right for her and Star at the time. Emma remembered all too well how when people were young, they thought differently, and unfortunately, it sometimes took years for them to realize their mistakes.

"Now what?" Emma asked. "Are you going to tell Jan what your mother said?"

"Definitely. I'm nervous yet anxious to see Jan today. I need to tell him I'm sorry for losing it last week and calling him a liar, among other things."

Emma placed her hand gently on Star's arm. "I'm sure he'll understand and accept your apology. I'm also certain he'll be glad to know that you've spoken to your mother and have learned the truth."

"I sure hope so." Star reached into her jeans' pocket and handed Emma a folded piece of paper.

"What's this?" Emma asked, peering at Star over the top of her glasses.

"It's a song I wrote just for you. Wanted you to know how I feel about the way you've touched my life."

Emma opened the paper, noting that the song was entitled "You Saw Me."

"A lot of layers hide me," Emma read out loud. "Disguise me. . . A shell of sorts to work through my pain. A stack of stories guard me. . . protect me; a trail of tales to keep me safe. But you looked beyond my past and stolen soul. You saw me; you looked beyond the masks and mirrors. . . saw me, and helped me face my faults and fears. When I was hiding, lost behind myself, you saw me."

Tears sprang to Emma's eyes and blurred the words on the page. "Thank you," she said, giving Star a hug. "The words you wrote are meaningful and beautiful. I'm so glad you came to my class, and even happier that you've found your dad."

Star nodded slowly. "Yeah, me too, and I can't wait till he gets here."

Just then another car pulled in, and a few minutes later a knock sounded on the door. When Emma answered it, she found Paul on the porch holding two paper sacks, a manila folder, and his camera.

"It looks like you came with more than your quilting project today," Emma said, smiling up at him.

"That's right, I did." He handed her the manila envelope. "This is for you. Since today is our last class, I wanted you to have something to remember me by. I had my camera in the van last Saturday, and I took the picture before I headed home."

Emma opened the envelope and withdrew an eight-by-ten photo of her barn. Several of her goats were also in the picture, since their pen was near the barn. "This is so nice. Thank you, Paul."

"I have something else as well." Paul reached into the paper sack and removed a package wrapped in foil. "Here are some tamales my sister, Maria, made. I hope you'll enjoy them."

"Oh, I'm sure I will," Emma said, feeling a bit choked up. "I never expected to receive any gifts today." She motioned to Star. "She wrote a special song and gave it to me a few minutes before you arrived."

Star's face reddened as she gave a brief shrug. "It wasn't much."

"It was to me." Emma slipped her arm around Star's waist. "Maybe you'll get one of your songs published someday."

"That would be nice, but I'm not holding my breath, 'cause I've learned from experience that things don't always go the way I'd like them to."

Emma smiled. "Well, let's pray that this time they do."

"I brought this along, too," Paul said, pointing to the camera and moving their conversation in a different direction. "Since it's the last day of our class, I thought it would be nice to take a picture of everyone."

"You're welcome to do that, but I won't be able to be in the picture," Emma said.

"How come?"

"Posing for pictures is frowned upon in my church. We believe it's a sign of pride."

"That's okay," Paul said. "Maybe you could use my camera and take a picture of the six of us who've come to your class to learn quilting."

"That'd be fine. We can do that after everyone gets here," Emma said.

"Oh, before I forget, you'll never guess who sent Sophia a package this week," Paul said, beaming from ear to ear.

"Who?" Star and Emma asked in unison.

"My wife's sister, Carmen."

"Paul, that's wonderful." Emma smiled, thinking this day seemed to be getting better and better.

"Lorinda's folks will be coming to visit us in a few weeks, and I'm anxious to tell them the good news, too. While Carmen may still think I'm to blame for Lorinda's death, at least she's acknowledging Sophia now."

Emma could see how pleased Paul was about this. "You know, Paul, before you arrived, I was getting ready to tell Star that I believe God has a plan for everyone's life," she said. "We don't understand that plan all the time, but sometimes, later on down the road, we can look back and realize why things happened the way they did." Emma knew that applied to her, too.

"I know what you're saying," Paul agreed. "I'm going to keep praying for Carmen and trying to stay in touch. I'm also trusting God that she'll eventually come around."

"I'll be praying for that, too." Emma gave Paul's arm a light pat, and then hearing another car pull up, she went to the window.

Ruby Lee arrived next and gave Emma four beautiful thimbles. Each one had the name of a different season on it, as well as a painted picture—a flower for spring; a sun for summer; an autumn leaf for fall; and a snowflake for winter.

Emma thanked Ruby Lee for her thoughtful gift, and then Ruby Lee told how her husband had met with the church board the previous evening. "Gene agreed to set his plans aside for adding on to the church, and the board members were pleased to hear that," she said. "So for now at least, Gene's going to stay on as their pastor."

"That's a good thing, right?" Star questioned.

"I suppose, but it's going to be hard to put all this behind us." Ruby Lee frowned. "Too much gossip and hurtful things were said about Gene, and I still wish I could give a few of those people a piece of my mind. I've just been so crushed by all of this."

"Psalm 34:18 says, 'The Lord is nigh unto them that are of a broken heart; and saveth such as be of a contrite spirit,'" Emma said.

Ruby Lee nodded. "That's right, and the New International Version of that verse says it this way: 'The Lord is close to the brokenhearted and saves those who are crushed in spirit.' Guess I should take that verse to heart. Sometimes it's hard to forgive and move on, but I know that as a Christian it's what God expects us to do."

Paul nodded in agreement. "God chooses what we go through, but we choose how we go through it."

"I think I'd like to know more about this relationship you three have with the Lord." Star looked over at Ruby Lee. "Would it be all right if I visit your church sometime? Maybe bring Jan along?"

"You want to visit there even after all the negative things I've said about some of the people?"

Star shrugged. "So who says anyone's perfect?"

"You've made a good point," Emma said. "And another thing we need to remember is that anyone who has never tasted what is bitter doesn't know what is sweet. The bad times really do help us remember to appreciate the good."

Another knock sounded on the door. "Would you like me to get it?" Star asked. "It might be Jan."

Emma smiled. "If you like."

When Star returned to the sewing room a few minutes later, Stuart and Pam were with her. Emma was surprised to see that Stuart wore a splint on the index finger of his left hand, but even more surprising was that his other hand held tightly to Pam's.

"What happened to your hand?" Paul asked.

"I had a little accident with a hummingbird feeder. The broken glass cut the tendon in my finger, so now I'll be facing surgery next week." Stuart looked at Pam and smiled. "One good thing came out of it, though."

"What's that?" Ruby Lee asked.

"Pam started crying when she realized how bad my finger was, and I knew then that she really does care about me. We had a good long talk about some things, which also helped. And when we got home from the ER, she stayed up late finishing the quilting part of my wall hanging."

It was Pam's turn to smile. "That's right, and Stuart showed that he loves me, too, when he told me this morning that he plans to buy an RV we can all sleep in whenever we go camping."

Emma was pleased to see that things were going a little better in everyone's lives. Now if Jan would just get here and respond favorably to Star's apology, everything would be nearly perfect. Oh, Emma liked happy endings, and she hoped she would witness one today.

"Pam and I both have something for you," Stuart said. "Mine's some frozen wild berries I picked when I went camping last summer, and Pam's is a plant that she set on your front porch." He grinned and handed Emma a paper sack he'd carried tucked under his arm.

"That's really nice. Thank you both so much." Emma turned toward the kitchen. "I'll just put these in the refrigerator while you all find seats."

When Emma entered the kitchen, she glanced at the clock on the far wall and realized it was fifteen minutes after ten. Since Jan still hadn't shown up, when she returned to her sewing room, she suggested that they get started with the class and wait on taking their picture.

———————

As Emma showed everyone how to bind their quilted wall hangings, Star was barely able to concentrate on what was being said. She kept looking at the clock, and as time went on, she became even more concerned. *Where is Jan? Maybe he's not coming today. He's probably upset about the things I said to him last week and doesn't want to see me again.*

"I baked a couple of angel cream pies yesterday," Emma said at around eleven o'clock. "Should we stop for a break and have some now, or would you rather keep working on your wall hangings and have the pie at the end of our class?"

"I'm really not hungry," Star mumbled. "But the rest of you can do whatever you want." She was convinced that Jan wasn't coming. If he was, he would have arrived by now.

Emma smiled sympathetically and offered Star a few comforting words. The others did as well, but as much as Star appreciated their concern, she still felt miserable. All her life she'd wished she could know her father. Now, even though she knew who he was, she was certain that she'd never get the chance to really know him.

"I think we should keep working on our wall hangings and eat when we're done," Ruby Lee said.

Everyone nodded in agreement.

Each of them took turns using the battery-operated sewing machines, and Ruby Lee even tried out Emma's old treadle machine, commenting on how much harder it was to use.

"You're right," Emma agreed, "but once you get a feel for using the treadle, it won't be so difficult, and who knows—you might even think it's fun. I certainly enjoy using that old machine."

Shortly before twelve, everyone had finished binding their wall hangings, so Paul got out his camera and suggested they all gather for the class picture.

Star shook her head. "I'm not in the mood. Besides, Jan isn't here, and without him, it wouldn't really be a class picture."

"I'm real sorry he's not here," Emma said, "but wouldn't you at least like to get a picture of those of you who are here today?"

Star really didn't want to, but reluctantly, she finally agreed. She'd come here today without her hooded sweatshirt but wished now she'd worn it, because she was in a really black mood.

"Let's go outside to take the photograph," Emma suggested. "It's probably not light enough in here for a good picture." She opened the door, and they all stepped onto the porch and struck a pose. Star was the only one not smiling. She just couldn't force her lips to turn up when she felt so sad.

After Paul showed Emma what to do with the camera, she stepped into the yard and was about to take the picture when Jan came trudging up the driveway, huffing and puffing. His arms and face were sweaty, and his clothes were covered with splotches of dirt.

Tears of joy seeped through Star's lashes, but she didn't utter a word. Just waited to see what Jan would say.

"Sorry for bein' late," he said to Emma. "Stupid chain on my bicycle broke, and then I spun out in some gravel and fell off the bike. Fooled around with the chain awhile, but with no tools, it was pretty much hopeless. Since I was determined to get here, I just left the dumb bike there and started walkin'. Then some mangy mutt, who shoulda been home in his pen, chased after me for a time. But when a horse and buggy happened along, the dog gave up on me and started buggin' the horse. Things went from bad to worse after that. The horse was so spooked, it ended up pullin' the buggy into a ditch." Jan stopped and drew in a quick breath. "Well, I couldn't leave the poor Amish woman who was drivin' the buggy alone to deal with all that, so after I'd shooed the dog away, I led the horse outa the ditch and got the woman's buggy back on the road. By that time, I knew I'd missed most of the class, but I had to come anyways, 'cause I needed to see Star, even if it was for the very last time."

"It's okay. You're here now; that's all that matters," Emma said.

Everyone smiled and murmured words of agreement. They, too, seemed happy that Jan had made it before the class ended. But none was happier than Star. She was so glad to see Jan that she almost gave him a hug. Catching herself in time, she just smiled and said, "I'm glad you're here. I was worried you might not come."

Jan shook his head. "I'd actually thought about not comin', but no, I decided I just couldn't do that."

"I need to tell you something," Star said, moving slowly toward him, hands clasped behind her back. Her heart thumped so hard she feared her chest might explode.

"What's that?" he asked with a hopeful expression.

"I spoke with Mom last night, and she admitted that she was the one who took off."

Jan's face broke into a broad smile. "Really?"

Star nodded. "I'm sorry I didn't believe you, but I didn't want to think Mom would lie to me about something as important as this. Can we start over—maybe spend some time together and get to know each other better?" she asked, looking down.

"Yeah, I'd like that. I'd like that a lot." Jan raised Star's chin so she was looking into his eyes. "I'll be getting my driver's license back soon. Think maybe you'd like to go for a ride on my Harley then?"

"Sure, that'd be great. I'd also like the chance to meet your dog.

I've never had a pet, so it would be fun to see what that's like, too." Star went on to tell Jan that when the time was right, her mom would like the chance to make amends with him.

Jan, looking more than a little surprised, nodded and said, "No problem. I'd be glad to talk to Bunny again and try to make things right between us. I know we can never get back what we once had, but if we could be friends, that would mean a lot to me."

"It would mean a lot to me, too," Star said sincerely.

Star and Jan started talking about some other things they'd like to do together until Paul cleared his throat real loud. "Should we take our class picture now so we can have our refreshments?"

"I sure can't be in no picture," Jan said, looking down at the dirt and sweat on his clothes and arms.

"How come? Is it against your religion, too?" Stuart asked.

"Nope, it's nothin' like that, but just look at me, man—I'm a mess!"

"The bathroom's just down the hall," Emma said. "You can go there and get cleaned up, and I'll even let you borrow one of my husband's shirts."

Jan grinned at her. "I'd be much obliged."

"While you're changing and cleaning up, I'll bring out the pie and something for us to drink. Then I'll take a picture of the six of you, and after that we can enjoy the pie while we visit," Emma said.

"Sounds good to me." Jan looked down at Star, and tears welled in his eyes. "Never thought I'd hear myself say this, but somethin' good came from me losin' my driver's license."

"What's that?" she asked.

"Because I lost it and had to serve some time in jail, I was forced to see a probation officer, who said I should find my creative self. And if I hadn't seen Emma's ad and signed up for this class, I never would have met my daughter." Jan smiled at Star in such a special way that she really did feel like his daughter.

"Well, guess I'd better get cleaned up," Jan said, before heading down the hall. When he was halfway there, he turned and called to Star, "Don't go anywhere now, you hear?"

"I wouldn't think of it!" she hollered. Star didn't know what the future might hold for her musical career, but she knew she was grateful for the chance to get to know her dad and was happy that her future would include him.

———◦———

After Emma found one of Ivan's shirts for Jan to wear, she hurried to the kitchen and was pleased when both Pam and Ruby Lee followed.

"What can we do to help?" Pam asked.

"Let's see now. . . . The pie's on the counter, so if one of you would like to cut it, I'll get out the plates, silverware, and napkins."

"I'll cut the pie," Ruby Lee offered.

Emma looked at Pam. "There's some iced tea in the refrigerator, and glasses are in the cupboard. So if you don't mind, you can take those out to the dining room where we'll sit and eat our refreshments."

Pam smiled. "I don't mind at all."

"You can put them on here." Emma handed Pam a large serving tray.

"I'm going to miss coming here every week," Ruby Lee said as she began slicing the pie.

"I'll miss all of you, too," Emma admitted. "But you're welcome to stop by anytime you like—either for a visit or for help with another quilting project. I'd love to see all of you again."

"You've been a good teacher," Pam said. "And I, for one, have learned a lot coming here—and not just about quilting."

"Me, too," Ruby Lee agreed. "Getting to know everyone and sharing our problems has been good for all of us, I do believe."

"Well, throughout these last six weeks, I've learned quite a bit myself," Emma said. Pam's eyebrows lifted high. "About quilting?"

Emma shook her head. "About people, and how each of us is special in God's eyes. I've also learned to accept help from others whenever I have a need."

"You mean like that nice man who filled in for you when you were sick?" Ruby Lee asked.

"Yes. Lamar's been a big help in many ways, and last night he stopped by with something he made for me."

"What was it?" Pam asked.

"He made a very special table. I'll show it to you after we've had our snack."

"This is ready now." Ruby Lee motioned to the pie she'd cut into equal pieces.

"Then let's get back to the others." Emma led the way to her sewing room, where Stuart, Paul, Jan, and Star sat visiting around the table.

"Can we take the class picture now, before we eat?" Star asked.

Emma nodded. "Let's go outside on the porch."

Pam and Ruby Lee put the pie and iced tea on the dining room table, and everyone filed out the door.

Paul showed Emma again which button to push and reminded her that the camera could focus itself. Then Emma's six students gathered together on the porch while Emma stood in the yard with the camera.

"We may be just a bunch of half-stitched quilters," Jan said as he stood next to Star and smiled, "but we've sure learned some lessons here while gettin' to know and understand each other, and I think we've also learned quite a bit about love."

Star looked over at him and grinned. "I'm really feelin' it right now.

How about you? Are you feelin' it, too?"

Jan gave her a high five. "Yep. Sure am, and I never wanna lose you again." Hesitating a moment, he reached up and put his arm around Star's shoulder. He looked happy when Star moved a bit closer.

Emma held the camera steady and snapped the picture. She planned to place an ad for another quilting class soon and couldn't wait to meet the next set of students God sent her way.

"All right now," she said, smiling as she stepped onto the porch. "Who wants a piece of my angel cream pie?"

EPILOGUE

One year later

I t's a nice evening, jah?" Lamar said to Emma as they sat on the front porch eating a bowl of homemade strawberry ice cream.

She smiled. "You're right about that, but what makes it even nicer is having someone to share it with."

Lamar's eyes twinkled as he gave her a nod. "Does that mean you're not sorry you married me this spring?"

"Of course not, silly." She reached over and patted his arm affectionately. "The only way I'd ever be disappointed is if you stopped loving me."

He shook his head. "No worries there, 'cause that's never gonna happen."

Emma pushed her feet against the wooden boards on the porch and got the hickory rocker Lamar had given her as a wedding present moving back and forth.

A year ago, she'd been determined never to marry again. But that was before Lamar had won her heart with his kind and gentle ways. She was grateful to have found love a second time and felt that Ivan would be happy for her, too.

"Is there anything you need me to do to help with your quilting class tomorrow?" Lamar asked.

"I was hoping you would show my new students the quilt design you came up with the other day," she replied.

"Jah, sure, I'd be happy to show 'em."

They sat quietly, watching the fireflies rise from the grass and put on their nightly summer show, until a noisy *Vr. . .oom! Vr. . .oom!* shattered their quiet.

When Emma saw two motorcycles coming up the driveway, she knew immediately that it must be Jan Sweet and Star Stephens. They dropped by frequently to visit, as did the others who had come to her first quilting class. Star and Jan may have been cheated out of knowing each other during Star's childhood, but Emma was glad to see how happy they both were now, as they spent a good deal of their free time together. They'd made a trip on their motorcycles to Disney World, and through the help of one of Ruby Lee's friends, Star had gotten two of her songs published. Star's mother, Nancy, now living in Fort Wayne with her husband, Mike, had contacted Jan, and they'd finally made peace. Emma thought the best news of all was that Jan and Star had attended Ruby Lee's church a few times together.

Pam and Stuart Johnston seemed happier, too. According to Pam, since Stuart had purchased an RV, they were spending more time together as a family, which in turn had helped their marriage. They, too, had gone to church several times this past year, which Emma felt certain had also strengthened their marriage.

Paul Ramirez had finished the baby quilt his wife had started before she'd died, and he'd brought little Sophia by on several occasions to see Emma's goats and play with the kittens that had been born earlier this spring. He, too, seemed happy and content and kept in touch with his late wife's family in California. The best news he'd shared was that his sister-in-law had finally come to terms with Lorinda's death and no longer blamed Paul for the accident. Carmen was even planning a trip to Elkhart to see Paul and Sophia sometime this summer.

Ruby Lee Williams, whose husband still ministered to their congregation in Goshen, had stopped by recently and told Emma that their church had grown and its finances had improved so much that the board was now talking about adding on to the building. Emma was glad Ruby Lee and her husband had stuck it out and trusted God to meet the needs of their church. Ruby Lee was glad, too, for she'd admitted to Emma that her faith had been strengthened because of the ordeal.

Emma waved as Jan and Star parked their cycles and headed for the house. Even though she'd taught several more quilt classes over the course of a year, she knew there would always be a special place in her heart for the students from that first quilting class.

She looked over at Lamar and smiled. "Isn't it nice to know that love looks beyond what people are to what they can become?"

He reached for Emma's hand and gave her fingers a gentle squeeze. "That's right, and I'm so glad that the Lord can use us at any age if we're willing."

Recipe for Emma Yoder's Angel Cream Pie

Ingredients:
1 cup half-and-half
1 cup heavy whipping cream
½ cup sugar
⅛ teaspoon salt
2 tablespoons (slightly rounded) flour
1 teaspoon vanilla
2 egg whites, stiffly beaten
1 (9-inch) unbaked pie shell

Preheat oven to 350 degrees. In a saucepan, combine half-and-half and whipping cream. Warm only slightly. Turn off heat and add, beating with a whisk, sugar, salt, and flour. Add vanilla and fold in stiffly beaten egg whites. Pour into unbaked pie shell. Bake for 45 minutes or until filling is a little shaky.

About the Author

Wanda E. Brunstetter is a bestselling author who enjoys writing Amish-themed, as well as historical novels. Descended from Anabaptists herself, Wanda became deeply interested in the Plain People when she married her husband, Richard, who grew up in a Mennonite church in Pennsylvania. Wanda and her husband live in Washington State but take every opportunity to visit their Amish friends in various communities across the country, gathering further information about the Amish way of life.

Wanda and her husband have two grown children and six grandchildren. In her spare time, Wanda enjoys photography, ventriloquism, gardening, reading, stamping, and having fun with her family.

In addition to her novels, Wanda has written two Amish cookbooks, two Amish devotionals, several Amish children's books, as well as numerous novellas, stories, articles, poems, and puppet scripts.

Visit Wanda's website at www.wandabrunstetter.com and feel free to e-mail her at wanda@wandabrunstetter.com.

Discussion Questions

1. Although Emma appreciated help from her family, she didn't want to be a burden and looked for ways to be more independent. What are some things we can do to help family members or friends who have lost a loved one without making them feel as if they're a burden?

2. Sometimes after a person loses a spouse, they shut themselves off to the idea of another marriage, thinking no one could take the place of their deceased loved one. Was Emma too closed to the idea of having a friendship with Lamar? How long do you think a person should wait after the death of a spouse to remarry?

3. Due to the problems they were having at their church, Ruby Lee wanted her husband to get out of the ministry. Is leaving always the best answer when a pastor feels that the congregation is displeased with him? What are some other choices a minister might make instead of leaving a church he has felt called to shepherd?

4. Did Ruby Lee support her husband enough, or was she feeling so much at the end of her rope that she saw no possibility of a positive outcome? What are some ways we can keep our faith strong when going through trying times?

5. Jan, having been deeply hurt when his girlfriend left him, chose not to make any commitments to a woman after that. How can a person deal with rejection and not let it affect future relationships?

6. Pam hid her childhood disappointments from Stuart. Is there ever a time when a person should keep information about their past from their spouse? How did Pam's childhood affect her as an adult? How can a person deal with a scarred childhood and not let it affect their marriage?

7. Communication is important in marriage. Did Stuart and Pam have an honest relationship, or were there too many unspoken feelings? How important is honesty in marriage? What are some ways a married couple can learn to be more honest with each other?

8. In the beginning, Stuart had no understanding of Pam's dislike for camping and fishing. What might he have done to make her more comfortable with the idea? Should he have been willing to stay home more and do other things with the family?

9. Star, having grown up without a father, had abandonment issues and low self-esteem. She also felt that her mother cared more about her own needs than she did Star's. What are some ways a single parent can make sure their children feel loved and secure? How can an adult who grew up with only one parent help themselves to feel more secure?

10. Paul sometimes felt guilty when he left his baby daughter at daycare or with a sitter. How can a parent—especially one who's raising a child alone—deal with feelings of guilt when they have to leave their children with a sitter? Paul also struggled with the fact that his sister-in-law blamed him for his wife's accident. What are some ways we can deal with the pain of being unjustly accused?

11. How do you feel that the Amish people view others outside of their community? Do you think Emma's response to her students was typical for an Amish woman teaching a quilting class? Do you think there's ever a problem of prejudice among the Amish?

12. Was there anything specific you learned from reading this book? Were there any verses of scripture that spoke to your heart?